AB

I had only one excuse left, but it was a solid one. "You want a real detective, Barbara. Not me. You want someone who knows what he's doing."

"I don't have any money for detectives, Mr. Keane. It'll be years before I earn enough to hire someone. But then it'll be too late. I have a feeling that I have to ask these questions now. You can help me. I know it."

"How do you know?"

"Because you're afraid, too. Afraid to help me, I can tell. And it isn't because you think you'll fail. You're afraid you'll find the truth."

———————— ★ ————————

Terence Faherty
Prove the Nameless

WORLDWIDE.

TORONTO • NEW YORK • LONDON
AMSTERDAM • PARIS • SYDNEY • HAMBURG
STOCKHOLM • ATHENS • TOKYO • MILAN
MADRID • WARSAW • BUDAPEST • AUCKLAND

PROVE THE NAMELESS

A Worldwide Mystery/April 1998

First published by St. Martin's Press, Incorporated.

ISBN 0-373-26269-8

Printed in U.S.A.

A HAUNTING

It was too hot to sleep. And too noisy. Somewhere nearby, one of my neighbors was having a party. I could hear half a dozen people or more talking at once and, from time to time, laughing. The voices were only noise, though, loud enough to bother me but too soft to be intelligible. The irritation I felt at being kept awake was countered by curiosity. I strained to understand the overlapping conversations, but I could only pick up random, meaningless words.

As I listened, I noted two odd things about the party. One was the absence of music, an interesting concession to the early hour by people too rude to keep their voices down. I decided that I'd dozed through the musical portion of the evening. I was now hearing the breakup of the party. The guests were standing at their cars, calling out protracted good-byes. In a moment, I would hear their car doors slam and their engines turn over. Then I'd certainly sleep, heat or no heat.

But the doors never slammed, and the good-byes, if that's what they were, never stopped.

The second odd thing about the party was that first one and then several of the voices sounded familiar. I hardly knew my neighbors, but soon each almost-voice seemed to be one I recognized. Almost recognized. I tried to picture the speakers, but their faces, like their words, floated just out of focus.

I'd almost given up when, from the jumble of familiar noise, I picked up the same words being spoken over and over again. The chant the voices had taken up was my name.

I sat up in bed. The movement was abrupt, electric, but the voices anticipated it, stopping in the very same instant. I sat in the hot darkness, waiting to hear my name again or the sound of the speakers sneaking away. I heard instead my neighbor's wind chime as it tolled for each second of the long night.

Lured by the breeze the chiming promised, I left my bed and then my house, stepping out onto the cool concrete of the drive. There was no moon, but here and there above me stars shown faintly through holes in a black overcast. By their light, I looked for the party goers, then for strange cars, then desperately for empty glasses and cans or any other sign that the speakers had really been there.

Finally, I admitted to myself that I'd been dreaming. I was embarrassed and surprised, too, surprised that it had taken me so long to recognize a dream I'd been having on and off for ten years. The competing voices were its standard climax. Always before, they'd been preceded by the flight of a mystery plane. In the early years of the dream, the plane had been something I'd chased after, first across sunny fields and then through a nightmare forest. More recently, the plane and I had reversed roles. It had chased me to the accompaniment of the laughing voices, coming so close that its black wings became my sky.

I scanned the real sky, wondering why the dream plane had failed to appear. I couldn't believe that it had become so familiar a terror that I could wake without remembering it. The dream had evolved again, I decided; I'd moved that far from the events that had inspired it. The plane that had changed from grail to demon was now gone completely. I told myself that this was a healthy step, that in time the voices calling my name would also fade away.

I had myself nearly convinced when I heard a new sound

in the night, a bass tone that slowly rose beneath the tin-kling of the chimes. It was the rhythmic droning of a plane. I stepped away from the house so I could better see the reassuring red and green lights of a real plane, lights my phantom never showed. But, though the droning grew louder, no lights appeared. I told myself that the plane was above the same black clouds that had all but obscured the stars, even though the force of the approaching sound made this impossible. I didn't believe the lie in any case. Before I'd finished telling it, I'd begun retreating toward the house.

As I fumbled with the screen door's simple catch, the droning arrived directly above me. The door rattled in sym-pathy with the sound waves or with my panic. Then I was inside the house, and the sound of the plane dropped away unnaturally. I stood in a corner, willing myself to wake again from the dream. I didn't wake, or sleep again that night.

ONE

THE SEARCH for lost families is a common pastime in our unraveling age. We re-create our families in the time-honored biological way, if we're able. If we're not, we replace them using likely strangers. In my wanderings, I've often observed children searching for parents, and I've been told, by a person whose opinion I respect, that these lost children eventually begin to search for sons and daughters of their own. I know from my own searching that replacement siblings are sought after, too.

One brother I'd acquired in a moment of need was a newspaperman named Tim Gleason. At a critical point in a critical investigation, I'd stumbled across Gleason. I'd pretended to be a fellow journalist to gain his trust. Later, to gain the trust of someone who trusted Gleason, I'd pretended to be Gleason's relation in fact as well as need. This course was suggested to me by the man I was trying to fool, who had noted my physical resemblance to Gleason: a hungry thinness; a dark, searching look; a wealth of nose. I had to settle for passing myself off as a relation and not Gleason's brother because I'd made the mistake of giving my true name. That name, incidentally, is Owen Keane.

Pretending to be Gleason's kin had gained me only exposure as a liar and the opportunity to wander around a pine forest as night came on. A little later, when I'd been working on another, related case, this same Gleason had done his best to have me arrested. For those unhappy reasons, I'd gone years without seeking him out again.

In the end, he'd sought me out. By that time he'd traded in his editorship of a weekly paper in a Jersey shore town for a position with a daily in *the* Jersey shore town, Atlantic City. I was living nearby, in quieter Mystic Island, and I'd come to the attention of Gleason's new paper, the *Atlantic City Post*, as the result of yet another of my investigations, a particularly unsuccessful one. Gleason had remembered my name and come to see me. Not everyone looks for help from their substitute brothers. Some look for brothers who need help. That was the case with Gleason. When he'd learned that I was supporting myself by tending bar in a casino, he'd offered me a job at the *Post*.

I'd studied English in college, and then theology during a disastrous stay at a midwestern seminary. Both majors intrigued Gleason, the first because he thought it qualified me to edit copy and the second because he thought it explained me, explained my avocation, I mean, the solving of mysteries. He was wrong on both counts. I'd majored in English literature, not English grammar, with which I had only a nodding acquaintance. Gleason's second misconception was subtler but more serious. I hadn't taken up my search for answers because I'd failed in the seminary. I'd failed there because I hadn't been able to control a constant need to question. It was a subtle distinction, as I said, but one that might have made Gleason more cautious about hiring me. And about sending mysteries my way.

It was July 1990, the height of the paper's busy time, the tourist season at the shore. I was seated at my desk on "the rim," the circle of copy editors' desks that surrounded "the slot," the desk of the news editor—"slot editor" in our local parlance. The furniture arrangement was an anachronism, dating from the time when the slot editor distributed sheets of copy by hand to a ring of scribbling copy editors. Now copy was distributed by the press of a button to editors typing away at computer terminals, but we were still circled like a wagon train expecting an Indian attack.

A Native American attack, according to the stylebook I'd
been issued by the paper.

It was the end of my shift, a very late Tuesday night
about to give way to a very early Wednesday morning. That
day's paper was done, as far as the copy editors were concerned. "Put to bed" was the way newspaper people on
television said it. The slot editor, Suzie, preferred "in the
can." Suzie's chair in the slot was empty at the moment,
as were most of the chairs along the rim. I decided to do
one more story before calling it quits, a Sunday feature with
a low priority that had risen patiently to the top of the
electronic queue. I was already logged on to the system and
attached to the queue, to use the strange, modern language
I was still picking up. A couple of keystrokes displayed the
story.

Twenty years ago this week, five members of a prominent Atlantic City family were killed while vacationing at their cabin in the Poconos in a senseless murder
that remains unsolved to this day.

I changed "murder" to "homicide" and struck out the
redundant "to this day" with my right hand while I groped
for my coffee cup with my left. I moved everything after
"Poconos" up in front of the comma, reread the sentence,
and then moved on.

The police in rural Lake Trevlac, Pennsylvania, and
here in Atlantic City worked hard to solve the case,
identifying no fewer than three suspects, including one
who subsequently killed himself.

After using a road atlas to confirm the unlikely-looking
spelling of Trevlac, I changed "killed himself" to "took

his own life," stared at it for a moment, and changed it back.

The suicide should have resolved the investigation. Instead, like every other "break" in the case, it deepened the mystery, perhaps making it unsolvable forever.

I sat up a little in my seat, typing "for all time" over "forever" without really thinking about it. Tired as I was, I was getting caught up in the story, which was bad news for my limited copyediting skills. But my interest was also inevitable—mysteries that grew more unsolvable with every new break and each new clue being a weakness of mine.

What is known for certain can be briefly stated. On the evening of July 11, 1970, the bodies of George Lambert, 32, his wife, Irene, 30, their two sons, Gerald, 8, and Paul, 7, and their daughter Ruth, 5, were discovered by a neighbor, Bud Switzer. Switzer was attracted to the Lambert cabin by the crying of a second daughter, six-month-old Barbara, who Switzer found in her crib. The other Lamberts were shot.

I changed the "who" to "whom" and recast the last sentence in the past perfect tense to eliminate the possibility that the curious neighbor had shot the bodies after finding them.

There were no signs of a break-in [changed to "forced entry"]. From the location of the victims, the police concluded that the killer had been admitted through the front door of the cabin by Irene Lambert, who's [changed to whose] body was found in the hallway.

George and his eldest son were found in the cabin's living room. Paul and Ruth were found in a bedroom closet, where they had tried to hide.

I added an "apparently" before the "tried to hide." The change actually made the sentence weaker, but the operation helped to make less real the picture of the terrified children huddled in their hiding place.

A noise that might have been gunshots had been heard by a second neighbor, Ralph Wirt, around two o'clock, four hours before the bodies were discovered. Wirt mistook the sounds for the backfiring of a motor on the nearby lake.

The first suspect to be identified was a local handyman, Samuel Calvert, 52. A few days prior to the killings, Calvert's only son had died in a traffic accident. Although the Lamberts were acquainted with the Calvert family, they did not attend a memorial service for the boy. Instead, George Lambert sent a small cash donation. This infuriated Samuel Calvert, who declared before witnesses that he would "see George Lambert in hell" before he would accept his money. Calvert had no alibi for the afternoon of the murders. He claimed that he had been working alone at an isolated farm.

The second suspect was Gary Geist, 26, a self-ordained leader of a small religious commune that had taken up residence in an old summer camp near Lake Trevlac. George Lambert had lent his name to a community effort to block Geist's request for a zoning variance. It was the only connection police could discover between the cult and the Lambert family, but locals still considered Geist the prime suspect. This sentiment was due in part to the publicity surrounding

the Manson murder trials in California. Geist's alibi
was not substantiated by anyone outside of the commune.

The notes inserted in the copy by the assignment editor
indicated that photographs accompanied the story. They
weren't in the last stack Suzie had given me. I found the
photos in a folder on her desk and carried them back to my
terminal. They were old glossies from the *Post*'s morgue
files, each made a little less glossy by a wide border of
thumbprints.

The photographs were labeled on the back with grease-
pencil notes. I didn't need any help identifying the subjects
of the first one. It was a professional portrait of the Lambert
family. George and Irene were seated a little stiffly on a
sofa, Irene holding Barbara in her arms. Paul and Ruth,
who had huddled together at the end of their lives, were
together in the photo, standing between their parents. Gerald stood to his father's right with his little hand on his
father's shoulder. It was a portrait I'd seen many times
before with different strangers in it. The Lamberts were a
handsome family, the father dark and prematurely graying,
the mother fair. The children all took after their father in
coloring, except perhaps for sleeping Barbara, who hadn't
declared herself at the time the photo was taken.

The second print in the file showed an older man, not
recently shaven, wearing a felt hat pulled low. The
grease-pencil notation said *Samuel Calvert*. He had held his
hand up toward the camera to shield his face, so the resulting portrait was of the outstretched open hand with the
man as background. It was a big hand, not entirely clean,
with thick fingers and the suggestion of calluses across the
palm. Behind this concrete thing, the man's face looked
much less substantial. One eye could be seen, and in that
eye an emotion: anger. Given the composition of the pho-

tograph, it looked like the unsubstantial man was angry at the callused hand.

The next photo was another group shot, although it was identified with a single name, *Gary Geist.* Geist appeared as the foreground interest of the photo, like Calvert's hand in the preceding picture. He had shoulder-length hair, very straight and very carefully combed, eyes given the appearance of depth by a bony brow, and a young man's feathery beard. Geist was smiling broadly, showing a full mouth of very straight, upper-class teeth. They were the only well-to-do thing about him. His shirt was a smock with wide, wrinkled sleeves, and his necklace was a twisted leather cord from which hung a roughly made wooden ornament shaped like a horseshoe. The figures in the background looked like clones of Geist. They wore their hair long and parted in the middle, and each sported a wrinkled, white smock. None came close to matching Geist's smile, though, or his confidence. Their small, out-of-focus eyes projected something else entirely: fear.

The last picture showed George Lambert and a second man, whose grease-penciled name was new to me. I set the photograph aside and went back to my reading.

The police had their own prime suspect, Russell Conti, 39, George Lambert's business partner. Although the investment firm of Lambert and Conti was thought to be a solid success by the Atlantic City business community, the police investigation revealed that the firm was in financial difficulty due to some risky speculations on the part of Conti. Conti stood to gain financially from George Lambert's death, primarily through a life insurance policy maintained by the firm for the partners. Conti had no alibi for the time of the murders. He claimed to have been attending a trade show in Philadelphia, but the police could find no one who saw him there during the five hours it would have taken him to drive from Philadelphia to Lake Trevlac and back.

Unfortunately, the police were also unable to find anyone who could place Conti or Geist or Calvert at the Lambert cabin on the day of the shooting. Nor could they locate the murder weapon. The physical evidence in the case consisted almost entirely of the bullets removed from the bodies and a cross drawn in blood on one interior wall of the house. Many Lake Trevlac residents believed that the cross pointed to Gary Geist and his cult. Geist maintained that it was a crude attempt to frame him. Despite an intense investigation, almost three years passed without an arrest.

As the third anniversary of the crime approached, the Mason County district attorney's office was on the verge of issuing an arrest warrant for Russell Conti. The DA, Myron Bass, was responding to intense pressure from two county detectives, John Ruba and Patrick Derry, who were confident that they could obtain a confession from Conti once he was in custody.

Somehow, Conti learned of the plan. Two days before the anniversary of the killings and only hours before the arrest warrant was to be served, Conti shot himself with his own gun, a gun the police had checked against the fatal bullets and returned. Conti's death might have settled the case, were it not for the note he left behind. In it, Conti maintained his innocence and claimed that he was hounded to his death by the police.

I stood the photograph of Lambert and Conti on my keyboard, sliding its curled edge in between two rows of keys so it would stand upright. Although older than his partner by seven years, Conti had affected a younger look. His black hair hadn't a trace of Lambert's premature gray, and he wore it combed low across his forehead and down over his ears in a greasy interpretation of the style young men had favored in the late sixties. Conti's attire was similarly dated: a white turtleneck decorated with a chain under a sports coat whose lapels were wide and pointed and outlined in contrasting thread. By comparison, Lambert's sedate suit and tie looked almost timeless.

I played with the irreverent idea that Conti had shot himself because bell-bottoms had gone out of style. That led me to wonder if I had any old photographs lying in wait to ambush me with proof that I had once backed the wrong fashion horse. I decided that, ironically, my congenital lack of style had spared me that cruel fate.

With the exception of his lower lip, which was heavy, Conti's face was lean and very angular, with a square, cleft chin begging to be caricatured and hollow cheeks. His dark eyes showed no emotion whatsoever, not Calvert's anger or Geist's unsettling cheerfulness. I slipped Conti back into the folder with the other suspects and the victims.

As the quiet newsroom grew even quieter, I read how the Lambert investigation had wound down after Conti's suicide. The murder cabin had been demolished and the land sold. Gary Geist's cult had disbanded, and Geist himself had completely dropped from sight. Samuel Calvert had died of natural causes in 1981. Russell Conti's widow had stayed on in the Atlantic City area, steadfastly believing in her husband's innocence. Barbara Lambert had been raised by her father's sister, Catherine Lambert, in a suburb of Philadelphia. Both Lamberts had declined to be interviewed for the anniversary story.

The story's author had ended with a little bit of the speculation and editorializing that are the journalist's real compensation.

Another possibility remains, which is that none of the three suspects killed the Lamberts. The family might have fallen victim to a subspecies of violence unique to our time: random, meaningless murder by a total stranger. There may have been no motive for the detectives to discover, no sense to be made of the tragedy, no orderly arrangement for the pitifully small collection of evidence. In fact, the only question we might profitably ask is whether the murder of the Lamberts, if reenacted today, would hold the public's attention for a week. If not, if we can no longer be shocked and outraged by such a crime, have we not all become victims of the same faceless evil that claimed the Lamberts?

I sat staring at the last sentence, wondering at it. The word *faceless* bothered me, but I didn't replace it in the text. I decided instead to counter it in the headline for the story, the creation of which was my final responsibility. Suzie had given me its specifications in a terse note: "4/ 60." A four-column headline in sixty-point type. I keyed in "Anniversary of a Nameless Evil" and commanded the computer to do the calculation that old-hand editors did in their heads, figuring whether the specified words set in the specified type would fit in the columns available. A message flashed on the screen, telling me the headline was too long. I typed "Killed by a Nameless Evil." Again, a rejection flashed on the screen.

My third try was cryptic, but the computer wasn't bothered by that. It accepted "Killed by the Nameless," and I was through for the day.

TWO

THE LAMBERT anniversary story appeared in the following Sunday's paper, but I didn't get the chance to reread it as I'd planned. In the warm months, I usually read the Sunday paper outside with my first cup of coffee. On the Sunday the Lamberts returned from the dead, I carried the paper and my coffee out onto the little dock in back of my little house in Mystic Island. It was actually my uncle's little house, my uncle who now resided in a nursing home outside of Cherry Hill. In theory, I was looking after the house for him. In practice, the house and my aged uncle were looking after me.

Mystic Island was an old vacation community built back in the days when wetlands were something you filled in to keep the mosquito population down. No nineties developer would be permitted to dredge out the lagoons that had been Mystic Island's original selling point, a system of canals that led to Great Bay and the Atlantic. Nor would they be permitted to use the dredgings to form the dry land on which houses like mine had been built.

The houses were small and flat-roofed and set closely together. They'd been sold to refugees from the crowded postwar suburbs around Philly and Trenton, and the buyers had consciously or unconsciously given their getaways the character of the suburbs they were fleeing. The houses on my lagoon were decked out in the kind of flashy colors that discount car-painting companies used, and their little, pebbled yards were overdecorated with religious shrines, pink plastic flamingos, and glass reflecting balls balanced on the bases of dead birdbaths. And there were lots of dogs, those almost artificial suburban dogs whose only joy is barking.

One such dog lived across the lagoon from my dock. She was a white toy poodle with a pink ribbon on the top of her head, and she hated me. Actually, we hated each other, but I was too dignified to show it. Whenever I appeared on my dock, the dog, whom I called Fluffy out of spite, would come down to the edge of her dock and bark at me. For perhaps the first year of our relationship, this had irritated me. Then I'd realized that my presence irritated Fluffy, and I'd started to draw a perverse pleasure from her yapping.

Fluffy was yapping now as I settled carefully into a chair whose plastic webbing had grown crisp with age. I saluted her with my coffee cup and opened the paper. Before I'd read the first word, Marilyn Tucci came down from the house to join me.

Marilyn was a weekend guest in Mystic, although her visits had become so regular that "weekend resident" was a better description. She was also an old friend. We'd met years before when we'd both worked in New York City. Marilyn was still there, in a publishing conglomerate's research department. I'd been a researcher, too, back then, before my personal inquiries had pushed my professional ones aside. In those days, Marilyn had had no time for my investigations, which she'd characterized as metaphysical, by which she'd meant pointless. The passage of ten years had gone a long way toward eroding Marilyn's old foundation of reason and common sense. She hadn't come around so far as to hope I'd someday find my answers, but she had acknowledged that my search was important.

"You're up early," I said.

"I'm leaving, Keane," Marilyn said, using her pet name for me.

She was half sitting on the peeling railing of the dock, wearing her traveling clothes, presumably. If so, the toll takers on the Parkway were in for a treat, as her outfit consisted of a bathing suit worn under a pair of my gym shorts. She uncrossed her legs to give them equal access to the sun. Recently she'd been dieting aggressively as part of a makeover that had included cutting off most of her auburn hair. I'd regretted that step from the first, Marilyn's hair being a special fascination of mine. Prior to the redesign, it had been long and thick and capricious. Saying her hair had a mind of its own was shortchanging it by thousands, perhaps tens of thousands of minds, for every strand had seemed capable of independent action. Now her hair was only slightly longer than my own, and the shock of that seemed to have broken it. Fresh out of bed, formerly its most creative time of day, Marilyn's hair was now unnaturally quiet.

So was Marilyn herself. She held her face toward the sun for a moment, letting me admire her shallow profile and the way her long lashes lay against her cheeks. Then she opened her eyes and shot Fluffy—still barking—a look that should have turned the dog into yet another lawn ornament. To me, Marilyn said again, "I'm leaving."

I knew what she meant by that. I'd known since she'd arrived the previous afternoon, sensed it throughout our perfunctory, old-married-couple lovemaking and the long, quiet evening. I'd been waiting for the announcement during our last few weekends, in fact, but I still pretended not to understand her.

"Something going on at home?"

She leaned over to take my coffee from me and drank some, grimacing a little at its sweetness. "I'm leaving for good, Keane. This isn't working out."

It seemed an odd thing to say of a relationship that had bumped on for so long on such modest expectations. I thought back on our last discussion of any length. It had been a familiar one about the inequities that had crept into our long-distance affair.

"I can come up to New York more often," I said. "I know I should."

"It isn't that."

"What is it, then?"

"Nothing," Marilyn said, meaning, I thought, "I don't know." But she repeated the word a few times as though she were exploring a complex idea. "There's nothing here," she finally added. "What I need isn't here."

It was a difficult pronouncement to soften, but Marilyn tried, redirecting her fire toward innocent Mystic Island. "Why won't you move back to New York? Why do you want to stay in this backwater? I'd think an investigator would want to be where things are happening. This isn't the place to search for answers. This is a place to hide from them. That's what I've been doing down here, hiding."

Her real charge, of course, was that I was hiding in Mystic Island when I should have been turning over garbage cans in New York or some other place where things happened. I had an answer ready for that, one I'd worked out during long sessions on my dock. I'd told myself then that the clues I sought were echoes and whispers that could barely be heard against the tumult of a New York, whispers that sounded clearly in a backwater like Mystic. That answer had satisfied me once, but I didn't try it on Marilyn. The memory of how I'd arrived at it, sitting in my fragile chair and staring at the lagoon when I should have been out searching, seemed to support her indictment.

I might have done better by attacking the idea that Mystic Island was a place where nothing happened. I could have reminded her that I'd almost gotten myself killed in sleepy Mystic, when one of my mysteries tracked me there. Marilyn herself had saved me, but we seldom mentioned that complex subject. It had happened shortly after she'd reestablished contact with me following her unsuccessful marriage. I said earlier that the passage of years had eroded Marilyn's faith in the rational, but the damage had really been done by her marriage. She'd turned to me for a way out of the resulting tangle, a move I'd found more intimidating than any of her earlier skepticism.

"I told you when you first came down here that I didn't have any answers," I said.

"And I told you that knowing the answers wasn't as important as believing they were out there."

That was the real charge, then. Not just that I was hiding from my quest, but that I'd lost faith in it altogether.

I tried to make a joke of the idea. "Turning forty has slowed me down a little, that's all."

"Bullshit," Marilyn said, sharply enough to make Fluffy pause for breath. "Turning forty has nothing to do with it. You've been forty for as long as I've known you. You were probably born forty. You've just stopped trying. I don't know why."

Neither did I, although it might have had something to do with the subject Marilyn and I seldom discussed: our brush with death. For a year or so after that event, my investigations had all been half-efforts and failures. There had followed a long dry period that I'd attributed to a lack of material. One of my rationalizations for accepting a job at the *Post* had been the hope that I'd hear of new mysteries in that clearinghouse of the sordid and strange. Now I foolishly tried to palm that idea off on Marilyn. She didn't hear me out.

"That's bullshit, too, Keane. That job is just another distraction." She poured what remained of my coffee into the lagoon. "Another concession."

"Concession to what? Material wealth?" I made a sweeping gesture that took in a block of clapboard castles, buckled seawalls, and faded fiberglass boats.

Instead of conceding the point, Marilyn batted it back at me. "Not material wealth," she said. "Just the material. The ordinary. I'm not interested in the ordinary."

She handed me my empty cup. "It'll only take me a minute to pack."

THREE

TWO DAYS LATER, when Tim Gleason called me into his office, I had a premonition that the summons involved the Lambert case. This was due in part to the teasing—pimping, my fellow journalists called it—that I'd been taking over my "Killed by the Nameless" headline. I'd even received a note from the author of the story, a reporter I barely knew named Kate Amato. The note was written on a yellow, gummed-back slip of paper stuck to my terminal, and it read, "Thanks for icing my story." I initially thought the "thanks" to be sincere and "icing" to be a colloquialism for topping something off, as in icing a cake. Then I remembered that the word was slang for killing and I reinterpreted the note to mean I'd done the story in.

My premonition that Gleason's invitation involved the anniversary article was reinforced by a feeling I'd had since first reading the Lambert story, an old, familiar sense of something unseen lurking just beneath the surface. Once, in my youth, I would have gone after that unseen thing. Now I waited, fatalistically, for it to come for me.

Gleason's office was a very modern cubicle of steel-framed panels, some holding glass and others covered with a carpetlike material. Like the terminals scattered around the newsroom, the architecture was a bit of self-delusion, the newspaper's attempt to convince itself that it wasn't one step removed from stone tablets and headed for the same ash can.

The man behind the plastic desk still looked a little like a lost brother of mine, although the years had softened the resemblance. Gleason had acquired eyeglasses and a slight paunch, and, unlike me, he'd avoided graying hair. The gut was surprising given Gleason's defining characteristic, his nervous energy. It was a testament to the amount of time he now spent trapped behind a desk. Another point of difference was attire. Gleason dressed more fashionably than I did, today in pleated pants and a loose shirt whose print was vaguely Hawaiian. I wore the white shirt and dark suit pants of a fortyish man—my swaddling clothes, according to Marilyn.

Seated on a swiveling pedestal chair opposite Gleason was a young woman. I guessed her to be a teenager, although she seemed different somehow from the paper's occasional intern. Though she was seated, I could tell that she was tall. The way she sat, leaning slightly from side to side in her chair, suggested that she wasn't comfortable with her height, that it was something new she hadn't gotten used to. Her head was inclined forward, but her blue eyes met mine. They were clear and steady and her best feature, the others being regular but ordinary. Two exceptions to this ordinariness were her ears, which stood out from her head at near right angles. Instead of hiding her ears, she displayed them, wearing her fine brown hair drawn back behind them and secured with a ribbon. The ribbon was a very pale pink, the same color as her dress.

The woman looked toward Gleason as he began the introductions. "Ms. Lambert, I'd like you to meet Owen Keane. He's one of the editors who worked on the story. Owen, this is Barbara Lambert."

The survivor. I had missed the woman's age on the low side. She'd been six months old when her family had been killed, which meant that she was just shy of twenty-one now. I took the other swivel chair, turning it a little Lambert's way. She hadn't smiled or nodded in greeting. Her hands were busy squeezing the life out of a folded newspaper. I recognized it as the features section of our most recent Sunday edition, and I jumped to another wrong conclusion: that she'd come to complain about the story. Again, it was Gleason who set me straight.

"Ms. Lambert is interested in reopening the investigation into the murder of her family, if reopening's the right word. The case was never solved, so I guess it was never closed. Anyway, she's been to see the police and gotten a cold shoulder. So she's come to talk to us about doing a follow-up to the anniversary article."

In the course of his opening remarks, Gleason's nervous fingers had completely unraveled two paper clips. He pointed to Lambert with the straightened bit of wire that was all that remained of the second victim. "Would you mind running through your idea again for Owen?"

"No, I wouldn't mind." Lambert's voice was light and it wavered a little until she got it up to speed. "My family's...the case, I mean, was never resolved. Solved, I mean. I think it would be interesting for your readers, I think it would be important to them if it was resolved."

"Why important?" I asked.

She nodded toward the folded newspaper in her lap. "You said that the deaths had affected everyone. That their not being explained had affected everyone."

"I didn't write the article," I said for Gleason's benefit as well as Lambert's. "I only edited it."

"And gave it its headline," Gleason said. "Ms. Lambert was particularly taken with the headline. It struck a chord for her. That made me think you might be just the person for her to talk to. I've told her a little about you and the investigating you do on the side."

I gave Gleason a long look while I tried to figure out what he was really up to. As I watched, he smoothed a stack of paper, tapped his various desk ornaments with a pencil, and took a long drink of cola he didn't need. Over the top of the soda can, his large eyes watched me back.

They were registering boredom. He didn't want anything to do with Barbara Lambert's follow-up story, I decided. Instead of just politely telling her so, he was trying to pass her to me.

Lambert also seemed to sense Gleason's lack of interest. "It has been twenty years, I know," she said.

"That's not a problem," our host replied. "Old mysteries are Owen's specialty. Yours wouldn't even set the record for him. How old was that Carteret case when you tackled it?" Gleason asked me, naming the business that had first brought us together. "Thirty years?"

That mystery had been forty years buried, but I didn't want to sound immodest. "Something like that," I said.

"Tell you what," Gleason said. "Things look quiet on the rim for the moment. Why don't you take Ms. Lambert out and buy her a cup of coffee?" To the woman being lateraled, he added, "If there's a name to be put on this nameless thing, Owen's the man to do it. What I mean is, if there's anything to be learned after all this time, Owen will ferret it out.

"He won't be representing the paper," Gleason added, giving me a significant look. "But he'll let me know if he finds anything. Then maybe we can talk about more articles."

He stood, or rather sprang, from his chair on that line, bumping the edge of his anachronistic desk blotter and scattering the papers he'd just straightened. Lambert and I stood, too. On the subject of her height, I'd guessed right for once. She easily topped me, or would have if she'd stood up straight.

I held the door to the newsroom open for her and said, "I'll meet you at the elevators. I have a quick question for Mr. Gleason about the bulldog edition."

After I'd closed the door, Gleason asked, "What the hell is a bulldog edition?"

"That was my question. I'd also like to know what's going on here."

Gleason was already back in his seat, attempting to restore order to his desk. "For starters," he said, "one of us is being damned ungrateful. I thought you'd jump at the chance to add Ms. Lambert to your collection."

"What collection would that be?"

"Hopelessly lost people. Didn't you sense that about her? But I should have said add her mystery to your collection. *The Casebook of Owen Keane*, or whatever you're planning to call it. I swear, Owen, you're making me feel like an insurance salesman. I thought you'd be anxious to turn over this rock. Unsolved murders that are none of your business. Aren't those two irresistible qualities for you amateur sleuths? Plus a lady in distress, plus..."

"Plus what?"

"I don't know exactly." Gleason sat still for a moment and thought about it. "Something not right. Something I can't put my finger on. Something."

"The Nameless?" I asked.

Gleason laughed. "Right. Where the hell did you get that, anyway? Kate Amato wants your grizzled scalp over it."

"I found it in a poem."

"Don't tell Kate that or she'll take off your whole head."

"Why aren't you interested in a follow-up story?"

"Because, A, that cow's been milked. I don't think there'll be any follow-up, just a rehash of the original article. Contrary to what I told Ms. Lambert about your gifts, I don't think there's anything new for you to find, not with two of the suspects dead and the third missing in action. Kate didn't just read through a file of clippings, you know. She's still gung ho enough to have driven around interviewing human beings. Kate would have stirred up the embers herself, if there'd been any embers left to stir and if stirring is what you do to get embers going. Maybe you fan them.

"Reason B is that the story's only a story because it is unsolved. Nobody gives a damn about twenty-year-old solved murders."

"You mean you wouldn't print a solution if you had one?"

Gleason's hands made a short, nervous flight, fluttering up from his desktop and down again, a gesture that always reminded me of our first meeting. "You know damn well I don't mean that. If you can get somebody charged with multiple homicide, and if it doesn't happen to be the weekend of the Miss America pageant, I'll get you page one. I should have said hopeless, not unsolved. That's what gives the Lambert case the little fascination it has after twenty years—its hopelessness. Take that quality away from it, and we wouldn't have run that anniversary article in the first place. The answers that can't be known are the ones people want to know the most."

He took off his wire-rims and began polishing them on his flowered shirt. Without the glasses, his billiard-ball eyes looked sharper, but that may have been a side effect of the way he was looking at me just then.

"Is there a reason C?" I asked.

"Yes, Ms. Lambert herself. There's something not right about that girl. I should say woman, according to our up-to-the-minute stylebook, but that doesn't seem to fit her somehow. Did you get that impression? The problem's more than immaturity, though. She's balanced a little too delicately for my taste. Take my word for it. Sitting behind this desk you develop a real eye for the type, people who come in to complain about a story or to bring you a big story of their own. People who take things way too seriously."

"What things?"

"Doesn't matter. Parking meters. Saving the whales. Things the rest of us laugh at and things the rest of us believe in. Only these people believe in them way too much. When I was as young as Kate Amato and working back at that weekly in Toms River, I looked forward to talking with people like Lambert. I got a sympathetic rush from their intensity. Now I look for concealed weapons."

"And send for me."

"Yeah, well, you look danger in the eye and make it blink. Besides, Lambert's not the violent type."

"What type is she?"

"Damned if I know. *That* may be reason C."

FOUR

Some people will tell you that easterners are reserved and even unfriendly as a result of overcrowding. I've sometimes wondered if that explanation didn't get the cause and effect reversed. We easterners may jam together in subways and elevators and tiny restaurants because we're naturally reserved, because we're trying to substitute physical proximity for emotional intimacy, because we find the rub of a stranger's shoulder comforting somehow.

I remembered that unlikely theory as Barbara Lambert and I squeezed our way into Benelli's, a little lunch counter a block or so from the paper. The restaurant was old enough to be the place for which the sobriquet "greasy spoon" was originally coined. Its interior was mostly wooden counter, heavily stained. On one side of the counter was a parallel stove top, which was just as dark and almost as long. Four tables stood along the dim window that backed the customer side of the counter. The tables were so tall in relation to their diameters that they looked like giant golf tees. At some time in the past, there might have been enough stools for each table. If so, three or four had since dissolved in the overheated atmosphere of the room. The surviving stools were prizes in a game of musical chairs without music and, therefore, without end.

One such prize stood at the table Barbara Lambert and I were lucky enough to claim. None of the stools at the other tables was free. I offered Ms. Lambert our seat.

"Oh no," she said. "You take it, please. I was an hour driving over here, so I'd really rather stand."

I almost asked her how old she thought I was, but that

sort of question always backfires. I climbed the stool instead. It was proportional to the table, so, at its summit, I was high enough to look straight across into Lambert's very young eyes. She was standing straighter now, a side effect of a rigid defensiveness she'd assumed the moment we'd left the *Post*. Her shoulder bag was pinned to her side by her left elbow. Her right elbow was also drawn tightly in, protecting the folded newspaper she still carried.

I gave her a little time to get used to the noise of the place. Then I asked, "You drove in from Philadelphia?"

"No," she said. "Riverton, across the river from Philadelphia. Your article called it a suburb of Philadelphia, but I don't see how it could be, since it's in New Jersey. We are right next to the Tacony Palmyra Bridge, though, so maybe the article was right."

Before she could give me the annual rainfall in Riverton, a counter person of great antiquity and uncertain gender called out for our order. I called back "two coffees," after consulting my guest, and then climbed down to retrieve them. By the time I was back on my perch, my companion had relaxed a little.

"Everybody here seems to know everybody else," she said a little wistfully.

"They just pretend to," I said. "It's part of the ambience. What do you do in Riverton?"

"Nothing there." She put the newspaper down on the table and used her free hand to check for stray hairs escaping from her headband ribbon. "I'm a student at Hickory Hill College, a little school on the Pennsylvania side of the river. I'll be a senior in September."

"Studying what?"

"History. You'll ask me next what I'm going to do with it. My Aunt Catherine always does. The answer is I don't know. Is it that important to have your future worked out?"

I didn't think so, but I was a poor source of career advice.

"Let's talk about your family history," I said. "Why do you want the case reopened?"

"I want to see justice done," Lambert said in a tone that suggested I'd asked a very silly question.

"Is that possible after all these years? Assuming the police identified all the likely suspects, the odds are two to one that the murderer is dead. If the cops missed somebody, some passing madman without a motive, it's even more hopeless."

Lambert's head bowed under the weight of something I'd said. I thought the hopelessness angle had done it, so I didn't ask for an explanation. I only had a second to think about it anyway. Then she looked up and said, "What is the Nameless?"

"I don't know. That's the short definition. It's everything you feel is out there somewhere but you can't put a name to."

"The things that go bump in the night?"

"In my experience, they're a little noisier than that."

I was trying to get a smile out of her, and she obliged, in a tentative way. I sipped my coffee while I waited for her to get back to the subject of her dead family. Instead, she did another side step.

"Tell me about the Carteret case."

"Why do you want to know about that?"

"I'm a history major," she said and smiled nervously again.

I thought she was still stalling, avoiding my original question about her reason for reopening the case, but I played along.

"Carteret was a millionaire banker who lived like a hermit on Long Island. Forty years before I met him, his brother and the brother's fiancée were killed in a plane crash in the Pine Barrens. Have you ever been there?"

"I don't think so."

"It's the big pine forest in southern Jersey. You might have driven through the edge of it on your way over from Riverton."

"Did the *Post* run an anniversary piece about the crash? Is that how Mr. Carteret found you?"

"I wasn't with the paper back then. I was working for a law firm in New York City."

"You were a lawyer?" she asked, her expression a wrestling match between admiration and incredulity.

"Not a lawyer, a camp follower. I was asked to write a report on the plane crash. Something like an anniversary article."

"Was the plane crash an accident?"

"No, as it turned out, it wasn't."

Lambert seemed relieved to hear that. "And you solved the mystery?"

"I think so. I worked out an answer that satisfied me. That's what I'd really been hired to do. To find an explanation that could bring Carteret some peace of mind."

Lambert took a half-step forward and bumped the table, almost toppling her untouched coffee. "That's what I'd like, too," she said. "An explanation." Her intensity embarrassed her and she looked away again. "I'm frightened, Mr. Keane. You've probably noticed."

"Call me Owen. I'll feel ten years younger." No smile this time. "What are you frightened of?"

"The Nameless. I hadn't thought of it that way until I read your headline, but I've always been afraid of it. Ever since I heard about the murders when I was ten."

"You were ten before you knew how your family died?"

"Yes. Aunt Catherine thought it would be better to keep the truth from me. When I was little, she would only tell me that my family was in heaven. She'd show me pictures and tell me how wonderful they'd all been. Especially my father. He was her brother, but you already know that from the article. When I was a little older, she told me they'd died in an accident. Not an automobile accident, just an accident. I used to picture them all together in an avalanche," she added, embarrassed again. "It was an idea I'd gotten from a movie. I've always liked to think of them all being together. With their arms around each other.

"I don't know how Aunt Catherine thought she could keep the truth from me. I have other family, cousins. One of them, my cousin Joan, sent me your article. She lives just south of Atlantic City. In Ventnor City. Anyway, it was inevitable that one day one of them would mention the murders. Ever since that day, I've been afraid."

"The murders happened a long time ago," I said in case she'd forgotten that small detail. "There's no threat to you now."

"I know that. I'm not afraid the murderer is out there somewhere. I may be afraid that he isn't. That there isn't any murderer, I mean, at least not the kind you read about in books, the kind who has a logical motive for what he does. I read a lot of mysteries," she added as though she were admitting to a nasty habit.

It was a vice I shared, but it seemed a macabre pastime for her. "Murder mysteries don't bother you?"

"No," she said. "It's silly, I know, but they've always made me feel a little better. I like the older ones. The English ones. The Agatha Christie ones. You wouldn't understand."

"It's because the mystery is always solved in the end," I said. "And the murderer is always caught."

"You do understand."

"Ms. Lambert..."

"Call me Barbara. It will make me feel older. I've been feeling like a little girl ever since I knocked on Mr. Gleason's door."

"Okay, Barbara. I was going to say that, outside of

books, it's possible to solve a mystery and still not know all the answers." That outcome was more than possible, in fact. My own career had shown it to be damned likely.

"That wouldn't happen to me," Barbara said. "If I knew who murdered my family and why he did it, I'd have all the answers I need. I'm frightened of never knowing the answer, but that's not true exactly. I'm frightened of knowing for certain that there isn't an answer. Of knowing for certain that there wasn't a reason for what happened. You said it yourself just now. You said my family may have been killed at random by a passing madman. That's what frightens me, the idea of randomness.

"There has to be a reason, Mr. Keane. Owen, I mean. It all has to have happened for a reason. That's what I need to know, that there was a reason."

"Suppose it turns out to be a petty reason or an ugly one?"

"It would still be a reason. The murderer would still have a name. And I could stop being frightened all the time."

"Back when you thought your family had died in an accident, you weren't frightened by the idea?"

"No. I was lonely, but I wasn't frightened."

"How is not knowing why your family was murdered any worse than believing they'd died in an avalanche?"

"An avalanche would have been an act of God, not an act of the Nameless."

"The Nameless is another way of saying God for some people."

"Not for me. My Nameless is a mindless thing. A mindless, random God wouldn't make any sense. My Nameless is the opposite of God. I don't mean the devil. I mean the absence of God. No plan, no design, no goal. Just things whirling around in the dark, hitting each other for no reason. Sometimes missing each other for no reason. That idea scares me, too."

"Because you were spared."

"Yes. I need to know why I was spared, Mr. Keane. Why I wasn't killed with my family."

I couldn't tell whether Barbara felt guilty over her escape or somehow cheated by it. I thought about her childhood daydream of an avalanche, wondering if she hadn't imagined herself huddling with her family when the clean, white snow swept over them.

Barbara took a step away from the table. "Excuse me for a moment, please," she said.

She weaved her way through the crowd and disappeared through a swinging door marked REST ROOMS.

I wouldn't have recommended Benelli's facilities to her, but the break gave me time to think of other, more important, advice I might give her. In Barbara's questions I'd recognized an old enemy of mine; my Moriarty, as I sometimes called it: the idea that the universe was a godless, mindless accident. Calling my enemy Moriarty was more than a nod to my lifelong obsession with mystery stories. It was also a reminder of warnings I'd been given about questions that cannot be answered, only wrestled with throughout an endless fall.

Having Barbara address me by my first name hadn't made me feel any younger. I felt very much like an older person when she returned to the table, her nose red and her blue eyes no longer quite so clear. In fact, I felt a little like an uncle, a person brimming over with good advice he couldn't foist on anyone. That didn't stop me from trying.

"I'm a stranger, I know," I said, "but if you don't mind a stranger's opinion, reopening the case might not be the best thing for you. I'm not saying you'll ever be able to forget that the murders happened. But you might be better off accepting the fact of them and moving on."

"I've been thinking that you sound like the policeman I talked with," Barbara said. "But you really sound more like a psychologist, Mr. Keane. Is psychologist another job you've had?"

It was another of the professions to which I'd briefly appended myself. I guessed that Barbara was even more familiar with it. "Have you been in counseling?" I asked.

"On and off since I was twelve. It was Aunt Catherine's idea, one of her ways of being overprotective. I've heard a thousand reasons why it would be better for me not to know the truth. I've never believed one of them."

She picked up her newspaper and tucked it under her arm again, ready to turn on her heel if I repeated one of her thousand rejected reasons.

"I don't think finding the truth would be bad," I said, "if the truth is out there to find. But it may not be. And investing too much hope in finding the answers may be a bad thing. You could end up another victim of the murders if you let your life be darkened by them."

I was speaking from experience, for once in my life, and hoping it gave my advice a little authority. Instead, it gave Barbara an excuse to examine my experience in more detail.

"Why did you leave the law firm in New York?" she asked.

"A difference of opinion between me and the lawyer I worked for."

"Over the Carteret case?"

"Yes. He wanted me to drop the investigation. I was getting his firm into hot water. And he thought I was too involved in the case emotionally."

"But you kept at it until you had an answer."

"I had an answer, Barbara, but it wasn't *the* answer. It didn't solve all my problems or make my life wonderful.

In some respects, not taking that lawyer's advice has made a mess of my life."

"I'm not asking you to make my life wonderful, Mr. Keane. No one can do that for me, I know. I'm asking you to give me a chance to *have* a life. You said I should put the murders behind me. I want to, I really do. If you'll help me find the answers, I'll put them behind me happily."

I had only one excuse left, but it was a solid one. "You want a real detective, Barbara, not me. You want someone who knows what he's doing."

"I don't have any money for detectives, Mr. Keane. I'm not inheriting any when I turn twenty-one, either. My parents didn't leave anything but bills. It'll be years before I earn enough to hire someone. By then it may be too late. I have a feeling that I have to ask these questions now. You can help me. I know it."

"How do you know?"

"Because you're afraid, too. Afraid to help me, I can tell. And it isn't because you think you'll fail. You're afraid you'll find the truth. I think you will, too."

FIVE

BARBARA LAMBERT was an unusual client in that she couldn't give me any firsthand information about the mystery she wanted investigated. She had that quirk in common with Robert Carteret, the man whose story seemed to fascinate her. I'd started that long-ago case with no more information than the fact of the plane crash and the date on which it had happened. Barbara came equipped with a little more data than that, but she'd gotten it all from the newspaper article I'd edited myself.

I parted with my client outside the lunch counter, promising her only that I'd do some poking around. Barbara told me she would be staying with her cousin Joan for a few days. She gave me the cousin's last name, Noll, and her phone number in Ventnor City and asked me to call if I poked anything substantial. Actually, she said, "Call when you find something." She said it with a confidence that made my shoes feel heavy.

I returned to the *Post* to look for Kate Amato, the reporter who wanted my scalp. The odds were against finding Amato at her desk, the paper's newsroom being understaffed and overworked. But I knew she'd be there because I wasn't looking forward to speaking with her. Keane's law of perverse probability, I could have called the feeling. Sure enough, Amato was on duty, pounding away at a plastic keyboard as though it were a cast-iron Remington from the original production of *Front Page*.

All I knew of Amato I'd gotten from the office grapevine. I'd heard that she was one of the paper's Young Turks—another term banned from the pages of the *Post* by its politically correct stylebook but still current at the paper's watercoolers. She was a recent hire, in other words, still aglow with the inner fires they stoke in college journalism courses.

The copy editors who labored on the rim were sometimes chastised for cherry picking, that is, for selecting a specific story to edit instead of taking the one waiting at the top of the queue. The editors who practiced this art preferred wire copy to stories written locally. No wire service ever called to complain about butchered prose. The next choicest picks were local stories by seasoned reporters too cynical or weary to fight a pitched battle over every changed word. Young Turk copy was the least desirable because it always turned out to have been written in sweat and blood, materials that were messy to edit. The result of trying could be bad feelings or an argument or even a shouting match.

I arrived at Amato's desk prepared for all of the above. But when she looked up from her typing, she smiled.

"Owen Keane," she said. "How nice of you to stop by."

She was almost as young as Barbara Lambert, but Amato's youth had a quality that my client's lacked. I thought it might have been the false but powerful sense of her own immortality, but that guess later proved to be wrong. The difference was probably nothing more than a sense of style. Amato's very black hair was as short as Marilyn's, but it had a wispy, unstudied elegance that gave it a completely different look. She had turned bad eyesight into another fashion statement by wearing glasses whose square lenses were far too big for her slender face. The resulting imbalance focused a viewer's attention on the eyes within the giant frames. The eyes were small and dark and too intelligent by half.

"I'm told you're after my scalp," I said by way of hurrying the process along.

"Now that I see your haircut close up," Amato said, "I think I'll settle for a piece of your hide."

I wasn't sure my hide would pass a close examination either, but I was too shy to broach the subject. "I liked your story," I said.

"What was left of it, you mean, after Gleason made his thousand cuts and you exercised your literary ambitions on it. You must have gotten caught up as you read, though. I noticed you didn't hack away very much in the last half or so."

Amato pushed her chair back from her desk. She wore white slacks, a T-shirt, and a generously cut khaki vest with big, button-down pockets. She was extremely thin, and her watch hung loosely around her wrist like a leather bangle.

"What did Gleason cut?" I asked.

"Just about everything interesting. Including a reference to one of our local employers. The mob."

"How were they involved?"

"Gee, Owen, I thought you knew that. I thought maybe they were the nameless guys from your headline. I studied headline writing in school. I thought yours might be an example of what my old professor called the intriguing type. The reader can't figure it out, so he reads the story looking for the answer. The funny thing is, I wrote the damn story and I still don't know what the headline meant. Could you give me a hint?"

Tim Gleason had told me what not to say on that subject, so the fatal words were waiting on the tip of my tongue. "It was something I found in a poem by Tennyson."

"Damn," Amato said. Her exclamation got us the attention of the one or two people in the newsroom who hadn't already stopped their work in the hope of seeing a copy editor dismembered.

"Would you mind reciting for us?" Amato asked. "I love poetry readings."

I disliked them myself, for very old and very good reasons. "It's a long poem," I said. "I don't know it by heart."

"Just give us the part about the Nameless, then. You have to know that by heart. Or do you keep a copy of Tennyson by your terminal in case you get stuck for a snappy headline?"

Given the size of our audience, I thought Amato was asking for a rather large piece of my hide. But I didn't see a way around it. I took a deep breath and recited:

> "'Thou canst not prove the Nameless, O my son,
> Nor canst thou prove the world thou movest in,
> Thou canst not prove that thou art body alone,
> Nor canst thou prove that thou art spirit alone,
> Nor canst thou prove that thou art both in one.
> Thou canst not prove thou art immortal, no,
> Nor yet that thou art mortal—nay, my son,
> Thou canst not prove that I, who speak with thee,
> Am not thyself in converse with thyself,
> For nothing worthy proving can be proven,
> Nor yet disproven.'"

I bowed to acknowledge the room's mocking applause. Amato wasn't clapping or even smiling. She signed off from her terminal with enough force to make the carnations on her desk dance in their vase. "Come on," she said to me.

She led me out of the newsroom, past various editorial offices, the lavatories, and the break room, to a doorway marked FIRE STAIRS.

"Where's the fire?" I asked her back.

"I'm about to light one."

Once in the stairwell, she climbed. And climbed. We finally reached a door whose crash bar was wound with bright orange tape. An orange-and-white sign on the door read, EMERGENCY EXIT ONLY, ALARM WILL SOUND. I was too short on breath to repeat the warning aloud. Amato was through the door too quickly in any case. I paused on the last step, listening for bells and horns.

"There's no alarm," Amato said. "Alarms cost money. Signs are cheap."

Beyond the doorway was the roof of the paper's little building. It was covered with white pebbles like my back-yard in Mystic Island, but the *Post*'s yard had a much better view. We were facing the ocean and what the locals liked to call the world's most famous boardwalk. That was the official nickname. The boardwalk was called the Hotel Underwood by the transient teenagers and homeless people who slept beneath it. Not that Amato and I could see much of the boardwalk or the ocean. Between those marvels and us were Atlantic City's new claim to fame—the casinos. I could see all ten of the boardwalk casinos from our vantage point, from the Showboat at the northern end of the row to the Grand in the south, tall, shining buildings that might have been mistaken for the headquarters of banks and insurance companies were it not for certain architectural eccentricities, the Showboat's awnings, for instance, and the Taj Mahal's minarets. As it was, they looked like office buildings vacationing at the shore, wearing the colorful, god-awful clothes of vacationers.

In the foreground was Atlantic City itself, or what was left of it after urban renewal: blocks of old commercial buildings and row homes that reminded me of Trenton, my hometown. Almost every block contained a parking lot marking the grave of a building too old to be renewed. In the blocks to the north, many of these gaps hadn't been paved for parking. They stood vacant and rubble strewn, whole blocks of them in some cases, patiently awaiting the new businesses legalized gambling was supposed to attract.

Amato wasn't interested in the view. As soon as we'd reached the roof, she'd set about starting the fire she'd spoken of, first by digging out a pack of cigarettes. Now she was searching the pockets of her safari vest for a light.

I offered her my old steel Zippo. In exchange, she offered me a cigarette.

"I quit years ago," I said.

"Why carry the lighter, then? So you can be gallant to ladies?"

"Just sentimental."

I watched her take a long drag, thinking, for the thousandth or so time since I'd given up smoking, that a cigarette wouldn't be half bad. Before I could weaken further, she said, "You shouldn't have done that."

"I'm sorry about the headline," I said. Sincerely sorry, since it had brought Barbara Lambert my way.

"No, I meant just now in the newsroom. You shouldn't have humiliated yourself like that."

"Wasn't humiliating me the whole idea?"

"I didn't think you'd go along with it. Not you."

It was an odd remark, coming from a virtual stranger, and it reminded me, belatedly, of the office grapevine. Amato had studied up on me the same way I'd researched her. I wondered what category I was classified under. Certainly not Young Turk.

The reporter's source turned out to be better than the rumor mill. "Tim Gleason told me about you."

"He's been talking me up a lot lately. Or was it down?"

"It was sort of sideways. He thinks a lot of you, but he doesn't have you figured out exactly. Sometimes he makes you sound like a down-on-your-luck detective. Sometimes like a down-on-your-luck mystic."

"He has a short memory. I was a down-on-my-luck bartender when he hired me."

"Is it true you were a priest once? And that you've been in and out of jail?"

"I never got as far as ordination. Never even got very close."

"How about the jail time?"

"Isn't this a lonely spot to be asking a question like that of a man you barely know?"

"I ask questions for a living, Owen, often in lonely spots. And I'm almost always asking tougher-looking birds than you. I only say 'almost always' because I occasionally interview children. Are you going to tell me about jail?"

"Gleason was exaggerating. The police have sometimes held on to me until a responsible adult could come and take me home. It's usually been a lawyer named Ohlman, by the way. Now can I ask you a few questions?"

"I'm twenty-four years old. I graduated magna cum laude from Rutgers. I'm single. I like windsurfing and karaoke bars. I live in Somers Point in a second-floor apartment above a couple named Ray. They drive a Corvette and they had a little sign made for their parking space that says 'The Rays' Stingray.' Any questions left?"

"Yes. Why would you want to sing in front of a lot of strange drunks?"

"You're not interested in karaoke or me, Owen. You want to ask about the Lamberts. The case intrigues you. Do you think it was an act of God?"

"Or someone in the same union."

"Come on, what's the hook?"

"There isn't one for me," I said, sounding sincere to my own very tin ear. "The case intrigues Barbara Lambert. She's asked me to look into it, thanks to a referral by Mr. Gleason."

"Damn," Amato said. "Why is she suddenly confiding in you and Gleason? She wouldn't even talk to me."

"That was probably her guardian's decision. Barbara's

aunt. She has a history of being overprotective. I don't know that I blame her, if the Mafia's involved. What's the story on that?"

Amato gave the question a dismissive wave of her cigarette that left a swirl of smoke for the breeze to clear away. "One of the suspects, Conti, the business partner, was a nephew-in-law of a local mob figure named Frank Botticelli. He was known as Smiling Frank and he died a few blocks from here one evening when his Cadillac exploded. Nobody knows if he died smiling."

"Did he die before or after Conti?"

"Years after."

"Could the Lambert killings have been a professional hit?"

"It isn't very likely. For one thing, the job wasn't exactly professional. The killer got in and out of the Lake Trevlac area like a pro, assuming it was an outsider. But the actual workmanship was pretty sloppy. Multiple wounds for almost all the victims. The youngest boy survived for hours and your friend Ms. Lambert was overlooked completely."

"Or spared," I said.

"Unprofessional either way. The biggest thing against the murders being a hit, though, is that Conti, the guy with the mob connections, didn't have an alibi. You don't order a hit on somebody and then disappear for five or six hours. You arrange to have lunch with the archbishop."

"I'll try to remember that. How about the firm of Lambert and Conti? Could the Mafia have been pulling the strings there? Maybe George Lambert tried to sever the relationship."

"That has the same problem as the hit theory, which is that it fails the professionalism test. The Mafia's legitimate businesses tend to be very liquid, since one of their functions is to launder an endless flow of cash. Lambert and Conti was very nearly on the rocks. Anyway, nothing turned up in the postmortem audit except bad business sense. Most of it Conti's.''

"So the mob probably wasn't involved?"

"Not directly. But I picked up something when I talked to one of the original investigators from the Pennsy end, a guy named Ruba. He wasn't happy with the cooperation he got from the Atlantic City police. He thought Conti may have had some kind of special protection. That doesn't mean Conti was the murderer, of course. Even an innocent man would use whatever pull he had to shake a multiple homicide charge.

"Anyway, Gleason wouldn't let me mention any of that. The *Post* is a little timid where organized crime is concerned. When Smiling Frank's Fleetwood blew up, we probably ran an editorial against unleaded gasoline.''

She paused long enough to cheat the breeze out of a little of her cigarette's smoke. "The *Post* didn't do a very good job on the Lambert anniversary, either, to get us back to the agenda of this meeting. I mean, the story I wrote was good, or started out good, but one article wasn't enough. We should have given it a bigger treatment. I have enough material for a series of articles, stuff I might as well toss.''

"How about tossing it my way?"

"That would be cheating, Owen, don't you think? Besides, I'd like to find out which one of us is the better investigator. Why don't we compare notes, after you've done some looking around?"

"How about spotting me some points, in deference to my age?"

She dropped her cigarette and then ground it into the pebbles. I noted that the smashed filter had plenty of company. "I'm listening,'' she said.

"Give me a list of your sources on the Lambert article."

That was on the order of asking a priest to discuss his

last shift in the confessional, but Amato didn't bristle or laugh me off the roof. "What do I get in exchange?"

"An exclusive story."

"Are you that sure you'll solve it?"

"We say 'crack' in the trade."

"I'll tell you what. I'll hand the list over on two conditions. One is that I get a story."

"If I solve it."

"Crack it, you mean, and there's no 'if' about it. I get either an exclusive on the Lambert solution or the complete history of Owen Keane."

That would make for one very long serial, I thought. "What's the second condition?"

"Dinner. Say tomorrow night. I'll pick the place."

SIX

THE NEXT DAY, I cashed in a little vacation time and left the shore, armed only with Kate Amato's list of contacts and my own vague sense of dread. Before setting out, I used the list to make a call to John Ruba, one of the original investigating officers on the Lambert case. He agreed to talk with me, which justified my investment in time and gasoline. My little red Chevy Cavalier and I headed west on the Atlantic City Expressway, reversing Barbara Lambert's drive in from greater Philadelphia. The traffic around the City of Brotherly Love was unloving, as usual, and my route was complicated, as usual, by Philly's never-ending road repairs. Not for the first time I wondered how it would feel to work on a road crew and to watch your handiwork being beaten into rubble faster than you could patch it. It was a cruel form of job security, and one that was all too familiar to me. *The Casebook of Owen Keane*, as Tim Gleason had laughingly called my career, seemed to me more and more like a volume whose early pages were crumbling while the ending remained unwritten.

I finally left the concrete barricades and flashing yellow lights behind me and started north on the Pennsylvania Turnpike. I wasn't on the turnpike proper, the old east-west highway that had once carried me to the seminary and then home again in record time. My road was the turnpike's Northeast Extension, which ran roughly parallel to Pennsylvania's eastern border, the Delaware River. If Russell Conti had snuck away from a Philadelphia trade show to murder the Lamberts, he had surely taken this road, back when the pavement was relatively new and the old industrial centers along it, Allentown and Bethlehem, still had a spark of life.

Around Allentown, the ground began to rise gently to meet some of the worn green hills that pass for mountains in the eastern part of the country. What they lacked in stature, these little ranges made up for in nomenclature, each good-sized bump having its own identity. In less than an hour's driving, I saw signs for the Blue Mountains, the Broad Mountains, and the more interestingly named Pohopoco, Penobscot, and Moosic Mountains. At Scranton, another old city whose reason for being had moved to the Sunbelt, I left the turnpike and headed northeast into the Poconos on State Road 191.

Before long, I spotted a turn for Lake Trevlac, but I passed by the exit. My first stop was Hartsdale, the seat of Mason County. John Ruba had been unsuccessful with the Lambert case, but it hadn't held him back. Despite that blot on his résumé, he'd risen to the lofty rank of county sheriff. Or maybe the career move had been a direct result of the old failure. I'd learned on an earlier case that sheriffs in Pennsylvania weren't policemen in the strict sense. They worked for the courts, serving papers and transporting prisoners.

I found Sheriff Ruba at the county courthouse, not far from Hartsdale's principal feature, the intersection of 191 and U.S. Highway 6. I was expecting the courthouse to be old, perhaps even colonial, but it turned out to be a disappointingly modern building whose modest cornerstone bore the year 1923. Sheriff Ruba's office looked even more modern than that, or rather it sounded more modern. The inside of the large white room was a droning chorus of hums and buzzes supplied by banks of fluorescent lights, a copying machine, a desktop computer, and a window air conditioner.

At the center of the noise sat the sheriff. He didn't rise

to greet me, but he did reach across his cluttered desk to shake my hand. His hand was big, as was everything else about Ruba. It was difficult to judge his mood. His eyes were hard to read, as they were squeezed between heavy black brows and broad, fat cheeks that glistened a little with sweat in spite of the conditioned air. Ruba's short, curly hair also glistened, but with some oily preparation that smelled like a flower garden.

"You're from the *Post,* are you?" Sheriff Ruba asked as he leaned back in his chair.

"Yes," I said as I sat up very straight in my chair.

"You've got some kind of identification, I expect."

"Yes." Sometime late in the moment of silence that followed, I realized that Ruba was waiting for me to produce the identification. Luckily I had something to produce—a press card issued by the New Jersey State Police. When I'd hired on at the *Post,* Tim Gleason had casually asked me if I wanted one. The cards were issued to reporters routinely and to editors as a courtesy. I'd taken Gleason up on the offer, perhaps unconsciously anticipating this opportunity to abuse the privilege.

Ruba nodded at the card and handed it back. "I was surprised to get your call," he said. "Ms. Amato, that other reporter I spoke to, was nice enough to send me a copy of the article she wrote." He held up a familiar clipping. "I have to tell you that I was disappointed with it. It was more than our local weekly, the *Courier,* ran, but that was only because the *Courier* ran zip. I was expecting a lot more from Ms. Amato, based on the amount of time I made available to her and on the background work she'd done, which seemed damn thorough. When I read what the *Post* actually printed, I felt as though I'd wasted a lot of time on the project."

I might have said something conciliatory and vague about Amato's article being a teaser, the first in a series on the Lamberts. Instead I said, "Is the feeling you've wasted your time a reaction to the article or a flashback to the Lambert investigation?"

Ruba's shiny face darkened slightly. Then he smiled grudgingly. "You got that right. I wasted my youth on that mess. And I was lucky to get off so cheap."

"What do you mean?"

"Nothing, just talking to hear myself. I do that from time to time. And not because of the Lambert case. Believe it or not, I can go quite a while without thinking of that. I'm not saying I would have forgotten the anniversary if Ms. Amato hadn't called. But the old frustration is pretty much under control. Back in the seventies, though, it was a different story. I wasn't that far from being a rookie in those days. I still expected to solve them all. Since then I've learned to solve the ones I can and to let the others go. A cop has to learn that or else he loses it. In my own defense, it would have been hard to let the Lambert murders go, even if I'd been seasoned. A whole family murdered like that."

"Not the whole family."

"Right. I was forgetting the baby. She's college age now, I guess."

"You haven't spoken with her recently?"

"I've never spoken with her that I know of. Why would I?"

"She came to the paper yesterday to ask us to do a follow-up article on the murders. She's hoping they still might be solved."

"So that's why you're up here." Ruba shook his big greasy head. "The poor kid."

"Ms. Lambert said she'd spoken to the police about reopening the investigation and been turned down."

"She didn't talk to me," Ruba said. "And the DA's office is on the floor above us. If she'd been there, I would have heard about it. She has to mean the Atlantic City police. I'm not surprised that those guys showed her the door. They weren't much help back when there was still a decent chance of solving the murders."

"In fact, didn't you think they were actually protecting Conti?"

"You got that bit straight from Ms. Amato, I assume, because it didn't make it into her article. The Mafia angle, I mean."

"It made it in, but her boss took it out."

"Just as well. I was blowing off some very old steam when I said that. Still, it's what I believed happened. Either the AC cops were shielding Conti or some politician who signed their paychecks was. Not that there was any outright noncooperation. Just a whole lot of foot dragging and requests for duplicates of lost duplicates of lost paperwork. That sort of thing. Velvet-glove questioning of Conti and worse."

He paused, trying to decide whether to tell me what the worse thing was. He decided against it. "My partner, Patrick Derry, was convinced that he could get a confession from Conti if we could just get him away from the guys who were running his interference. That's why he pressured our boss, an old-timer named Myron Bass, into issuing the warrant. It was a gamble, but, after three years, we were ready to gamble."

"You didn't have enough evidence to convict Conti without a confession?"

"We couldn't have convicted him of trespassing on what we had. Not even with a jury of locals who thought people from New Jersey were only one step removed from illegal aliens."

"The Lamberts were from New Jersey. Were they illegal aliens to the locals?"

"Maybe they felt that way about George Lambert, but

not the rest of the family. Irene Lambert was a local girl. Her maiden name was Miles. Bob Miles, her father, was a big developer of vacation property after the war. That's how the Lamberts happened to own their cabin. They inherited it when Miles, who was a widower, passed away.''

''From natural causes, I hope.''

Ruba's brief smile was accompanied by a grunting sound. ''Not counting what happened to the Lamberts, natural causes is mostly what people around here die from.''

''You have accidental deaths, too. Samuel Calvert's son, for instance.''

''Right. Drunk driving in young Calvert's case. We've got way too much of that, God knows.''

''Nothing unexplained about the accident?''

''Nope. Straightforward case of teenager in pickup truck meeting an immovable object. An oak tree, I think it was. Nobody to blame for it but the kid himself, but that wasn't how Sam Calvert seemed to feel about it. He blamed everybody but Sam Junior.''

''Did you and Derry practice your third-degree treatment on Calvert?''

This time Ruba grunted without smiling. ''I assume you're using the term *third degree* loosely, in a generic kind of way, to mean all forms of interrogation. I assume you don't think we were using rubber hoses on people in 1970. I assume you're just referring to the kind of aggressive interrogation techniques that have always been a valuable part of police work.''

I assumed my interview would end dramatically if I said no, so I said yes.

''The answer is that we did question Calvert, pretty damn aggressively, and he held up under it. That old guy was one hard case. He had a drinking problem, which may have run in the family. A lot of times, drying a guy like that out will loosen his tongue. It didn't work with Calvert. The drier he got, the harder he got, like a bucket of cement. On the subject of the Lamberts, he was a slab of rock.''

''How about Gary Geist?''

''Just the opposite of Calvert, as far as our interrogations went. Geist was a blubberer, a real bag of bean dip. He was scared of me and terrified of Derry. Hell, he was even afraid to drink the water we set out for him. Afraid it was spiked with truth serum or something. Back in the seventies, a lot of people thought policeman was another name for storm trooper, but Geist had it bad.''

That didn't match the mental image of Geist I'd already formed. ''The picture we ran with the story showed Geist smiling away like he didn't have a care in the world.''

''Yeah, that picture really took me back to the old days,'' Ruba said, looking down at the clipping on his desk. ''Geist was a showman in front of the cameras, and he had that little flock of his snowed completely. Behind closed doors, he was an entirely different guy. When it came to maintaining his innocence, Geist was just as convincing as Calvert, but for the opposite reason: He broke down into such tiny little pieces. If there had been any guilt in the pile, it would have been easy to spot.''

Ruba's conclusion assumed that Geist had squandered all his acting ability on the news photographers. ''What about the bloody cross you found in the Lambert cabin?''

''It turned out not to be a very good tie to Geist, in spite of what the locals felt. None of them really knew much about the workings of the commune. They only knew they didn't like living near a bunch of hippies who smoked grass but never mowed it. They assumed Geist was a Jesus freak because he wore his hair and beard like the original. Geist's actual message didn't have much to do with Christianity or any other faith. If you ask me, the only thing those kids worshiped was a good roll in the hay. Geist always claimed

that the bloody cross was an attempt to frame him by someone who didn't know very much about his philosophy."

"Russell Conti?"

"Right. We figured it like this. Conti heard from George
Lambert that he'd had some kind of run-in with a religious
commune over a zoning issue. That's all Conti knows about
it, but it's enough to give him the idea of throwing suspicion Geist's way."

"What was the zoning issue?"

"Geist wanted to buy a property that adjoined his camp
and expand his operation. He needed a zoning variance,
and the community was organized against it. The Lamberts
were involved because Mrs. Lambert's father had been one
of the developers of Lake Trevlac. A lot of the landowners
looked to her and her husband for leadership.

"Look, Mr. Keane, motives like Calvert and Geist had,
which were pretty much just grudges, look good in a book
or a movie, but don't hold up in the real world. In my
experience, only two motives for murder are really de-
pendable: love and money. Russell Conti stood to gain financially from George Lambert's death. In fact, it was the
only thing that kept him out of bankruptcy court. If we'd
really gotten the chance to square off with Conti, we would
have gotten the bastard."

"But you never got the chance."

"No. Conti screwed us out of it. And he did it just hours
before we got things moving on the Jersey end. For me,
that's the only real mystery left about the Lambert case.
How did Conti know we were coming for him? Somebody
leaked it, but we never found out who."

"Somebody on the Atlantic City police? Is that the accusation you stopped short of making just now?"

"I wouldn't have put it past those guys to have slipped
the word to Conti, but you still have to explain how they
found out."

"They didn't know? You needed the Jersey cops to make the arrest."

"Right, but we were holding off telling them until the last possible moment, for fear of tipping Conti. And that did us no damn good. We ended up with a dead suspect and a suicide note that made it sound like we'd been leaning on the guy. If only we could have."

"So even if the AC police were protecting Conti, you still had to have a leak on your end?"

"Right. Pat alienated damn near everyone working on the case trying to find the stoolie. I did some hard looking myself, for a reason of my own."

His reason was easy to guess. "Derry even suspected you?"

"Yes. Because I'm Italian. Pat always saw things as pretty black and white, the dumb mick. Anyway, I never found the leak, so I never cleared myself in Pat's eyes. That was the last time we worked together."

Ruba's big hands searched through the papers on his desktop while his narrow eyes gazed into a spot in the buzzing air just above my head. Finally, after his hands had shifted their search to the pockets of his shirt, he looked down at them in surprise. The moment brought to mind Amato's search for a match, and that, in turn, reminded me of the way I'd half-considered her offer of a cigarette. "When did you quit smoking?" I asked.

"Too damn recently," Ruba said. "For a guy who looks like he's daydreaming half the time, you don't miss much."

Buoyed by that compliment, I decided to try another deduction. "When you said earlier that even a seasoned cop would have had trouble with the Lambert case, were you talking about Derry?"

"Yes. Pat had already chalked up twenty years back then, as a uniformed officer down in Scranton and a county detective up here, but all that experience didn't do him much good. He never could let go of the case. The trouble was, he didn't really go on working on it either. Pat was convinced that Conti was our man, so after the suicide he was stymied but good."

"What about the note Conti left maintaining his innocence?"

"Pat never believed it. I didn't either. We knew Conti was lying in the note about being hounded by the police, so it wasn't hard to figure the whole note as a lie. Pat saw it as a last swipe at us. He thought Conti withheld the truth as his revenge against us for tracking him down. We might have gotten him, or been about to, but we'd never have the satisfaction of being sure, of knowing for certain that we had the answer."

"If Conti was that clever, why didn't he plan a better murder?"

Ruba shrugged. "Whether or not Conti intended it, his suicide note hit Pat right between the eyes. He was never the same cop afterward, from what I heard. That's what I meant earlier about having to let go of a question when there's no knowing the answer. It's the only way to keep your head on straight."

I recognized the advice I'd given Barbara Lambert. It had probably sounded as useless coming from me as it did now from Ruba. "What happened to Derry?"

"He ended up taking early retirement. You'll never guess where he bought his retirement property."

"Lake Trevlac."

"Right," Ruba said, slightly put out. "I thought it was a lousy place for him to pick, sort of like Napoleon retiring to Waterloo."

Never one to quit while I was ahead, I made yet another deduction. This one was based on Derry's name being missing from Amato's list of contacts. "When did Derry pass away?"

"He hasn't. Not the man, anyway. The cop died in seventy-three."

"Do you have his address?"

"No. Ms. Amato had it. Didn't she share it with you?"

"Must have slipped her mind."

"Well, like I told her, you don't really need a house number or a street name to find a person in a little place like Lake Trevlac. Just ask around down there for Pat, you'll find him. I also told Ms. Amato that he probably wouldn't talk to her. Pat developed a real dislike for reporters during the Lambert case."

I wondered how he felt about phony reporters. It kept me from dwelling on the fact that Amato had held out on me.

"Anything else?" Ruba asked.

"You said your local paper didn't do an anniversary article. Why not?"

"Because the *Courier*'s not really local. It's one of half a dozen county papers owned by a company in Scranton. The only really local stuff they run are the ads for the Shop 'n Save and pictures of the Little League teams. The kid who runs the *Courier* probably never heard of the Lamberts. Most of the people who live around here now probably haven't. Hard to believe, but it's true."

I thanked the sheriff for his time and stood up.

He waved his newspaper clipping at me. "I've been meaning to ask, did Ms. Amato write this headline?"

"No," I said. "That was some desk jockey. Silly, isn't it?"

"Not to me," Ruba said. "To me, it's way too right. I've been looking over my shoulder ever since I read it."

SEVEN

ASKING FOR PAT DERRY at Lake Trevlac turned out to be more complicated than John Ruba had made it sound. The lake was large, to begin with, and the wooded hills around it had been subdivided into a number of little neighborhoods, each with its own tangle of winding gravel roads that dead-ended on the water. After wandering in and out of several tangles—and scanning mailboxes and bothering strangers—I spotted a small real estate office that also claimed to be headquarters of the Lake Trevlac home owners' association.

The A-frame building was staffed by two people, one of whom was teething. That individual was blond and chubby and strapped into a car seat perched atop the counter that - split the cabin's single room. She was chewing away on something resembling a dog biscuit, patiently reducing it to a grainy pap that ran down her chin. She paused long enough to give me a toothless smile that made my day. The nonteether was slightly less blond and a good deal less friendly. She smiled, too, but promptly undermined the gesture by getting up from her desk and walking over to retrieve the baby.

"Madison likes the view from up there," the woman said. "Don't you, Maddy?"

While she carried the baby to safety behind the counter, I turned to look out through the A-frame's picture window, which displayed half a dozen browning pine trees and my own dusty Cavalier. It didn't look like much of a view to me, but then I'd been around.

Blonde number two was back at the counter by the time

I'd tired of nature. She lost a lot of the interest she had in me when I told her I was after directions. I gave her Derry's name, and she searched for him in a large metal box crammed with index cards. While she searched, I waved at Maddy, trying to get the baby to wave back. At one point, she took the biscuit out of her mouth and dirtied her forehead with it, which I counted as a wave to keep our relationship alive.

"Mr. Derry's not in one of the lakeshore communities," the real estate agent finally said. "He's in Trevlac Hills, a more affordable area not far from the lake."

The low-rent district, in other words. "Could you point me that way?"

She took a photocopied map from a stack of photocopied maps and drew in my route with a yellow highlighter. "Eleven Trevlac Trail," she said.

The map showed the lake as a wavy outline roughly the shape of an arrowhead pointed due north. Each separate community on its banks was set off with heavy black lines that looked like aerial views of broad moats. Derry's neighborhood, a little south and east of the lake, had no symbolic moat. No need to keep the riffraff out of its own neighborhood, I thought.

"Which community did the Lamberts live in?" I asked.

"The Lamberts?" The woman repeated, reaching out for her card file.

"The family that was murdered in 1970."

Her hand dropped to her side. "Oh yes, right. Their cabin was in Northwood, I think. It was torn down a long time ago."

"Could you find the address in your records?" I was going to volunteer the names of the neighbors mentioned by Kate Amato in her article, but a cold front sweeping through the office told me not to bother.

"Our residents don't want that kind of attention," the agent said. "Northwood is our most exclusive area."

The old punch line "People are dying to get in there" came to mind, but I stopped short of speaking it aloud. Patrick Derry could give me a tour of the murder site, if I managed to find him.

I thanked the agent for her time and said good-bye to the baby. This time, Maddy really did wave her soggy biscuit at me. The biscuit didn't look all that bad, which told me that lunch was a real priority.

Unfortunately, I didn't happen upon any fast-food restaurants between the real estate office and Derry's neighborhood. The upper crust in Northwood probably wouldn't allow them. Without my copied map, I might have driven right by Trevlac Hills, as there was no sign at the entrance. The development's winding roads were covered in the area's standard gravel, though it seemed to have been replenished less recently than the stone in the neighborhoods I'd visited earlier. In addition to winding, the little roads did some serious climbing and descending. In a level stretch between a descent and a climb, I found Derry's cabin.

The log structure—set back from the road and fronted by a rutted crescent drive—was roughly the size and shape of a house trailer. Its gable roof was covered in wooden shingles that were themselves covered in moss. In one particularly thick patch, a pine seedling had taken root. The cabin's front lawn was less green than the roof. It was carpeted with pine needles and dead leaves and decorated with an overturned aluminum rowboat painted in a peeling camouflage pattern.

I sat in the Chevy for a while, listening to the ticking of the hot engine, or rather to the stillness against which the engine's ticking was audible. I was also experiencing the unsettling feeling of somehow remembering Derry's cabin, a place I knew I'd never seen before. It took me a moment to explain away the déjà vu—longer than it should have, given Tim Gleason's recent resurrection of the Carteret case.

Derry's cabin reminded me of one that had once belonged to Jim Skiles, a professional storyteller and resident of the New Jersey Pine Barrens. A professional character is what Skiles had really been, a self-styled combination of garrulous old hermit and shaman. It was to Skiles that I had tried to pass myself off as Gleason's relation when, at the editor's recommendation, I'd followed the Carteret trail to Skiles's retreat. The old hermit had seen through my act and had responded by stranding me in a haunted stretch of his forest. Later, we'd overcome that shaky beginning and become friends. Skiles had been an important person for me, one of the few who had taken my searching seriously. He was now out exploring dark mysteries himself, or so I liked to think. He'd made a joke to that effect before he'd died, consoling me in advance.

I climbed out of my car and stood in the heat of Derry's cluttered yard, remembering how Skiles had come out to greet me on my first visit as though he'd been expecting me. Derry evidently lacked that kind of second sight or else he'd used the forewarning to make himself scarce. After a few minutes of standing and remembering, I crossed to the cabin's door and knocked.

Seen up close, the cabin's logs turned out to be a veneer, thin strips of wood tacked onto the building's plywood siding. The plywood had once been painted white to create the illusion of mortar between the logs, but only a few flakes of the paint remained. One strip of log near the door was loose, and it vibrated each time I knocked.

That was the only response my knocking produced. No replacement sage appeared to lead me. Or to mislead me, as Skiles had sometimes chosen to do.

In my jacket pocket, I found an envelope addressed to me by my admirers at the electric company. I emptied the envelope, wrote my phone number under my address, and added the postscipt "Regarding the Lamberts." I slipped the envelope between the door and the frame at the height of the knob. Then I set out again.

EIGHT

THIS TIME I DROVE until I found a restaurant. Actually it was an antique ice cream stand in the town of Lake Ariel that had diversified to meet challenging economic times. I placed my order at a screened front window staffed by an earringed kid whose entire being radiated an intense desire to be somewhere else. I was surely radiating a fair amount of that myself.

The old stand's seating consisted of three picnic tables set in a grove of beech trees whose trunks were scarred with thousands of initials. I carried my hot dog, fries, and birch beer to the shadiest table. Its top was also decorated with generations of initials, professions of undying love, and other, less uplifting messages. I scanned the resulting mosaic while I ate, on the off chance that the Lamberts had once stopped there for frozen custard. It was also possible that the murderer's initials were somewhere in the tangle before me. Picking out a pair at random seemed as likely a way of identifying the killer as driving around asking questions. I decided to try it, scientific investigator that I was. I closed my eyes and waved my finger around in the air above the table, finally stabbing it down when the planets felt sufficiently aligned. Then I opened my eyes to confirm what my sense of touch had already told me: My finger had found a square inch of smooth, undamaged wood, miraculously preserved in the midst of the giant cipher.

"Of course," I said aloud, "the Nameless doesn't have initials."

My next stop was a nearby town called Gravity, where Kate Amato had interviewed Samuel Calvert's daughter,

Rebecca Topley. Mrs. Topley lived on the town's main street in a white Victorian cottage whose bright yellow gingerbread trim seemed almost fluorescent in the midday sun. A hand-painted sign hung from the roof of the front porch, advertising SCULPTURED NAILS. I had visions of ten-penny nails bent to form barnyard animals or stick-figure humans representing various professions and hobbies.

That deliberate misreading was dispelled by the appearance of Mrs. Topley herself. The hand she used to wave me into her parlor was adorned with very long, very pink nails. I spent so much time admiring them that I was sitting down before I really noticed the lady herself. She was in her thirties, I guessed, but I might have been guessing low based on her size, which was extremely petite. When she sat in an armless upholstered chair across from my sofa her feet didn't quite reach the hooked rug. She had a round, pleasant face touched here and there with faded freckles. Her eyes were a light blue that might also have faded from some more striking color. They came to life somewhat when she smiled at me.

I'd used my press card to introduce myself at Mrs. Topley's front door, and she was now misinterpreting the card and me at a brisk pace. "You're working on the same story as that Italian girl, Miss Amaro?"

"Amato."

"Yes. I can't understand why a girl that age dyes her hair. Do you? The story about my father is what I'm talking about, and how the Lambert business ruined his life."

I might have pointed out that the "business" hadn't done the Lamberts a world of good either if I hadn't still been reacting to the news that Kate Amato dyed her hair.

"That's the story I'm interested in," I finally said. "I'm here to verify Ms. Amato's research. If you don't mind re-covering old ground." By that, I meant reviewing what she had already told Amato, but Mrs. Topley took it to mean the murders in general.

"No, Mr. Keane, I welcome the chance. I'm not naive enough to think that my father's name will ever be cleared, not after all this time. But it's important to me to have his story told. When he's seen from the point of the view of the Lamberts, my father comes across as a drunken old hillbilly right out of the Hatfields and McCoys. The Calverts and the Lamberts—the Calverts and the Miles, I should say—might have had their little feud, but the fault was as much on their side as ours. And while my father had been reduced by circumstances to doing odd jobs, he wasn't uneducated or backward. He'd had dreams and hopes of his own. Too many dreams."

Sometime during those revelations I almost blew my cover as Kate Amato's trusted co-worker. Perhaps I'd blinked once too often or unconsciously licked my lips. When I asked about the feud between the Calverts and Irene Lambert's family, the Miles, Topley frowned.

"Didn't Ms. Amato tell you about that?"

I smiled. "My editor only gave me the outlines of Ms. Amato's story. Our method at the *Post* is to have a second reporter cover the story independently. Then the two compare notes." And fight it out in the alley, I added to myself. "We get different points of view that way, like the new view of your father you mentioned."

"Exactly," Topley said, pacified—for the moment at least. "That's the point I want to get across. Where should I start?"

She asked the question of the parlor in general, glancing around for the answer. I glanced around, too, noting that the room was decorated in layers of antiques. Ornate Victorian pieces with burl walnut inlays were covered in lace doilies that were themselves covered by china knickknacks and framed photographs. Mrs. Topley found what she was looking for next to a statuette of a fat child bending over to kiss a goose. She hopped up from her chair and went to retrieve the answer: a photograph of a smiling man in a soft-collared shirt and a bow tie. She sat down again, holding the picture on her knees facing me.

"This is my father, Mr. Keane. This is the way I remember him being before the Lambert business. Not all the time, of course. He had his disappointments, as I said. But with me, it was always smiles."

"What disappointments did he have?"

"As you know—or maybe you don't—the Calverts were a very prominent family in this corner of Pennsylvania. One of our ancestors was an officer on Washington's staff during the Revolution. He was wounded at Monmouth Court House, one of Washington's famous victories. My father's grandfather was a member of Congress and a judge in this county for years. He founded the town of Calvert, which used to be the county seat.

"There's a town named Calvert?" I asked. "Is it near Lake Trevlac?"

"Very near it," Topley said. "In fact, it's under the lake. When Robert Miles and his partners flooded Calvert Valley back in the forties to make the lake, they covered the town. Not that there was much town left by then. The county seat, along with most of the businesses and the people, had moved to Hartsdale when the federal highway was built. But Calvert House, the judge's house, still stood there. It was the largest brick house in the county once. Nowadays a house like that would be protected as a historic structure, but not back then. Robert Miles bought it and the rest of the town and drowned it."

"Why did your father sell? Or was it your grandfather?"

"It wasn't either one of them, Mr. Keane. The Calverts had some reverses after the judge died. Before he died, really, since he lost most of his fortune in the Panic of

1884. His son, my great-grandfather, lost the rest, including Calvert House. That's why my father couldn't stop Robert Miles, for all his trying.''

''The feud started when the valley was flooded?''

''Yes, but it wasn't really a feud, just hurt feelings. You can understand that. My father couldn't forget the glory days of the Calverts. He always thought that things would turn our way again, but he ended up a day laborer and the house he was born in ended up at the bottom of a lake. My father hated that lake, especially the name Robert Miles gave it, which was just a slap in the face to us.''

I thought of the lake's strange name, finally making the connection I should have made back at my desk at the *Post*. ''It's Calvert spelled backward.''

''Yes. My father hated having to explain that to new-comers, people who had never heard of the Calverts. If Miles had named the lake after himself, it would have been easier for my father to swallow. But the joke, the name Trevlac, always reminded him of everything that had gone wrong with the family and how the Calvert name was going to die with him.''

''After your brother was killed in the accident.''

''Yes.''

''What can you tell me about that?''

''I can tell you how it felt, which was like the world had ended. My brother Sam was seven years my senior. I started trailing along after him as soon as I could walk. After the accident, when I didn't have Sam to follow, I was just lost.

''It was even worse for Daddy. He'd given up hoping that he'd be the Calvert who would bring the family back. His drinking had seen to that. He'd moved all his hopes over to Sam. That might have been why Sam was a little wild, because Daddy loaded him down too heavy too early. But he was only a little wild. Nothing like some of the kids back then. Sam was just unlucky.''

"How did your father react to the accident?"

"You know that part of the story, I'm sure. You wouldn't be here otherwise. Daddy had too much to drink. He said some things he shouldn't have about the Lamberts because they didn't come to the funeral. Because they sent money instead. 'Miles money,' Daddy called it."

"Did your father actually say he'd see the Lamberts in hell?"

Topley turned the picture of her father away from me and wrapped her arms around it. "I knew you'd heard about that. It's the only part anyone ever remembers. Yes, it's true. I heard him say it myself. When he talked about being in hell and seeing all the Lamberts there, all I could think about was my brother Sam, burning forever. It made me so upset I was nearly hysterical for a time. I had to stay in my room. I was in my room when I first heard the news about the Lamberts. I was lying on the floor, listening at the heating register to a conversation going on downstairs. Someone had come to the house to tell my father about it. That was before the police came to question him for the first time.

"I forget how many times they questioned him. He always told them the same thing, that he didn't do it. I don't remember him ever saying he was sorry it had happened. I remember feeling bad about that. I think it would have helped Daddy with the police if he could have said it."

"Do you remember any of the policemen in particular?"

"Two of them, the two who came most often, I remember. One was a big man with curly black hair. A giant, he seemed to me. The other man was smaller, almost dried up compared to the giant. He seemed pretty old, but he might not have been. Every adult seems pretty old to a ten-year-old. I remember he smoked a lot and once he burned a hole in our rug. My mother was fit to be tied."

"Who did your father think killed the Lamberts?"

"I never heard him say. When he talked about it at all, he always made it sound as though they'd died in some natural disaster, like a tornado or an earthquake. An act of God almost."

"How about you? Did you think about who might have done it?"

Topley's faded freckles faded even further as she blushed. "I thought I could solve it. I tried to, in fact. Too many Nancy Drew books, I'm afraid."

I was familiar with a related condition involving the Hardy Boys. "Did you have any hot leads?"

"Not really. I just wore out the tires on my bike, bothering people and watching for strangers. The only local suspects the police had besides my father were the young people at the old summer camp."

"Gary Geist's commune."

"Yes. I pedaled out there half a dozen times to spy on them. But I never saw anything. I was too frightened of the place to get very close. My mother thought those kids were devil worshipers. Somehow, I mixed them up with the nightmares I was having about Sam being trapped down in hell."

"It must have taken a lot of courage to have even gone out there."

Mrs. Topley dismissed my compliment with a wave of her pink-tipped fingers. "I was driving over toward the lake just the other day and I was surprised to see the old camp up and running again. As a summer camp, I mean, not as a commune. I don't know who's running it now."

"I don't remember seeing the camp," I said. "Is it near Lake Ariel?"

"It's not on that road. It's on the shortcut between Gravity and Lake Trevlac. I can direct you right to it."

Listening to Mrs. Topley describe turns and intersections reminded me of the tour of the lake I'd hoped to get from

Pat Derry. When she'd finished, I asked, "Back when you were investigating the murders, did you ever bicycle to the Lambert cabin?"

"Yes. That frightened me more than the trips I made to the camp. The front of that cabin had two big picture windows that looked like eyes staring back at you. I wasn't sorry when they tore it down."

"Could you tell me where it stood?"

"I could show you on a map, I think. If I had one."

I had one, the photocopied map I'd gotten from Maddy's mother. I went out to my car to retrieve it, Mrs. Topley following me as far as her front steps. She spread the map out on a sunny stretch of her front porch railing.

"It was right there, I think," she said, fixing a spot on the paper with one of her fabulous nails. I half expected it to leave a pink mark on the paper. It didn't, so I drew a pencil X myself.

When I thanked Mrs. Topley, she waved at me again. "I'm sure Ms. Amaro took it all down correctly the first time. About my father being more than a drunken handyman, I mean."

If Amato had gotten Judge Calvert and the rest of the clan into her first draft, Gleason had red-penciled them, along with references to the Mafia and God knew what else. Not that the editing had really hurt Samuel Calvert. If anything, he seemed to me a more likely suspect now, a man who had lost his past and his future and might have seen the Lambert killings as an eye for an eye.

The biblical allusion made me think of a certain cross drawn in blood. "Was your father a religious man?" I asked.

"No," Topley said. "He found his consolation in other ways. I wish I could have solved the mystery for his sake. It would have made his last few years a little easier."

She could still provide that service for Barbara Lambert,

who had more than a few years of useless wondering ahead of her. I thought briefly and wistfully of palming Lambert off on Detective Topley and her trusty bicycle. If nothing else, the two survivors would surely have laid to rest the old family feud.

"Thanks again," I said and left.

NINE

CAMP PAUPACK'S FRONT GATE was open and unguarded, but I knew right away that beyond it someone was home. I could hear voices as I drove beneath the gateway's stone arch. So many voices, in fact, that they blended together and formed a continuing rush of noise like a waterfall, though in a different key. The source of the noise turned out to be a body of water at the end of the camp's short drive. It was a small lake supporting a wooden raft and edged with a sandy beach. On the beach and the raft and in the water between them were children, perhaps fifty, yelling like five hundred.

I parked the Chevy in the shade of a tulip poplar and climbed out to enjoy the show. I already felt tired and sweaty after a day of driving around in the heat, and those feelings only increased as I watched the children churn the sunlit water into a dazzling light show.

I might have nodded off, leaning back against the Cavalier in the shade, if my presence hadn't finally been noticed. A heavyset woman in an official camp T-shirt and cutoff jeans came around the back of my car and startled me into an upright position by asking if she could help me. The woman had red hair that would have gone well with Rebecca Topley's freckles, and glasses whose thick lenses were tinted blue. On her left arm, peeking out from beneath the sleeve of her shirt, was a tattoo of a rose.

I asked for the owner of the camp, and the woman indicated herself with a thumb pointed at her broad chest. "That's me, Beverly Simzack. I'm also the cook."

I introduced myself, mentioning the name of the *Post* in passing.

"You're the second *Post* reporter who's been up here," Simzack said. "The first was a young woman with black hair."

"Dyed," I said before I'd thought better of it.

Simzack wasn't surprised to hear it. "She asked about some guy who used to own this place and what had happened to him. I told her I didn't know, that I'd bought it ten years ago at a sheriff's sale for back taxes. I didn't ask too many questions about the previous owners. When you're taking advantage of someone else's bad luck, it's easier if you don't know them too well."

"Did the other reporter ask you about the Lambert murders?"

"Are you her supervisor or what?"

"We're thinking about a series of articles. The surviving Lambert child has asked us to reopen the case."

"Oh." Simzack hitched up her shorts. "To answer your question, your co-worker didn't really ask much about the murders. She asked how long I'd owned the camp and then left. She wasn't here but a minute or two. I know about the murders, of course. As soon as I moved up here, the locals started dropping pumpkin-sized hints about them. You'd think the killings happened here at the camp instead of over at Lake Trevlac. Not that it would have hurt my business if they had. These kids have all seen a dozen slasher movies set at summer camps. I think they come up here expecting to witness a murder or two at least."

She looked out toward the ringing water. "I'm afraid it would be old news for some of them if they did see something like that."

"Where are they from, Beirut?"

"Philadelphia, my hometown. I didn't grow up in one of the better neighborhoods either." She turned her arm over to display her tattoo. "But I came through it. Most of these kids will, too."

"Do you tell them the Lambert story around the campfire to scare them?"

"No way," Simzack said. "Maybe in another fifty years it will be aged enough for that. We tell them about the ghost of Chief Paupack coming back in the dead of night to avenge injustices committed against Native Americans. It's trendier."

"You can scare a city kid with that?"

The owner and cook laughed. "Get a kid away from electric lights, a kid who's never heard a cricket before, much less an owl, and you can scare him with *Hiawatha*. Take my word for it."

I did, shaking her large, moist hand before I climbed back into the Chevy.

It was only a short drive from the camp to the western shore of Lake Trevlac. I circled the lake to the north, until I came to its most exclusive neighborhood: Northwood. No one stood guard at its entrance either, but that's where the similarity to Camp Paupack ended. Certainly no echoes of happy children screaming their lungs out reached me. I didn't even have the crunching of my tires on gravel for company; Northwood's roads were paved in flawless asphalt.

My limp little map told me to follow the neighborhood's main road, Northway, down to the edge of the water. I did, passing "cabins" that would have been called mansions in my neighborhood. Some were either brand new or very recently remodeled in the curious nineties school of architecture that looked like Cape Cod mated with strip mall. Most of the cabins were older, though, and reflected the neighborhood's birth in the fifties. They were stone and unpainted wood, darkened with age, with flat roofs tilted at odd angles and windows that were bleak expanses of glass—dark glass in the shade of the heavily wooded lots.

When I spotted the water through the trees, I slowed the Cavalier to a crawl. All the properties along Northway were big—two to three acres at least—but at about the spot Rebecca Topley had indicated on the map I came to a gap between cabins that was unusually wide. I pulled over to the grassy shoulder of the road and switched off my engine.

I was listening for sirens or watch dogs as I got out of the car, but all I could hear was a motorboat out on the lake. A fisherman, perhaps, about to snag his line on the remains of Judge Calvert's fine brick house. At least the judge's house was still somewhere, though the somewhere was very damp. The Lambert cabin hadn't even been given a watery grave. It was simply gone. After all the years that had passed, it was difficult to guess where it had stood. I walked toward a little rise that seemed like the most likely spot, walking slowly through the ferns and weeds and making a wide detour around a hedge of wild blackberries. A slow, reverent pace was appropriate for the place in any case, and appropriate for the hot afternoon.

At the top of the rise, the ground was mossy and strewn with flakes of dark red stone, each the size of a dinner plate. I couldn't make out the outlines of a foundation or any surviving pieces of it, unless it had been built up from the red chips. Of the house proper, not a board or nail was visible. That left the invisible, the psychic vibrations, things to which I was singularly unattuned.

From the rise I got my first good view of Lake Trevlac. It was even bigger than I'd imagined and bluer than Camp Paupack's little pond. The far shore was a blue-green blur of wooded hills, but the distortion was due as much to the hazy air as the distance.

I stood gazing out at the peaceful water, thinking not of the Lamberts but of Jim Skiles, the Pine Barrens storyteller, and of the Carteret case. The idea of psychic vibrations had brought them to mind. I was reliving again the time I'd let Skiles talk me into a walk into the woods so I could see the spot where the Carteret plane had crashed. He'd wanted the atmosphere of the place as background to the ghost story he was telling me. I'd played along in the hope that the ground where the thing had happened would somehow slip me the missing clue, perhaps through a hole in my shoe. As it turned out, all I'd found in the forest was what I'd brought in with me, including the demons that had chased me out of the place.

Those demons were quiet on this sunny afternoon. Too quiet, Marilyn Tucci would have said. No brilliant insight into the Lambert murders popped into the resulting void inside my head. I was saying good-bye to Lake Trevlac when I heard a muted crashing sound coming from the trees to my right. I turned quickly—Skiles's ghost story still fresh in my mind—and saw a man walking in a straight line toward me.

It was an old man who didn't share my feeling of reverence for this stretch of woods. Not that he was moving quickly. His noisy progress was determined and dramatic, but very slow. He pumped his arms as he walked, occasionally swinging out at a branch or bush in his path with a stick he carried, but swinging so slowly that he barely moved the offenders out of his way.

When he saw that I had spotted him, he called out, "Stay where you are! Don't even think about moving!"

I almost laughed aloud at his warning. I could easily have walked to the Chevy, gotten my tire iron out of the trunk, and made it back to the rise before the old man had covered the thirty yards that separated us. That precaution seemed unnecessary, though, so I stood and waited to be captured.

As he drew nearer, I noted that he wore dark green trousers, carefully pressed but sprinkled now with several va-

rieties of clinging seed pods. His navy blue cardigan, worn
buttoned against the warm afternoon, was also liberally
covered. He had reached the age at which the shape of the
skull becomes a person's most prominent feature. His was
somewhat square, much longer than it was wide, and covered with white hair, brown spots, and blue veins in roughly
equal proportions.

"You're trespassing on private property," he said when
he finally drew near me. He stopped ten feet away, not the
least bit out of breath. "Don't you know that?"

"I know it."

"What?" The old man shouted back, raising the bulbous
head of his blackthorn stick to one ear.

I bit back another laugh. "Sorry," I shouted.

"You could have broken your fool neck. Then some rel-
ative of yours would have been after me faster than you
can say lawsuit."

"How was I supposed to have broken my neck? I'm way
past tree climbing."

"Look around behind you, wiseacre. No, over there by
the base of that dead pine."

I looked and saw a black hole in the floor of ferns. It
was about four feet across and unnaturally circular. "What
is it?"

"It's a well. Dug by hand in the last century. Early in
the last century. You tumble into that, you'll break your
neck without trying." He picked up a piece of rock and
tossed it toward the well. It landed short by a good three
feet. "Damn," the old man said.

"If you're worried about liability, why don't you fill it
in?"

"What?"

I shouted the question.

"It's a piece of history. You don't shovel dirt into a piece
of history."

No, I thought, in this part of the country you flood it.

"The well is from one of the oldest farms in Mason County. Belonged to an officer on Washington's staff."

"Name of Calvert?"

"Yes," the old man said, his dislike for me moderating somewhat. "You some kind of historian?"

"You could say that." Robert Miles had done more than drown a town and make a joke of the Calvert name when he'd built his lake. He'd also put his own cabin on the original Calvert homestead. Did Rebecca Topley not know that, I wondered, or had she been holding out on me? Her sensitive father had surely known.

My host was still on the subject of the old well. "The previous owners of the lot had the hole covered over with a wooden cap, but it rotted away," he said. "I haven't gotten around to replacing it."

"The previous owners being the Lamberts?" I shouted.

The old man slowly turned away from me to gaze in the direction he'd come. Then he turned back to me and took a few teetering steps my way. "Keep your voice down; my wife might hear you. I don't want her disturbed."

"You lived here then?"

"Yes. Now you'd better tell me who you are and what business you have on my land."

I told him my name.

"Keane? I don't know any Keanes."

That was understandable, given the local property values. I decided it wouldn't do to flash my press card at the old man. He might just call the paper to complain, which would be awkward. "I'm looking into the murders for Barbara Lambert, the surviving daughter."

My captor did another slow-motion turn in the direction of his delicate wife. "The baby?" he asked when he'd made it back around to me.

"Yes. Do you remember her?"

"I should. My name's Wirt. Ralph Wirt."

I remembered the name from Amato's article. "You're the neighbor who might have heard the gunshots."

"I heard them," Wirt said. "There was nothing wrong with my hearing back then. Heard them when I was getting in my car to go to our club. I just didn't recognize them. I thought it was some boat out on the lake. Or some kids playing with firecrackers. There was no reason for anyone to be shooting around here. It wasn't hunting season. Anyway, this land's all posted against hunting, has been since the lake was built. There's too many damn hunters in Pennsylvania. The woods aren't safe in the fall."

Wirt's bout of rambling was a black hole more obvious than his precious well. I sidestepped it. "Did you see anyone come or go that afternoon?"

"Not a soul. We never had a stranger come back in here, not before the murders. Afterward, we had nothing but strangers. Policemen crawling all over the house. Searching the woods for the gun—twenty different times, I bet—dragging the lake for it, too. They even tore the cover off the well and sent a man down. That's probably why the boards rotted away. Damaged, probably.

"If it wasn't the police bothering us, it was the reporters and photographers. And just plain gawkers. You wouldn't believe it, but people would drive here from all over the county just to see the cabin. It was so bad on Sunday afternoons that we had to post a security guard down at the end of Northway to turn them back."

"Is that why you tore the cabin down?"

"There wasn't anyone going to live in it after what happened. Bud Switzer, the neighbor on the other side, he and I bought the place and demolished the cabin. We split the land between us."

With the lucky Switzer getting the piece that didn't have a hole in it. I recognized his name: He was the neighbor who had discovered the bodies. "Does Mr. Switzer still live over there?" I asked, gesturing over my shoulder toward the next cabin.

"No," Wirt said. "Bud moved to Florida in 1980. Died in eighty-three. Brain tumor."

So much for my estimate of Switzer's luck.

"You'd better be moving along now," Wirt said. "We don't want to be disturbed."

He started to make another shuffling turn toward his cabin, but stopped early in the process, perhaps because I hadn't moved. I was intrigued by the old man's excessive concern for his wife's peace of mind. I approached the subject obliquely.

"Was your wife fond of the Lambert children?"

"No, she wasn't. She never liked the noise they made. We never had children ourselves, so we never got used to that part of children, the noise. The Lambert children were noisy. Very noisy." Wirt heard the stony echo of his words and added, "God rest them," to soften it.

"Now get in your car and go. And don't even think about coming back to bother my wife. I'm here every day and I won't permit it." He raised his stick again over the course of a long ten count. It was the slowest threat I'd ever received.

"Why do the Lambert murders still bother your wife so much? It's been twenty years."

"That's none of your damn business."

"In that case, I can't promise that I won't be back to ask her myself."

Wirt lowered his stick as slowly as he'd raised it. The veins on his skull had become its primary decoration, eclipsing the wispy hair and the age spots. "It's because of the little Lambert boy, Pauly."

"I thought your wife didn't like kids."

"Be quiet and listen. Pauly didn't die right away. He

bled to death slowly in a closet where he and little Ruthie had hidden. He was probably unconscious—a bullet had grazed his forehead—but he was still alive. If the shooting had been noticed earlier, if help had gotten there earlier, he might have been saved. But he wasn't. My wife blames herself for that."

"Did your wife hear the shots, too?"

"No. She heard something else."

Wirt's rounded shoulders were very rounded now. He held the head of his stick in both hands and rested his weight on it. He had to raise his head to glower at me.

"Bud Switzer discovered the bodies. He got home from fishing around six o'clock and heard the baby crying. So he walked over to see what was wrong and found the front door ajar. Irene Lambert was lying just beyond it. Bud called the rescue squad, but it was too late by then to save Pauly.

"That's what my wife heard that day: the baby crying. Edna listened to it for an hour at least before Bud came home, but she didn't do anything about it. It was just the noisy Lamberts, she thought, being bad neighbors again. She went to the phone half a dozen times to call Irene and complain, but she never made the call. That was Edna's way. She never spoke up when something was bothering her; she just stewed about it."

I didn't pick up right away on Wirt's use of the past tense, but I fell in step with it. "Why have you stayed here all these years if those memories bothered her so much? Why didn't you take her somewhere where she could forget?"

"Because I didn't know," Wirt said, shouting again as he'd done when he'd made his entrance. "Edna never told me. She kept the whole business locked up inside her. That's what she always did. Eighteen months ago, she had a mild stroke. There was no paralysis or loss of speech. No memory loss, either. Just the opposite of that. The stroke brought the Lamberts back to the surface for her. She started talking about them like they still lived over here.

''That's when I found out that Edna's blamed herself all these years for Pauly's death: eighteen months ago. It was too late by then to sell out and move away. We're too old to start over somewhere else. I can't do that for Edna. I can't. But I can protect her. I won't have you or anybody else questioning her about the Lamberts.''

"I won't bother your wife," I said.

Wirt tried to straighten himself as he looked around the forest, blinking back tears that embarrassed us both.

"Maybe Bud and I made a mistake when we split up the lot. Maybe if we'd built a new place and brought new people in, my wife could have forgotten the Lamberts.

"We did it for the peace and quiet. And now it turns out it's never been quiet. Not for Edna. All these years, she's been hearing that baby.''

TEN

I OFFERED TO WALK Wirt back to his cabin, but he didn't want me anywhere near the place. I left the old man teetering at the lip of his historic well, his stick holding him upright. I was almost that tired myself, but I had one more stop to make before I said good-bye to Pennsylvania.

I drove back to Scranton and headed south on Interstate 380. In just under two hours of nodding and searching the AM dial for ball games that had all moved to television, I arrived in a little city named Easton. It looked on the map as though Easton might be the high-water mark of the old industrial area centered around Bethlehem, so I expected to see the characteristic signature of a high tide: the jumble of odds and ends tossed up by the last wave, in this case boarded-up factories, stores to let, and prefab neighborhoods whose warranties had expired.

I found instead a going concern with a fast-food franchise on every corner and too much traffic on its hilly streets. I parked on one of them, a particularly steep street named Grinslade, the Chevy's parking brake groaning as it took up the strain. My space was directly in front of a one-story limestone building with grassy alleys on either side. The word INSURANCE was cut into the stone above the front door. I admired the carving as I paused to retie my tie, or rather I admired the confidence of the person who had been willing to chisel his or her hopes for the building into its stone. It might have been misplaced confidence, because the gold lettering on the front door read, BRUCE SOMERS, CERTIFIED FINANCIAL PLANNER.

Somers was the man I'd come to Easton to see. He was

identified on the list Amato had given me as "cult member." All twelve of Gary Geist's disciples were listed, but "Somers, Bruce" was the only name with an address next to it. He hadn't been mentioned in Amato's story, though, so he'd either declined an interview or been considered expendable by Tim Gleason.

Beyond Somers's front door was a small reception area whose air was cold enough to keep milk fresh. The air temperature matched the interior decoration, which was white on white. A young woman sat behind the igloo desk, poking numbers into a mammoth old adding machine. I toyed with the silly idea that she dated from the same lost time as the machine, that she was really a grandmother, miraculously preserved by years spent in the ice-box office. That wise use of my time left me unprepared for her "May I help you?"

I collected my thoughts and asked for Somers. The secretary looked first at a white wall clock, which showed that we were stretching the bounds of the business day, and then at the closed inner door before asking, "And you are?"

"A recent lottery winner, looking for a place to put my millions."

The old building had an old intercom system. It consisted of the frozen secretary getting up and crossing to Somers's door. She knocked and opened the door wide enough to lean her head through for a private conversation. The part of her still in the room with me was wearing a short, tight skirt, which wasn't white. I discreetly checked for goose bumps. Remarkably, none were visible.

I was checking the ceiling for icicles when the secretary reemerged and told me to go in. The inner office was larger and paneled in a deceptively warm-looking cherry. There was nothing warm about Somers's handshake, but his smile seemed genuine enough.

"You're the lottery winner?" he asked. "May I congratulate you on your disguise?"

He waved his cold hand in the direction of my suit coat. His own crisp pinstripe hung in a corner. His white shirt looked like he had just put it on, and his yellow tie was unmarked, except for its decoration of tiny tear-shaped dots. Somers had the kind of skin that looked shiny and dry at the same time. It was especially waxy on the top of his head beneath what remained of his brown hair.

"Speaking of disguises," I said, "don't you normally wear a white robe and sandals?"

"I beg your pardon?"

"That's how disciples dress, isn't it? Or did you call yourselves apostles?"

Somers smiled. "For me, the correct term would have been lemming. If you're referring to a certain episode from my youth, that is. What can I do for you?"

"I'd like to ask a few questions about Gary Geist. I believe you've spoken with a colleague of mine, Kate Amato. She gave me your name."

"She forgot to give me yours."

"It's Keane."

"Have a seat, Mr. Keane."

He pointed to a wing chair, and I sat down, barely making an impression on its icy blue vinyl. Somers walked around to the door and told the secretary she could finish her calculations in the morning. I wanted to see if she melted when she stepped out of the polar office and into July, but Somers shut the door securely before returning to his seat.

"I talked with your colleague on the condition of anonymity," he said. "It wouldn't do me any good professionally for my clients to know that I'd once spent a summer on a different astral plane."

I readily agreed not to publish Somers's name, having nothing in which to publish it.

"Is this for the same article?" He glanced down at a desk calendar that was the size of a family Bible. "The anniversary of the murders has come and gone."

"I'm approaching the story from a slightly different angle."

"Which is?"

"The surviving Lambert has asked us to identify the killer."

"You're kidding." He waited a polite moment and then said, "You're not kidding."

"No."

"Well, what should I say to that? Good luck? Don't look at me? The latter, I guess. If you're checking alibis, I can tell you that I was way too out of it that summer to pull off a perfect crime. Or even to be a reliable witness to one, God help me. I spent the month leading up to the murders shoeless and stoned, living in one pair of jeans that I washed in a little lake Geist owned. I had a change of underwear, but I was saving that for the apocalypse."

"You've come a long way since," I said.

"Too conformist for words, right?" Somers said, extending one arm so we could both admire a monogrammed gold cuff link. "This all represents a reversion to type, not a change of character. I grew up in the most normal, Ozzie-and-Harriet household you can imagine. I was a Cub Scout, Little Leaguer, Sunday schooler, you name it. Now I'm Ozzie himself. I coach the Little League and pass the basket at church. My life's a straight line with one little twist in it: Gary Geist."

"What brought you two together?"

"It was a girl I met at Lehigh University back in seventy. Betty Bartalow."

I thought Somers was going to sigh, but he managed to

hold it in. While he was picturing her, I slid Amato's list out of my pocket and found Bartalow's name.

Meanwhile, the drifting Somers had recaptured enough of his past to fall into its terminology. "I had the hots for Betty in no uncertain way, but not much hope of doing anything about it, with the spring semester ending and the two of us going our separate ways. Then Betty attended some lecture Geist gave in a campus coffee house. 'From Earth to End Time,' I think Geist called it, 'A Journey to Consciousness.' Unconsciousness is more like it.

"Anyway, Geist spotted Betty in the audience, which required only average eyesight, and invited her to come up to the Poconos for a summer of spiritual experimentation. She was afraid to go by herself, so she asked me to tag along. It meant trading my guaranteed summer job in my uncle's pencil factory for a slight chance of sex with Betty. Naturally, I went like a shot."

Somers paused to muse again. I said, "So what happened?"

"Between me and Betty? Aren't you afraid you'll shock your readers?"

"They're a pretty tough bunch, but I was referring to what happened between you and Geist."

"That part is more embarrassing than shocking. It embarrasses me, anyway, to remember how easily Geist handled me. I knew he was a con man from the start, but I figured the only thing he was after was Betty's body, same as me. That made us rivals, of course. Geist got around that by sharing her. Hell, he had eight women in his coven, and I figured he was bestowing his blessings on at least four of them, so he could afford to be generous. Share and share alike might have been the only philosophy Geist had. He was even more generous with his pot. That's how he really manipulated me, although I didn't realize it at the time. I'd tried marijuana once or twice at Lehigh, but I don't think

I'd ever gotten a buzz from it. At Earth, I perfected the technique."

"Earth?"

"That's what Geist called this broken-down old summer camp he'd latched on to somehow. That's where the 'Earth to End Time' slogan came from. He was supposed to be a mystic, waiting in his private microcosm of the planet for the end of the world to arrive, which, we gathered, would be any minute.

"That dream of the apocalypse was the secret of Geist's phony messianic appeal. He had his troop convinced that the world they'd grown up with was passing away. I almost fell for it myself, it seemed that logical. I mean, what teenager doesn't think he's the culmination of human history? I remember the feeling that an era, at least, was coming to an end. It may have just been a sense of my own childhood ending. Or it may have been a subconscious mourning for the dead sixties, the feeling that nothing could follow that crazy time."

"Disco did," I said.

Somers laughed an easy, prosperous laugh. "Right, but who knew that that was waiting in the wings? Or that we'd all survive to get old and fat and bald?"

"Even Betty?"

"Damn, I hope not." This time Somers actually did sigh. "Not that she would ever give me the time of day again. I turned out to be a lousy bodyguard. As I said, I thought that Geist only wanted sex from Betty, which seemed like a natural enough thing to be after. It turned out that Geist was also after Betty's money. Some rich relation had set up a trust that she could draw from. It was supposed to be for college. Geist had her drawing money out as fast as she could and passing it on to him. That came out during the police investigations after the murders. He'd been bilking several of the kids at the camp. The rest of us were just dress extras in his farce, although we didn't know it.''

"Did any of the victims have Geist prosecuted?''

"Not as far as I know. It would have been a hard case to make, since Geist never twisted anyone's arm. And it would have meant testifying in court about what we'd all been up to that summer. I know for certain that Betty and her folks didn't go after Geist. She seemed to blame me more than Geist anyway. I don't know that she ever really blamed him. Not even after the cops investigating the Lambert murders let us in on what a crumb Geist was. He had a police record, it turned out.''

"Any violent crimes?''

"No, only very nonviolent ones. Petty theft mostly. And some bunco stuff. I think he would have had a better chance of holding our esteem if he had been guilty of something serious. Bank robbery, say, or bombing a draft office.''

"Or murder?''

"Well,'' Somers said, suddenly less breezy, "maybe not that serious.''

"Could Geist have killed the Lamberts?''

"I don't think so. Geist's philosophy, such as it was, was pretty passive. He wasn't training us to go out and make the apocalypse happen. That would have meant getting our heads straight and keeping our pants zipped. As I remember it, we were all lying back, waiting for the end of time to roll over us like a wave at the shore.''

"What happened on the day of the murders?''

"I really don't remember it all that well. I was pretty far gone by that point. I was with Betty, I remember that. We were out in the woods behind the lake. It was our little spot. Only my head was so screwed up by then that I'd almost lost interest in her company.''

Somers had told me that his memories of the cult embarrassed him, but this was the first time he actually sounded embarrassed. "Do you believe it? Betty Bartalow having to ask me twice. More than twice, that afternoon."

I stepped on his next sigh with a question. "You weren't with Geist on the day of the murders?"

"No."

"Who was his alibi?"

"A couple of the others. Two of the women." I handed Somers my list of Geist's followers. He glanced at it briefly and handed it back. "None of those names looks familiar, except for Betty's and mine. Sorry. It was twenty years ago, remember. And we didn't use our real names at Earth. Geist gave us all nicknames. Adam got to name everything in the garden, and Geist claimed the same privilege. They were real seventies nicknames, too. Betty's was Sunrise. Mine was Stone. Probably short for stoned. Geist really had my number."

"How good do you think his alibi was?"

"I think it was the original junk bond. Geist took me into his sanctum sanctorum shortly after the police made their first visit and asked me to back him up. Specifically, he asked me to lie to the police about seeing him around the camp that afternoon."

"And that didn't make you think he might be guilty?"

"No. I figured he was just looking for a little extra insurance. He was convinced that someone was trying to frame him because of something the police found at the murdered family's place. It was a cross drawn in blood. But Geist never used a cross or a Star of David or anything like that. His symbol was omega." Somers drew an upsidedown U in the cold air between us, and I remembered the wooden ornament Geist had been wearing in the *Post* photograph. "Last letter in the Greek alphabet. It stood for the end of time.

"That little interview with Geist was a real revelation. I had him figured for a con man, but I still had a kind of screwy, adolescent respect for him. Who wouldn't respect a guy who could thumb his nose at convention *and* get Betty Bartalow into the sack? But that day, I saw how scared Geist was. And I saw that he didn't believe his spiel about the end of time. Not the littlest part of it. I should have been grateful, but I was disappointed.''

"Why should you have been grateful?"

"If Geist had believed his own line, I might not be sitting here now, late for a Rotary meeting. I've done a lot of thinking about Geist over the years, as you might expect. And I've read up on people like Charles Manson and Jim Jones. I've come to the conclusion that a con man is really only dangerous when he starts to believe his con. Then his followers can end up serving life terms in prison or guzzling poisoned Kool-Aid.

"Thanks to Geist being a total sham, I came through that summer intact."

Somers's rosy confidence was back. It irritated me. "The Lamberts didn't do quite so well," I said.

"Not because of anything that happened at Earth. I sincerely believe that." He all but placed his hand over his heart. It was probably the tone he used when recommending mutual funds.

"Do you have any idea where Geist is now?"

"Not the slightest. The murders were a wake-up call for me and the rest of the troop. As soon as the police let us, we all scurried home to our families. If the other eleven were like me, they stuck to the straight-and-narrow after that.''

Somers stood up and crossed to the corner where his suit jacket hung. "I never heard of or from Geist again." He put on the jacket, shot his sparkling cuffs out the sleeve ends, and buttoned a single button. "Sometimes, though, when I'm watching late-night television, I half expect Geist to come on. During the commercial break, I mean, selling miracle car polish or steak knives.''

He moved a step closer to the door and then waited for me to take the hint. I stood up. ''Maybe he'll be selling financial planning,'' I said.

Somers laughed his Rotary Club laugh again. ''That would be perfect. 'Buy short-term bonds. The end of the world is at hand!'''

ELEVEN

I GOT BACK in time for the best part of Atlantic City's day, the last few seconds of dusk. Sunrise is usually the big moment at the Jersey shore, given that the sun always sets way out west in someone else's ocean. Dawn on a clear day brings with it the sun's spectacular resurrection and the attendant illusion of pristine possibility. That same sense of an unspoiled chance comes to Atlantic City at dusk, when one by one the casinos burst into light against the deep blue of the approaching night.

The Chevy and I were swept across the bay bridge by that evening's shift of anxious gamblers. They weren't the most comfortable people to share a road with, dreamers who might be seeing each approaching headlight as a nickel spilling from a slot machine. As soon as we were on the island, I parted company with them, making a quick left into an old Italian neighborhood called Duck Town.

I was there to pay off my debt to Kate Amato. The easy part of the debt, anyway—the dinner out. She had given me instructions to meet her at a place called Cleo's. I had a sleepy vision of a storefront restaurant with checkered tablecloths and pictures of fighters named Rocky on the walls. Sinatra would be singing in the background. Or Jerry Vale or Eddie Fisher. I would be the second youngest customer in the place, edged out of the title—by no more than a generation—by my date.

I got the storefront part right. Cleo's was the first floor of an old corner building whose upper story featured a turret. The restaurant's front door was set into the corner of the building and it opened onto a barroom full of people and smoke and a peculiar noise, the nasal chatter of New Jerseyans in conversation. A canned singer was competing with them, but it wasn't Sinatra or anyone who could even spell Sinatra. I was the second oldest person in the place, edged out of the top spot by an old woman in a stiff black dress who was seated at one end of the bar. It was Cleo herself, perhaps, or just some customer they'd remodeled the place around.

A few seats to the woman's left, Kate Amato was waving at me. She was wearing olive green—a short, loose-fitting dress with no sleeves.

"You're late," she said when I was close enough to pick her voice out of the maelstrom.

I needed a shave and a fresh shirt, too. Put your best foot forward, that's my motto.

"What would you like to drink?" Amato asked.

I suppressed the answer "anything" and checked her glass. It contained ice and a clear bubbling liquid garnished with a lemon slice. A vodka and tonic perhaps or a wine spritzer or maybe even a club soda. Not much inspiration there, so I glanced down the bar. A few feet away, a waitress was accepting a tray from the bartender. The tray contained half a dozen glasses of what appeared to be different kinds of beer. What caught my eye were the containers themselves, each no bigger than a juice glass.

"If that's the size of their beers," I said, "the bartender and I are going to become well acquainted."

"That's a sampler platter. This place is a restaurant and a microbrewery. You know what a microbrewery is, don't you? You were a bartender once, weren't you?"

I'd also been an English major. I put my old analytical training to work. "A microbrewery is a place where they brew teeny-weeny beers."

My ignorance pleased Amato. "A microbrewery is a small, independent brewery. It may or may not have a restaurant or bar connected with it. It differs from a brew pub in that it brews enough to sell outside its own place, either at other restaurants or through package stores. I did a story on them last year. Do you want to try the sampler? It's everything they're selling today, from that black stuff, which is porter, on up to pilsner on the light side."

The bartender arrived toward the end of Amato's recitation. "A pint of something in the middle range," I said. "Try to match my eyes."

He went away unamused, but Amato was still smiling. She lit a cigarette and asked, "So, did you crack the case?"

"Twenty-year-old murders usually take me two days," I said.

"Sounds like we'll have to get together again tomorrow night."

My reaction to that was covered by the arrival of my pint. The unsmiling bartender had erred on the light side by bringing me an amber ale. It was very cold and surprisingly smooth for a beer that wasn't much older than my relationship with Amato.

That relationship was going alarmingly well. No trace remained of her resentment over my clumsy editing. On the downside, there seemed to be way too much of the strange element I'd detected during our chat on the roof: misplaced admiration.

I wasn't too tired to do some admiring myself. Amato's jet black hair looked like it had been carefully combed and then tousled lightly. She'd traded her giant, square glasses for small oval ones. The change de-emphasized her eyes, giving all her delicate features equal time. The frames were silver with turquoise arms, and these two materials were repeated in her earrings, which dangled down almost to her shoulders.

"You're thinking of a question," Amato said. "What is it?"

It was my all-purpose "What am I doing here?" but that didn't seem like the right note to hit. My sleepy mind groped for a substitute and came up with something worse by far. "Why do you dye your hair?"

Instead of taking offense, Amato laughed into her drink, a vodka and tonic, I now knew, having heard her ask the bartender for another. "It's a holdover from college. A lot of the kids I hung with dyed their hair. Either some crazy color like purple or orange or else black. Black for most of the kids who did it. A heavy statement about mortality by people obsessed with it."

"Why would anyone that young be obsessed with mortality?"

I was thinking of Barbara Lambert and hoping that Amato had an insight to share, but she mistook my question for a straight line. "Everything's life and death for a teenager, Owen. Don't you remember being one?"

"No. I've always been forty."

It was Marilyn's charge, and it brought her to mind, a spectacular example of bad timing. Amato was gazing deeply into my amber ale eyes. "I find that hard to believe," she said.

This time the maître d' provided the respite. He was wearing a yellow shirt liberally adorned with pictures of fish. A subtle advertisement for the catch of the day, I thought as I followed him and Amato into Cleo's interior.

The dining rooms had probably once been part of an apartment behind the original bar. We shared a small, narrow room with two other couples. The first pair was holding hands across the candlelight. The second couple was eating in silence. Two stages of romance, I thought as we sat down, the peak and the subsequent plunge. It occurred to me that Amato and I might be mistaken for yet another stage, the first date. That idea brought with it a familiar sensation of events sweeping past me in a blur.

As a way of slowing down the scenery, I tried to get us back on the subject of the Lamberts. "Why didn't you have Pat Derry's address on your list? John Ruba told me you had it."

"Yep. Got it from the district attorney's office, same as you ended up doing."

"I ended up going door to door. Why did you hold Derry back?"

Amato grinned. She was having far too good a time. "I can't do all your work for you, Owen. I left him off the list because the old fart wouldn't talk to me. He said it was because I was a reporter and he hated reporters. He might have talked to an amateur detective, though, which would have given you an unfair advantage."

"I see."

"Did he talk to you?"

"He wasn't home."

"Good." More grinning accompanied by more vodka and tonic.

"I thought we were working together," I said.

"I thought we were working independently and comparing answers."

"All right, let's compare. Who's your favorite suspect?"

Amato leaned back and stretched in her chair, raising one half-bare shoulder and then the other. "I don't have one. That's what makes the Lambert story so good. At the moment I was researching any one of those guys, that guy seemed like the one who had to have done it. Then I turned to the next one, and he seemed just as good.

"I've always hated that about murder mysteries on television. Nine people at a dinner party where somebody's killed, and all nine have a motive. What are the odds of that? I always thought it wasn't true to life, but here's the Lambert case with three decent suspects, all of them halfway right for the murders, but each of them wrong for a different reason.''

The waitress came by for our order, and I hadn't opened my menu. That turned out not to be a problem. Amato ordered chicken carbonara for both of us and another drink for herself. I was still nursing my first beer, afraid I'd fall asleep in a second one and drown.

"What's wrong about Conti?" I asked when the waitress had gone.

"His suicide. He'd be my suspect number one if it wasn't for that note he left. Why would a guy lie in his suicide note? Why would he give up his last chance to make his confession?"

To spite the police, John Ruba thought. That didn't seem like a good enough reason to mention. "How about Samuel Calvert?"

"His motivation is weak. So the Lamberts passed on his son's funeral and sent a few bucks instead. I mean, would even a crazy old drunk get that mad over a social slight?"

"What about the way his family history was erased by Irene Lambert's father?"

"Trevlac for Calvert and all that? More slights, Owen. Would you wipe out somebody's family if he named a lake Enaek? On the plus side, Calvert's synchronicity is strong.''

"Synchronicity?"

"The theory that unrelated events are somehow linked. If you want to talk about unlikely odds, what are the odds of the Lambert family being murdered within days of Calvert's son dying in that accident."

"It seems to have really been an accident, too," I said.

"I know. That's a shame. I was hoping the kid had known the Lamberts. I thought maybe they'd corrupted him somehow. Maybe even given him the fatal six-pack. That would have propped Calvert senior's motive up big-time. But there was no connection.''

I nodded in sad agreement, as though I'd thought of that particular angle myself. At the same time, I wondered why I hadn't.

Amato took out a cigarette, looked over at the other diners, and put it away. "Another thing in Samuel's favor is his knowledge of the area," she said. "He could have gotten to and from the Lambert cabin without being seen.

"That trick would have been tough for Gary Geist. He looked and dressed like the lead in a Passion play. Only with Geist, the passions were carnal. He'd be Hollywood's pick for the killer. He'd be my pick, too, if he hadn't turned out to be such a wimp. You want your crazy messiahs to be above things like alibis. Geist was given a short lease on the best podium any preacher ever had. He could have gotten any message he wanted into every paper in the country. Jesus Christ should have had it so good. And all Geist could do was play Peter and deny himself. A big disappointment was Mr. Geist.''

She took a fortifying drink before adding, "You would have done better in his place, Owen.''

I needed a drink myself after that, but my bottomless glass had finally run dry. "I'm not a crazy messiah. I'm a crazy copy editor.''

Amato shook her head. "You're a searcher after the truth, Owen, same as me. You wouldn't deny the truth to save yourself.''

"It's hard to say, since I've never found it.''

"You've solved mysteries. Tim Gleason told me.''

"That's not the same thing as knowing the truth.''

It was the distinction I'd tried to make for Barbara Lambert. Amato was even less discouraged by it. "That makes carrying on even more noble.''

I thought of Marilyn again, feeling that my infidelity had

been magically doubled. Not only was I there with Amato—which, to be honest, Marilyn wouldn't have given a damn about—but I was also letting the reporter praise my devotion to a quest that Marilyn had accused me of forsaking.

Fortunately, we'd arrived at a break in the embarrassment. Our salads appeared, and Amato fell into a series of reminiscences about her tight-knit, all-American family. I always enjoy family stories, and, as Amato was an animated and insightful storyteller, I enjoyed hers especially. I was almost wide awake when we finally stepped out onto the street outside Cleo's.

We had the halogen-lit corner all to ourselves. I offered Amato a ride home.

"You think I'm too drunk to drive?"

"You've had a few."

She stepped up to me and took hold of my lapels. "Young reporters play hard, Owen."

"That would explain the shortage of old ones."

"Don't give me any grandfatherly advice, please. It would spoil the mood."

Before I could ask what mood she meant, Amato drew me down by the lapels and kissed me. Like all her features, her lips were small. And, in the evening air, very warm. Any grandfatherly thoughts I'd had didn't survive the experience.

She released me, still grinning away. "We'll continue this conversation tomorrow night," she said. "Your place. Don't worry about the directions. I'll track you down for practice."

TWELVE

EVEN SMALL New Jersey cities have bedroom communities, places where the city's day shift goes to hide at night or, to take the historical view, places to which businesses and people fled when the host city started to die of old age. Atlantic City's death turned out to be temporary, but, because it returned to life as a gambling center, its bedroom towns didn't suffer from the comeback. On the contrary, they swelled with diehard AC residents disaffected by the changes gambling brought and casino workers who couldn't afford to live on the island.

Just across the marshy bay from Atlantic City was Pleasantville, biggest of the satellite towns, and north of it, Absecon, a community of large, old homes built around large, old country clubs. I drove to Absecon the morning after my dinner with Kate Amato. It was the tail end of the morning, as I'd risen late, my sleep untroubled for once by bad dreams.

I was in Absecon to talk with the last person on Amato's list: Grace Conti, widow of Russell Conti. I'd telephoned her first, expecting and maybe even hoping that she would signal an end to my investigation by refusing to see me. Instead, she'd sounded as though a visit from Owen Keane would be the highlight of her week.

I found her house on a busy street called Bannon near Bannon's intersection with the even busier Route 9, the old shore highway. Mrs. Conti's drive was blocked by an iron gate, so I parked in the street. The house had its own protection, a screen of large, full willow trees. Beyond them, I found an antebellum Southern mansion built to three-quarters scale. Two-story pillars supported the roof of a veranda that spanned the full width of the house. The veranda's floor was flagstone, and the house beyond was white brick discolored by whatever car exhaust the willows couldn't filter. Suspended above my head as I stood rapping the brass knocker was a wrought-iron carriage light half the size of a diving bell.

The door opened as far as its security chain permitted. The resulting narrow gap turned out to be the perfect frame for the narrow face that peeked out at me.

"Mr. Keane?" the woman asked. She then began nodding before I'd had a chance to say yes or no.

"I'm Grace Conti," she said as she unchained the door. "Thanks for coming over so quickly."

The greeting made it sound like our getting together had been her idea. So did her next line, which she delivered in her kitchen. It was a big room decorated with shining copper cookware on overhead racks and copper molds in assorted shapes that hung in groupings on the walls like family photos. A spotless brick hearth occupied one wall and a bay window was set into another. The window had been intended to light the breakfast table, but the architect's scheme had been foiled by the landscaper, who had ringed the window with dark fir trees.

Mrs. Conti sat me down at the table and poured me a cup of inky black coffee. "I've been anxious to talk to you people again," she said.

I winced as I sipped my coffee, either because of its bitterness or because of Conti's "you people," a reference to the *Post*. I'd weakened on the phone and gone back to the pretense that I was representing the paper.

"I knew you wouldn't be satisfied with that little article you printed," she said. "Your readers weren't satisfied, I'm sure. I wasn't satisfied."

"Why not?"

"Because it was just a restatement of the old lies and rumors. You want the truth from a newspaper." Conti emphasized her words by patting the table lightly as she spoke each one. She was a small, thin woman with silvery gray hair and eyes as black as her coffee. Her skin was exceedingly wrinkled, especially around her mouth, and it had a sallow cast. "I want the truth," she said slowly, patting out each word.

The way she sustained the word *truth* brought Amato's flattery at Cleo's to mind. My long night's sleep suddenly seemed all too short. "Do you know what the truth of the Lambert case is?" I asked.

"I know what it isn't," Conti said. "I know that an article that makes my husband sound like a murder suspect couldn't be true."

"He was a suspect," I said.

"Was is right," she said, slapping the table this time. "Was was was. But he couldn't be now. He died to prove his innocence. Because that was the only way he could prove it.

"I found the body myself. Right in this house. Right in my husband's study. I can show you the desk where he was sitting."

She stood up abruptly and led me back the way we'd come, through the first floor's center hall toward the front of the house. On one side of the flagstone entryway were closed double doors. Conti opened them as wide as her arms would reach. She entered the study first, crossing to windows protected by venetian blinds. When she raised the blinds, I noted that there was no dust visible in the shafts of light that lit the room. Nor was there any on the centerpiece desk, a dark, pseudo-Spanish piece whose edges were decorated with the heads of brass nails. The room's walls were lined with bookshelves, but they contained few books, and most of those were investment guides. The rest of the shelf space was devoted to pictures of Russell Conti. I scanned them, taking in his whole life in the course of a minute or so. Conti as a baby, a formally dressed child, an undersized but determined football player, an infantryman, a bridegroom. His bride was a beautiful young woman with striking dark eyes. Now she was the keeper of his museum.

She was standing with folded arms, her back to the light. "I was away when it happened, visiting my mother. That was the biggest mistake of my life. I should never have left Russell alone. Not with the police badgering him all the time. I'll never forgive myself for that."

"How were the police badgering your husband? I've been told they were having a hard time even interviewing him."

"That's their guilty consciences talking. They don't remember things the way I remember them."

There was no arguing with memories that had had twenty years to dig themselves in, so I tried another line. "I understand you were related to Frank Botticelli."

"He was my uncle."

"I've heard he was an influential man in Atlantic City."

"He was," Conti said cautiously. She gave me an insight into how she'd gotten at least some of her wrinkles by pursing her lips down to the size of a dime.

"Could your uncle have used his influence to protect your husband?"

"He didn't even like Russell. And I won't have anything bad said about Uncle Frank under this roof. I wouldn't even have this place if it wasn't for him. Russell only left me with bills and mortgages. Uncle Frank looked after me."

Until the warranty expired on his Cadillac. "Could he have been looking after you earlier by shielding your husband from the police?"

Conti considered that question carefully, as though it was the first time it had ever been asked of her. I thought I had her, but she eluded me at the last second. "He couldn't have shielded Russell. If he had, Russell wouldn't have had any reason to kill himself."

That brought us back to the dispute over Conti's motive for killing himself. "Were you present during any interviews between your husband and the police? Did you see them badgering him?"

"There are ways of badgering a person besides interviewing him. You can plant seeds of doubt about a person in other people's minds. Then wherever he goes, he sees the doubt in their eyes. He maybe even starts to doubt himself, if he isn't strong. Russell wasn't strong. That's why my family didn't like him. You had to be tough to get Uncle Frank's respect. Russell wasn't tough. He just wanted people to like him. And look where it got him."

She looked toward the desk where her husband had died. I did, too. It was my second visit to a scene of violent death in connection with the Lambert case. As I had on the shore of Lake Trevlac, I tried to detect some residual psychic dissonance. All I felt was the summer heat sliding into the room on the dustless shafts of sunlight. Certainly the desk and the area around it showed no sign that a man had once shot himself there. Or eaten there or napped there or even worked there.

"You said your husband didn't leave you with much. What about his company, Lambert and Conti?"

"Atlantic City Investments, you mean. Russell changed the name after he took the firm over. He wanted to call it Conti Investments, but he couldn't. Not after people's minds were poisoned against him. It didn't matter what he called it, though. The business all went away. The police saw to that."

"Wasn't the firm in trouble before the murders?"

"Some of the investments went sour, but they weren't all Russell's picks. George Lambert was no financial genius, let me tell you. The way he ran through his wife's money showed me that. But you'd never guess it from the stories in the papers after he died. Don't speak ill of the dead, they say. But that's never applied to Russell. He's still a murder suspect to you people. That's all he'll ever be.''

She started to cry then, large tears slipping down one after another across her sunken cheeks.

I asked her the same question I'd put to Ralph Wirt. ''Why haven't you moved somewhere where you're not reminded of everything that happened? Why have you stayed here?''

''I've been waiting for you, Mr. Keane.''

It was an answer that made me look toward the nearest door. Conti was talking too fast to notice how she'd frightened me. ''I've been waiting for someone who could help me clear my husband's name. Someone who can print the truth.''

''Why me? Why didn't you ask Kate Amato, the reporter who interviewed you for the anniversary article?''

''I didn't know then that I'd have to talk about this. I never dreamt that people would still suspect Russell. Not after his sacrifice.'' She looked at the empty desk again.

''What is it you'd like to tell me?''

''I have proof that my husband was innocent, proof he couldn't use when he was alive.''

''I'll be happy to listen.''

''I don't need someone to listen to me, Mr. Keane. I have a priest who does that whenever I ask. I need more than that from you. I need a promise—no, a guarantee—that the *Post* will publish a retraction of their lies about my husband. Print it on the front page. A front-page story that says he was innocent all along.''

''If you'll tell me what your proof is, I promise to present it to the paper's editors.''

"That's not good enough. You go right back and tell them my conditions. First they promise to run the story. Then I tell them the truth about my husband."

"I don't think they'll go for that, Mrs. Conti."

"Then they'll never know the truth. I'll be breaking faith with Russell if I tell you. He died rather than have this come out. For twenty years, I haven't told a soul. Not even my priest. Before I tell you, I need your paper's solemn, solemn word that it will restore my husband's good name. Its solemn word."

THIRTEEN

I DIDN'T KNOW whether the *Post* had a solemn word to give Mrs. Conti, but I knew someone I could ask. Tim Gleason would be in his own office, I knew, because he was always in his office, bricked in there by his successful career. The trick wasn't finding Gleason; it was finding him free.

When I arrived at the *Post*, Gleason was in conference with the graphics editor. They were discussing how best to present a diagram of the colon in connection with an article on cancer. It wasn't my idea of eavesdropping material, so I went to look for Kate Amato. That was strike two, Amato's cluttered desk being unoccupied. I was considering a climb to her smoking lounge on the roof when the graphics editor breezed by me with computer-generated colon maps tucked under one arm. I hurried back to Gleason's office, narrowly beating out a pressman who doubled as shop steward for the employee union.

"Owen," Gleason said, "I thought you were on vacation. Get tired of the beach? Or did you just miss us? You're welcome to edit copy until the feeling goes away."

"I haven't been on the beach," I said. "I've been looking into the Lambert murders."

Incredibly, Gleason had forgotten that he'd palmed Barbara Lambert off on me. I could tell he had by the frost his eyeglasses developed as he remembered. "Right, right. So, what's up? I really only have a minute, Owen. Actually I don't have a minute. Benson the union rep is waiting to tell me that we've been printing more commas than our last contract allows."

"I've just come from Grace Conti." Gleason blinked.

"Russell Conti's widow." Gleason blinked again. "He's the guy who killed himself just before the police could haul him in."

"Right," Gleason said, tapping the side of his head. "It's all tucked away in here."

Never to be heard from again, I thought. "She claims to have proof that her husband was innocent. She'll hand it over if we promise to run a retraction of the story naming him as a suspect."

"No shit?"

"None whatsoever."

"Damn. Wait a minute. How did Mrs. Conti even know you worked here? Didn't I tell you to keep the *Post*'s name out of this?"

"I must have mentioned it in passing."

"Uh-huh. What kind of proof is she talking about?"

"She wouldn't tell me. She claims that she's never told anyone. Not even her priest."

Gleason's thin lips twitched a little. I could tell that he was working out a joke. Something about how telling me a secret was the equivalent of telling a priest. Or perhaps that learning Conti's secret would put me one up on the real priests. Whatever the joke was, he decided not to use it. "What did you tell her?"

"That the paper probably wouldn't go for it."

"Allow me to be more definite. The paper *won't* go for it. Personally, I wouldn't promise to run a retraction if I had the proof in my hands and knew it was solid. I'd consider another story, but I wouldn't promise one."

"Why not?"

Gleason glanced toward one of the glass panels near his door. Beyond it, his next appointment was beginning to huff and puff. "I told you before that the story's already gotten all the play it deserves. It didn't draw much of a response from our readers. In fact, if you exclude the Lambert kid and Mrs. Conti, it got no response."

"I'm not surprised," I said, "given the cutting Kate's story took. There's a lot more to the Lambert murders than we printed. I know; I've retraced Kate's steps."

"Kate? You two are on a first-name basis? How did that happen? Last I heard, she was writing your obit."

"Why did you all but kill the Lambert story? And why are you so anxious to avoid a follow-up?"

Gleason looked toward his door again and then shrugged. "Sit down, Owen. I didn't want to have to tell you this. I don't want to tell you now, in fact, but if I don't, you'll just keep digging till we're all in trouble. It may be less dangerous for you if I tell you. You'll have an idea what you're up against, at least."

I sat down heavily, Gleason's sudden gravity being contagious. It had certainly dampened his characteristic jitters. His hands lay lifeless on his desktop.

"The *Post* had a good reason for downplaying the Lambert anniversary. There's more to those murders than you know. More than Kate Amato knows. Powerful forces are at work behind the scenes. Dangerous forces."

"The Mafia, you mean? Kate told me you'd yanked a mention of them out of her story."

"They were involved."

"Because Russell Conti had married into a mob family?"

"No. That was just a coincidence. Russell Conti was entirely innocent. But we'll never print that."

"Why not?"

"Because it would narrow the field of suspects and direct attention toward the real murderer. The cult leader."

"Gary Geist?"

"Right. Haven't you ever wondered how he managed to disappear so completely? The mob arranged that. Mr. Geist

is currently sleeping away in the cement of some big north
Jersey construction project. The goons who planted him
there were avenging the Lamberts, though they probably
didn't know it. They were carrying out a request made by
a certain highly placed Catholic clergyman who had ties to
a Mafia family.''

Gleason was leaning across his desk, almost whispering
his story to me. His delivery made me think of Camp Paupack, Gary Geist's old stomping grounds, where counselors
whispered ghost stories to city kids made gullible by the
hypnotic dance of a campfire. My skepticism finally kicked
in. ''Why was the Catholic Church involved?''

''Armageddon. Part of what I edited from Kate's story
was her detailed description of Geist's philosophy. He was
an end-of-the-worlder, Owen. And he wasn't just predicting
it or hoping for it. He'd found a way to make it happen.''

Gleason read my expression correctly and picked up his
pace. ''The key was the Lambert family. They were sacrificial victims. Geist had picked the location of his commune because of its spiritual significance. He'd identified
the exact date and time of the sacrifice from some ancient
texts. He needed six victims, the exact mystical number, so
he selected the Lamberts. At the precise moment of the
precise day, he performed the ritual killings. Only he
missed the baby. That little slip saved the world as we
know it today. But it's also why the true story can never
be told. Barbara Lambert has to be protected at all costs.
There's this slim chance that Geist's incantation is just on
hold somewhere, waiting for the day when the last victim
is murdered. If that were known, every headcase with a
death wish would be trying to bump her off. And the whole
world with her.''

He was almost lying across his desk as he finished, his
thin face barely retaining its grip on his bulging eyes.

I waited until his face had turned red from the strain. Then I asked, "No shit?"

"No," Gleason said, pushing himself backward into his chair. "Definitely shit." He started laughing then. It took him some time to get it out of his system. "Damn, Owen, I had you going for a moment. I really did. I almost blew it right at the start when I couldn't remember that Geist character's name. Luckily, you filled in the blank for me. After that, I was in top form. I thought about working the pope in and pointing out that the name Lambert contains 'lamb' as in sacrificial, but that would have been overkill. The great ones always hold something back."

"Why the fairy tale?"

"Why not? It's been a bad day, and I needed a laugh. Sorry, Owen. I know I shouldn't be yanking your chain. But damn, sometimes you ask for it. It's amazing. A yarn like that, you'll swallow. Half swallow, anyway. If I'd had more time to work out the details, I could have dragged you along all the way to the end. But if I tell you the real reason Kate's story got shrunk, the prosaic truth of it, you won't believe me."

"Try me."

"All right. Stop looking at me like I just backed over your puppy, and I'll give you the facts of life. The first is that there are only so many pages in a newspaper. The number is roughly proportional to the amount of advertising we sell. You've heard of advertising, right? It's what pays your salary."

"I've heard of it," I said.

"Okay. Now to fill our finite number of pages, we have to select from an almost infinite number of stories. You've heard the phrase 'slow news day' I'm sure. Let me tell you, they're few and far between. We don't have an airliner crashing every day or an assassination or any of the other man-bites-dog things that people equate with news, but there's always plenty happening. More than we could possibly squeeze in. So we flat ignore some things and edit others down to the bone. That's what happened to Kate's story on the Lamberts. It was a full-page article that got squeezed into a column and a half.''

I interrupted the lecture. ''On the same page as the Lambert story, we ran a feature on Christmas-tree farming. Why didn't you cut that?''

Gleason shrugged. ''Now we're moving from Journalism 101-type explanations into the grayer area of my personal philosophy. I happen to believe that one legitimate function of the features section is to counterbalance the negativity of the news sections of the paper. And don't think I'm saying that we should avoid the hard, important stories, because I'm not. My take is this: If we let the *Post* become too negative overall, people will stop reading it and we'll end up with nobody to tell the hard, important stories to. We can't suppress a real news story just because it happens to be negative, which, incidentally, most of them are. So we balance the negativity with features and comic strips and horoscopes and anything else we can think of.

''That's another way the Lamberts got screwed. As features go, their story was anything but positive, and on Sunday we really needed positive. Too much real life hit the fan last week. We had that tour bus accident out on the Parkway and the shootings at the basketball tournament on top of the normal run of minor crap. The balance was off. So the Lamberts lost out to the Christmas-tree farmer.

''That's the whole dark secret, Owen, honest. No pressure from the mob or the Boy Scouts of America or anybody else.''

I got up from Benson the union rep's chair. ''What should I tell Mrs. Conti?''

''Tell her to call Kate if she wants to pass along any evidence that doesn't have strings attached. And cheer up.

What I told you before still goes. Identify the murderer, and we'll run a Lambert follow-up. Even if the archdiocese turns out to have really been involved.''

I turned back at the door with my hand on the knob. ''Aren't you afraid a story like that will tip your balance the wrong way?''

''Don't worry. Liza Minnelli is coming to the Sands. With her we could balance Pearl Harbor.''

FOURTEEN

KATE AMATO'S ergonomically correct desk chair was still empty. I sat down in it and used her phone to call Grace Conti. The widow had told me earlier that she'd spent the last twenty years waiting for me to show up. Her vigil was still on, it seemed. She picked up on the first ring.

"This is Owen Keane, Mrs. Conti. I'm sorry, but I wasn't able to get the promise you asked for. The *Post* is interested in hearing your evidence, but they won't guarantee a retraction."

"Oh," Mrs. Conti said and hung up.

As a method of sticking to a bargaining position, it was very effective. I sat holding the receiver to my ear, inhaling a residual trace of Kate Amato's perfume and listening for clues in the dial tone. It slowly dawned on me that my investigation was over. With the two exceptions of Pat Derry and Gary Geist, I'd spoken with everyone I'd hoped to when I'd set out. I'd visited the murder site and, as a bonus, I'd stood in the very room where one of the suspects had scattered his brains. Nothing had come of any of it. I would have felt relieved if there hadn't been one last obnoxious duty hanging over my head: I had to call Barbara Lambert and tell her I'd let her down.

I dialed the number Barbara had given me, the one belonging to her cousin Joan. The cousin answered the phone, or so I guessed. Certainly the voice was too bright to be my client's. I asked for Barbara and then passed the minute or two that followed by examining the personal touches on Amato's desk.

The centerpiece item was a group photograph of a large

family with a younger version of the reporter seated at its center. Her parents, if the family was in fact Amato's, looked happy and healthy and all too close to my own age. The other children were all boys, which accounted for Amato's place of honor at the center. She looked safe and secure there, naturally enough. Next to the photo was a champagne cork. It was an innocent enough sourvenir, a reminder of a brother's wedding perhaps or a romantic evening. But it hit the wrong note for me, reminding me of Amato's drinking the night before. Her hard playing, to use her spin. I was still trying to reconcile the two items, the happy photo and the trophy cork, when Barbara Lambert came on the line.

"Hello, Mr. Keane," she said. "Owen, I mean. What do you have for me?"

"I'm afraid it's bad news, Barbara. I've been up to Lake Trevlac. I've spoken with everyone I could locate who has any connection with the murders. I haven't turned up anything promising. I think—"

"Wait, Mr. Keane. Please don't say anything else. I don't want to hear this over the phone. I'd like to meet with you again, please. I can meet you tonight. Anywhere you say. I'd come right now, but my cousin and I were on our way out. We're going to visit my family. They're buried in the Methodist cemetery in Pleasantville."

A cemetery near Atlantic City was the logical place for the Lamberts to be buried, but for some reason it surprised me. "I have to stick close to home tonight," I said. "Someone's coming over." By a strange coincidence, it was yet another woman half my age who had an inflated opinion of me.

"Where is home?" Lambert asked shyly.

"Mystic Island, a little town about half an hour north of Atlantic City."

"May I come there? I'll come early, I promise, and I

won't stay long. I have to talk with you face to face. Please, Mr. Keane.''

She didn't say I owed it to her, which would have been a bad strategy. She just sounded scared, which was an excellent strategy.

''Okay,'' I said. I gave her directions to Lake Champlain, my grand-sounding street, and said good-bye.

That left the rest of my afternoon free. I could have used the time to haunt the Conti residence in the slim hope of learning the owner's secret, but that property was so haunted already that I would have had to stand in line. I also thought about researching a question Mrs. Conti had raised, namely whether her husband's bad judgment or George Lambert's had really scuttled their business. I couldn't think of a way of finding the answer, though, so I settled on a third plan, which was to go home and hide.

I had plenty of straightening up to do at the house anyway, old newspapers and the physical evidence of take-out meals to collect, dishes to wash, laundry to stash. For the last two years, almost all my cleaning had been inspired by Marilyn's visits, so it was natural enough for me to catch myself thinking over and over that she would soon arrive. It was a misapprehension that gave the approaching evening the flavor of a French farce. I imagined Marilyn and Kate Amato and Barbara Lambert all arriving within moments of one another. In the time-honored tradition of the genre, I would then shuffle them in and out of the rooms of my little house, keeping each oblivious to the others until the climactic moment when they all came onstage simultaneously and I was undone.

My daydream was only slightly more ridiculous than what was likely to happen between Kate Amato and me if I didn't exercise some restraint. I told myself to seize the initiative with her, to use my gray hairs and her unfounded respect for me to my advantage and slow things down. This lecture was undercut somewhat by the fact that I was changing the sheets on my bed as I delivered it.

I KNEW THAT Barbara Lambert had a lot of visiting to do at the cemetery, but she was still much longer at it than I'd expected. The summer day was starting to fade when she finally knocked on my door. She was dressed in late-summer mourning attire: black slacks and a black blouse still marked with suitcase creases. There was no ribbon in her hair today, which gave her both an older and a more relaxed look, but she still had a bagpiper's grip on her long-suffering purse.

"I'm sorry to be so late," she said as she looked around my tiny living room for hidden guests.

"Relax," I said. "You're the first to arrive."

"I couldn't come right after the cemetery. I had to get myself back together first. That took a while."

"Does it always affect you like that?"

"No. I mean, there haven't been any other times. This was my first visit. I'm ashamed to admit it, but I've never really wanted to go before. I've always felt that my family, that they were near me. So going to visit the spot where their graves happen to be, it's never meant that much."

She checked my expression to see how well that explanation had gone over and then looked away quickly.

"Let's take a walk out back," I said. "I can show you my water view."

Fluffy wasn't in her yard across the lagoon waiting to harass us, but the woman who owned her was there. She was poking at some steaks that were sizzling audibly on a charcoal grill. The aroma or the activity had attracted a number of gulls, who sat in a row on the roof of the house behind the woman like extras in a Hitchcock movie. The presence of the birds might have explained the absence of

Fluffy. Any one of them was big enough to carry the dog off by its curly hair, an event I'd visualized more than once.

Through some trick of the evening light, the lagoon actually looked beautiful. We stood at the edge of the seawall, looking down at our reflections in the almost-still water. The reflections were spoiled by the arrival of half a dozen panhandling ducks, but not before I'd imagined I'd seen a wavering darkness about Barbara's image, an aura that hadn't been visible inside.

I was phrasing a question about it when she spoke. "This afternoon on the phone you were going to drop the case, weren't you?"

"Yes."

"That's why I wanted to come to see you. I thought it might be harder for you to quit if you had to look at me while you did it. Silly idea, wasn't it?"

To borrow John Ruba's phrase, the idea was way too right. I turned to face Barbara, which obliged her to do the same. She certainly had been crying, but it hadn't made her face swollen. It seemed drawn and even strangely aged.

"If it helps," I said, "I can tell you everyone I've spoken to and what they told me."

She shook her head. "Just tell me you've spoken with everyone and there isn't anything you still need to know."

"I can't tell you that. I haven't found Gary Geist, the only suspect who may be alive. I haven't done much to try to find him. And the wife of Russell Conti, your father's old partner, is holding out on me. I visited her this morning at her home in Absecon, and she tried to make a deal with me. With the *Post*, actually. She wants the paper to whitewash her husband in exchange for proof she claims to have that he was innocent. I couldn't sell the deal."

Barbara's eyes had brightened dangerously, so I added, "Even if she really has the evidence, which I doubt, it wouldn't tell us who murdered your family. It would only tell us that Conti didn't."

"But don't you see? The police were convinced that Mr. Conti did it. Once he was dead, they lost interest. If we can prove to them that he was really innocent, they might re-open the case."

"You can't count on that, Barbara. Not after twenty years."

"It's worth a try, Owen. Anyway, it's one more piece of the truth we can know. Isn't that worth going after? Isn't there some way you can persuade Mrs. Conti to tell us? Can't we trick her into telling us?"

A possible resource came to mind, one due to arrive at my door anytime now. Kate Amato might talk Mrs. Conti out of the secret by pretending to be the paper's official spokesperson. Better still, she might be able to twist Tim Gleason's arm until he agreed to some compromise version of Conti's deal.

"There may be a way of getting it done," I said. "But I don't know if it would be worth the effort."

To tip the argument her way, Barbara fell back, consciously or unconsciously, on the tactic that had worked so well for her over the phone. "I'm frightened, Owen."

"You told me that the day we met."

She nodded. "It's gotten worse since then. But it's more than just being afraid. I have this crazy feeling that the Nameless is nearby somewhere, watching me."

She actually looked around for it, so I looked, too. I didn't see anything out of the ordinary, but that was exactly what you could expect to see if the Nameless were closing in on you. My skin crawled empathetically.

"Did you pick that feeling up at the cemetery?"

"I think so. I guess that was all it was, the cemetery getting me down. I know I felt it strongly when I was standing by the graves. It seemed as real a thing as the headstones. As real as a hand on my shoulder. I thought the feeling would go away when I left the place, but it hasn't.''

"It will," I said.

It was the same useless advice therapists and counselors had given her all her life: It will go away. She came close to tossing it back in my face. Instead, she did something almost as dramatic. She reached out and touched my arm. "Help me to find out what Mrs. Conti knows. If that doesn't lead to anything, I won't bother you again. I promise."

"I'll see what I can do."

We walked back through my now-dark house. I intended to see Barbara to her car, but she turned to say her goodbye on my front step.

"I'll be fine," she said. "Don't worry about me."

FIFTEEN

I CERTAINLY would have worried about Barbara Lambert, if I'd had the free time. As it was, I hadn't even moved very far from my front door before my next visitor began banging on it.

"Scheduling your assignations a little tightly, aren't you?" Amato asked as soon as she'd stepped inside. "I got here in time to see the last shift leave." She was wearing a watered silk blouse whose color might have been called tangerine. It was untucked and so long that it almost covered her jeans skirt.

"That was no assignation," I said. "That was my client."

"Barbara Lambert? Damn. If I'd known that, I would have left you hanging on the line and interviewed her instead."

"You're here to interview me?"

"Of course. You still owe me the Owen Keane story. What did you think I'd come for—sweaty sex?"

While I was wording a dishonest answer, she slipped past me, coming so close that my modest living room felt even smaller, about the size of a hip pocket. She stopped in my dining room—the carpeted end of my kitchen—and looked around.

"*Très, très* ordinary. Where's the Persian slipper with the tobacco in it and the coal scuttle full of cigars?"

"I moved them down to the Bat Cave."

"Ha." Amato the smoker's mention of tobacco and cigars had a predictable effect. She pulled a pack of cigarettes from her purse. "Any objections?"

"No." The New Yorker who would have made them was gone for good.

"While we're on the subject of permission, is it all right to ask for a drink? Or will that get me another lecture on my boozing?"

"I don't remember the first lecture."

"You conveyed it with your furrowed brow." She tried to do an imitation, but she didn't have the furrows for it.

"Is beer okay? I have scotch, too."

"Great. We can do boilermakers. Only kidding, Owen. Beer is fine." She passed on my offer of a glass and raised her bottle in a toast. "To soul baring."

We then competed to see who could swallow the most beer in the first gulp. Inspired by the reporter's toast, I was an easy winner.

"So what's your story, Owen? Start with your birth in the log cabin."

"I thought the story you wanted was the solution to the Lambert mystery."

"That was my first choice. Why, have you solved it?"

"I've made some progress. But I need your help." As I told her about Grace Conti's proposition, I was conscious of having switched sides on the issue. To Barbara Lambert, I'd made the lead sound like the original dead end. Now, to keep Amato from deconstructing me, I tried to pass that dead end off as the key to the case.

When I'd finished my pitch, she handed me her empty bottle. "Interesting. It's definitely worth another trip to Absecon. I'll go tomorrow."

"Thanks."

She crossed to my refrigerator. "Mind if I help myself? You can keep count. Damn, Owen, are you collecting milk cartons or what? You've got one in here from June."

I shut the refrigerator door firmly, but slowly enough for the reporter to extract herself and her new beer. The operation left us standing very close again as I'd cleverly trapped myself between Amato and the kitchen counter.

She didn't yield an inch. "This Barbara Lambert, are you two involved?"

"No. She's way too"—I paused fatally and then said, "tall."

"*Young,* you were going to say, right? That's considered an advantage in most of the civilized world. So there's nothing between you two?"

"No."

"Any women of your own advanced age I should know about?"

"Not anymore."

"On the rebound, huh? That has its pluses and minuses."

Before she could tally them, I said, "There's another favor I'd like to ask, a question Mrs. Conti raised. You told me that Russell Conti ran the partnership into the ground, but Mrs. Conti claims that it was George Lambert's doing. Can you think of a way of double-checking that?"

"I already have. We happen to work for one of the great fact-checking institutions of our time, the daily newspaper. I asked Sid, our business editor, about it. Sid has a contact on the chamber of commerce who's old enough to remember the firm. This contact was an investment guy, too, an old competitor of Lambert and Conti. There was no doubt in his mind that Conti was the liability. Couldn't spot an investment opportunity if it pissed on his pants leg was how the old guy put it."

"The colorful old guy."

"Right." Amato took a step back from me just when I was getting used to her body heat. "What's left on the house tour? Billiard room? Sauna?"

She made a right past the refrigerator and entered the bedroom with the freshly changed sheets. The room was almost hot enough to double as a sauna. I'd resorted to trying my old window air conditioner, but it was putting out more noise than cool air. Amato walked over to the unit and switched it off.

"I actually do like my sex sweaty," she said.

"Huh," I said.

She slowly unbuttoned her tangerine blouse and dropped it to the floor. "Still feeling old?"

I was thinking old anyway. Amato wasn't wearing anything under her blouse, and my first reaction had been to marvel at how firm her breasts were. "I'm getting over it," I said.

I'D FELT unfaithful to Marilyn before, when Amato and I had only been dinner companions. Now, as she and I reclined on unfresh sheets, the guilt lay damp and cool on my skin. I asked myself why I hadn't used the fact of the Lambert case to reestablish contact with Marilyn. I was working again, however unwillingly. I was in a position to answer her charge that I'd given up. Or was I? If Barbara Lambert had spotted how much her mystery frightened me, I'd never hide it from the all-seeing Marilyn.

Amato broke into my thoughts by running a toe down the length of my leg. "Frankly, Owen," she said, "you're not as focused as I'd like you to be right now."

She wasn't exactly of a single mind herself. She'd already made a quick trip into the kitchen for another beer. The bottle was balanced on her flat stomach, and it was sweating away like everyone else in the room.

"Sorry," I said. "I'm worried about Barbara Lambert." I might actually have been worrying, subconsciously. The lie came that easily. "Remember telling me how some young people are obsessed with mortality? Barbara Lambert definitely is."

"Can you blame her? At her age, some people haven't

even lost a grandparent or been to a funeral. She's the sole survivor of a massacre."

"What's your excuse? Too many funerals in your recent past?"

"Are we back to my drinking? Or is this another reference to my raven tresses? I told you that was just part of a pose. The whole Generation X thing. You've heard of Generation X, I know. Our mutual employer just ran a big article on it."

I remembered the piece, vaguely. "You're the post-baby boom generation."

"The post-*you* generation." Amato softened the remark by running her toe down my leg again.

I made an effort to concentrate. "You're pessimistic about the future because my generation has grabbed all the good jobs."

"Something no one could accuse you of, Owen. Anyway, that's just the materialistic explanation of Generation X. The newspapers like to print it, but I don't like to read it. It's too simplistic. It omits the spiritual screwing over of my generation. That was worse than any financial hit we've taken. The boomers trashed all the old verities, the old morality, the mainstream religions. But they didn't come up with anything to take their place, unless you count their narcissistic materialism. They left people like Barbara Lambert and me out in the cold. In the dark."

"Sorry," I said, sincerely this time.

"This isn't about you, Owen. It's about your generation. You're the last person I'd blame." She sat up and gazed down at me earnestly. Hot as it was, I considered pulling up the sheet.

"When you described Barbara Lambert to me, I thought 'X-er' right away. Lonely, haunted, searching for a spiritual solace society can't provide. That's X-er all over."

"She's that way because she lost her family," I said. "Not because of her generation."

"A lot of us have lost our families, Owen. We're the children of divorce, of broken homes. Lambert's only an extreme example, not an exception. We're all searching just like she is. For families. For answers."

"For truth?" I asked, remembering how Amato had classified herself at Cleo's: "a searcher after truth." She'd politely put me into the same category. I began to understand why the reporter had acquitted me of my generation's crimes. And why she'd taken an interest in me. But I hadn't guessed the half of it.

"Do you like movies?" she asked out of the blue.

"Detective movies," I said.

"How about science fiction?"

"Not really."

"Then you probably don't know the Mad Max movies. They're set in some future time after a big nuclear holocaust. Mad Max is an ex-cop who helps people out. Mel Gibson played him. You've heard of Mel Gibson."

"Yes," I said.

"The gimmick of those movies is the cars people drive. There aren't any new ones. All they have are bits and pieces of the pre-holocaust cars. So everybody's driving around in these crazy, patched-together things. Part truck, part limousine, part hay baler. Can you picture that?"

I tried, coming up with something very like a Volkswagen I'd driven for years. "Got it," I said.

"Well, I think that's how my generation is spiritually. We're living in a postdisaster time, but our big bang was the death of the old beliefs. So we're each cobbling together the spiritual bits and pieces we come across and making our own wheels, like the survivors in the Mad Max movies. The chassis could be Judeo-Christian or Islamic or whatever, with body parts from Buddhism or Taoism or communism, you name it. For chrome work, there might be odds and ends like tarot cards or channeling or UFOs. The possible combinations are limitless. I have a friend who believes that God is the zone she gets into when she runs. Most of your generation couldn't begin to understand that.''

The implication was that I did understand the runner theologian. When I opened my mouth to deny it, Amato lightly touched my lips with the neck of her beer bottle, signaling that she had something important left to say. ''In the real world, today's world, I mean, the Mad Max character wouldn't be a crazy cop trying to single-handedly enforce law and order. He'd be somebody looking for a new system. For something new to believe in.''

Mad Owen. Amato seemed as embarrassed by that conclusion as I was. She made a performance of finishing the last half of her beer, throwing her head back and arching her spine to get the last golden drop from the bottle. Then she slid off the bed and switched the air conditioner back on.

After its initial throat clearing had settled down to a death rattle, I said, ''You're leaving?''

''Yep. It's no reflection on you. I just hate morning afters. Besides, I promised to stop by the paper to sew up my latest butchered story. Nothing you'd be interested in. Effective time management in the nineties.''

That speech covered the process of collecting her clothes as well as her exit to the bathroom. A little later, she was gone, after promising to tackle Mrs. Conti in the morning. She'd also paused long enough to give me a tentative, first-date kiss.

Effective time management in the nineties, I thought as I watched her drive off.

I sat down at the dining room table facing the sliding glass doors and watched for UFOs in the sky over my backyard. If I'd gone down to the water, I could also have kept an eye out for mermaids, but that would have meant a longer walk to the refrigerator. I finished one beer and plunged right into another. There were no minors around to corrupt now with a bad example.

While I drank, I compared Amato's Generation X thesis with the questions that Barbara Lambert had put to me: Why had something horrible happened to her family and why hadn't it happened to her? Kate's assessment of her contemporaries and Barbara's questions fit together so well that I suspected the two women had been corresponding secretly. Certainly Barbara's fears of a mindless, violent universe were ones that people had always countered with spiritual systems. It was Barbara's bad luck—one piece of her bad luck—to have been born in an age short on spiritual answers. Or an age that had too many, if Amato's very inclusive list was an accurate indication. A generation that could find God in astrology and oxygen deprivation was at least as resourceful as it was desperate. It consoled me somewhat to think that, if I failed my client, she wouldn't be carrying on her search alone.

I was planning another trip to the refrigerator when my phone rang. It was Amato. I wasn't given the briefest chance to imagine that she'd called because she missed me. Her voice was that metallic from the start.

"Owen, something bad's happened. Really bad. Barbara Lambert was involved in some kind of traffic accident in Absecon. I don't know the details. She was DOA at the Atlantic City Medical Center."

I was aware for a time that Amato was saying my name over and over, but it didn't occur to me to answer her. I was looking out toward the dock where Barbara Lambert had stood so recently, frightened and alive. Now she was dead. Tim Gleason's wild story echoed through my frightened mind, the tale of an incantation on hold for twenty years pending the sacrifice of the final victim. I set the phone down and walked out into the hot night, watching for the first sign that the world was coming to an end.

SIXTEEN

BARBARA LAMBERT'S death didn't end the world or even get it down. A beautiful weekend began the next day, its flawless blue sky as jarring to me as a pink or green one would have been. I woke from an hour's sleep with the worst hangover I'd had in years, a headache and an unsteadiness way out of proportion to the evening's few beers. While this flashback to my youthful drinking dragged on, a phrase ran around and around in my head like a bit of a song or a jingle. The phrase lacked the rhythm of a jingle, but it did have alliteration going for it: "an awful accident."

The little I'd learned over the phone from Kate Amato appeared in Saturday's Post in a section reserved for late-breaking local news. The entire story wasn't much longer than its headline: HIT AND RUN KILLS WOMAN IN ABSECON. There were one or two additional details. The accident had been witnessed by Barbara's cousin, Joan Noll, who had been seated in Barbara's parked car. She'd watched Barbara start to cross busy Bannon Street in the middle of the block. Seconds later, she'd seen her cousin struck down by a large blue car that seemed to Noll to have come from nowhere. In place of useful facts, like the make and model of the car, the story gave the number of feet Barbara's body had traveled through the air—twenty-five—and the dehumanizing detail that her shoes had remained at the spot where she'd originally been struck.

The little article had no byline, but I was fairly certain that it hadn't been written by Amato. For one thing, it didn't mention Barbara's connection to the murders at Lake

Trevlac. A subsequent article might, if Barbara rated a subsequent article. Nor did the *Post* speculate on Barbara's reason for being on Bannon Street, which Amato had surely worked out. I had managed it even before I'd hung up on the reporter. Barbara had gone there after Grace Conti's secret. Either she hadn't trusted me to get it or she'd been too impatient to wait. Perhaps, in addition to sensing the presence of the Nameless, Barbara had foreseen that she was running out of time; perhaps sensing the Nameless was the same thing as running out of time.

My own time seemed limitless because I couldn't think of a single useful thing to do. I tried calling Joan Noll in Ventnor City, but her line was steadily busy. Noll had surely sat outside my house during my last interview with Barbara, supporting her cousin as she had in the cemetery. That explained why Barbara hadn't let me walk her to her car. She'd admitted to being frightened, but she hadn't wanted me to know how true the charge had been.

In between calls to Noll, I made equally frustrating ones to Grace Conti. In place of busy signals, Conti's phone gave me endless unanswered rings. I was soon tired of the phone and of my house. As on the evening before, too many women were coming and going, although now, like Marilyn, they only came and went in memory.

Joan Noll wasn't listed in the phone book. Barbara had given me her cousin's unlisted number, which might be worth having if Noll ever hung up her phone. In the meantime, it meant that I couldn't even visit her. I drove instead to an address I knew—Grace Conti's. I wasn't discouraged by the widow's failure to answer her phone. I saw that as a new tactic in her ongoing negotiations with the *Post*. Those negotiations were about to break wide open. I was going to do my own lying and promise Conti anything in exchange for her secret. It was too late for the secret to bring Barbara Lambert peace of mind, but I wanted it anyway. Perhaps for my own peace of mind.

Bannon Street had recovered from the accident. The traffic was heavy and schizophrenic: One lane was backed up from the Route 9 intersection and the other carried escapees from that highway still traveling at highway speed. I parked as Barbara and her cousin had done, on the opposite side of the road from the Conti house, and paced the shoulder looking for some trace of the accident. I found surprisingly little. An *X* was chalked on the pavement under the fast-moving lane of traffic. It was already well on its way to being erased. A few uncut diamonds of headlight glass lay in the gutter at my feet, but I couldn't tell if they'd come from the car that struck Barbara. Broken headlights had to be common on a street that took so little notice of a death.

I'd intended to cross Bannon at the point marked by the chalk *X*, but somehow I'd drifted a little to the west by the time a break in the traffic came. That act of cowardice led to another discovery. In the road near the far curb I almost stepped on the remains of a highway flare. The bit of gutted tube was stuck into the pavement on a pointed metal tip like the business end of a nail, and it made me think of a spent votive candle. I pulled it out of the pavement before I stepped onto the safety of the curb. As physical evidence, the flare was perfectly useless. That might have been why I felt brave enough to pick it up.

I put the bit of flare into my pocket when I rounded the weeping willow trees and saw a stranger on the porch of Mrs. Conti's house. He saw me at the same time and took his hand from the brass knocker. He also turned to face me, a move that forced me to finish my walk to the veranda.

I said hello when I was on the first flagstone step.

"Hello, Mr. Keane," the stranger said.

I froze at the sound of my name, and the stranger smiled. He was well under six feet and stocky, except for his arms, which were as thin as they were hairy. They hung limply from the broad, short sleeves of his burgundy dress shirt. The shirt was open at the neck, displaying more black body hair. The man's gray slacks were textured polyester and his black dress shoes had toes as pointy as cowboy boots. His head was slightly less pointy. It was the only part of him that wasn't doing well in the hair department. The stubborn tuft centered above his heavy brows and dark eyes had all the earmarks of a last stand.

"Nervous?" the man asked.

I finished the climb to the veranda but stayed close to the top step. "This morning I am," I said. "How is it you know my name?"

"Lucky guess. Mine's Fruscione. I'm an investigator with the Atlantic County prosecutor's office."

It was the same job John Ruba and Patrick Derry had held in a different county and a different state and a very different time.

"The young woman who was killed out there on Bannon last night," Fruscione said. "Her cousin told me that she'd come here to talk with a Mrs. Conti. The cousin also told me about visiting you last night. I was going to stop by to talk to you. You saved me a drive."

"Did the cousin also describe me?"

"She must have," Fruscione said.

I was too polite to point out that Joan Noll and I had never met. I was more interested in the investigator's reason for being there. Fruscione's boss was the top law-enforcement officer in the county. The prosecutor's office would take a leading role in any big case. A murder investigation, for example. But they wouldn't bother with a hit-and-run.

A newspaper bound up with a rubber band lay at Fruscione's feet. He rolled it over with the pointy toe of one of his shoes. The paper was the latest edition of the *Post,* the

one containing the description of Barbara's accident. It
didn't hold the detective's interest for long. He turned to
rap the knocker again. "Mrs. Conti doesn't seem to be
home. What were you going to talk to her about?"

He had to know that answer already, so I improvised a
substitute. "I was going to ask her if she drives a big blue
car."

That produced another lazy smile. "She doesn't. Doesn't
drive at all—I checked. Must be the only adult in New
Jersey without a license. It was a Lincoln Town Car, by
the way. The Absecon cops showed Ms. Noll some pictures
this morning and she picked it out. So did another witness,
a driver waiting to pull off of Nine. Probably an eighty-
eight or an eighty-nine Town Car. It was a flashy shade of
blue that Lincoln only offered those two years. Jersey
plates, maybe."

"Headed west," I said.

"Right. You knew it had to be west because of the traffic
pattern. Eastbound traffic gets too bogged down by the
Route Nine light to hurt anybody."

Actually, I'd known the car had been heading west because I'd wanted it to be heading east. Barbara had turned
west onto Bannon herself. If the car that hit her had been
eastbound—if it hadn't been following her—it would have
made it that much easier for me to believe in the "awful
accident" mantra that was still running through my head.

I had the unsettling feeling that Investigator Fruscione
could hear that mantra clearly. "Why would anyone want
to kill her?" he asked.

"No one would."

"Nothing in it for anybody. She wasn't an heiress or
anything."

"No."

"No. And there couldn't be a connection to those murders in the Poconos all those years ago."

"It doesn't seem possible," I said.

"I remember when they happened. I was ten. It stuck in my mind. A family being killed off like that."

I waited for him to add that the case had inspired his career choice. To help him along, I said, "And you recognized Barbara Lambert's name when you heard about the accident."

"Nope."

His tone said, "Guess again," so I did. "Do you specialize in old, unsolved murders?"

"Someone seems to think I do. Walk with me a ways."

He stepped past me off the porch and started up the drive. I fell into step beside him.

"What do you specialize in, Mr. Keane? You're not a licensed private investigator. You're not an investigative reporter or any other kind of reporter. Just what is it that makes you so fascinating?"

"Who finds me fascinating?" I asked. I was studying our feet, struggling to match his short, irregular strides. When I looked up, the detective was no longer smiling his lazy smile. I noted that he had a face made for not smiling. It was a heavy face, and it appeared to be slipping downward. The movement was led by his heavy eyelids, which had drooped noticeably. When we were abreast of the sheltering willows, he stopped walking and turned to face me.

"This Lambert woman must have seen something in you. She trusted you to solve her family's murder. She didn't go to a licensed PI, which would have been just a hair smarter. She didn't go to the police."

"She did try the police. The Atlantic City police. They turned her down."

That seemed to be news to Fruscione. He thought about it and shrugged. "Twenty-year-old, unsolved case. What did she expect?"

"A little empathy?" I asked.

"Empathy? That's like sympathy right? Only different."

"It means understanding another person's feelings."

"Huh. Is that what she got from you—empathy? Were you two fucking kindred spirits? More to the point, what did you get from her? Did you take money from her?"

"She didn't have any money."

"You sure?"

"Ask her cousin."

"Maybe you were after sex. Would her cousin know about that? A girl that young and vulnerable, she'd be an easy mark. You sleep with her?"

"No."

"How about Kate Amato?"

"What?"

Fruscione didn't answer me. His eyelids had slid down even more, so much so that he had to tilt his head backward slightly to see me.

"You didn't get all this background from Joan Noll," I said. "You got it from Kate. She called to tell you that this might be more than a standard hit-and-run. She's the one who described me to you."

"In pretty serious detail."

I fought an urge to swallow and asked, "You and Kate are friends?" Even as my questions went, it was a stupid one.

Fruscione stopped short of hitting me for it. "We're talking about *you* and Kate."

"What about the woman who died here last night?"

"She died crossing the street. In the dark. In the middle of the block. Wearing black, for Christ's sake. She was asking to get hit. It had nothing to do with any murders in Pennsylvania. It most especially had nothing to do with any article Kate wrote. Anyone who tries to fill her head full of that guilty shit is going to answer to me."

"Where is Mrs. Conti?"

"How the hell should I know? She's at the hairdresser maybe or sunning her old bones at the beach. Wherever she is, I'm going to find her. I'm going to prove to Kate that Conti's deep, dark secret is no more than a lonely old woman's sick imagination."

"I'd like to know that for sure myself," I said.

Fruscione didn't believe me, which meant that Kate hadn't told him everything about me. And probably not all that much about us. I decided to call his bluff.

"Let me know when you find Mrs. Conti," I said as I started down the drive.

"Where do you think you're going?" Fruscione demanded.

"To console a reporter."

SEVENTEEN

KATE AMATO had made a big deal of finding my house in Mystic Island, but, as we worked for the same company, it really hadn't been much of a feat. To track her down, I called the *Post* and talked to its one-person Human Resources Department, a woman named Gilbert and nicknamed Gibby. She began by telling me that she was giving up her Saturday to clean off her desk and not to do favors for me. Her words were forceful enough, but her enunciation of them was stilted, leading me to deduce that she had a cigarette in her mouth. I could even smell it, an example of the power of suggestion or part of my phone booth's subtle charm.

"I need Kate Amato's address," I said.

"She's not in the book?"

"This booth doesn't have a book. I'm going to report it as soon as we've finished."

"So what am I, Information? Is this business-related or personal?"

I'd found that the best way to lie to the Gibbys of this world was to tell them the truth and count on their contrary natures to reject it. "It's personal. She left a garter at my house last night."

"Sure she did. A pup like Amato wouldn't know what to do with a garter. She'd wear it as a choker probably." Gibby then started laughing or coughing, or both. When she'd finished, she read off Amato's address and hung up.

I ended up back in Duck Town, the Atlantic City neighborhood where Kate and I had dined together. I parked very near Cleo's, there being no competition for spaces early on a Saturday afternoon, and searched for the reporter's apartment on foot.

The apartment turned out to be the upper floor of a double. That is, the tall, skinny house would have been half of a double if a matching bookend house had stood next to it. Its neighbor was actually a vacant lot, which gave the surviving house an incomplete and even forlorn air, like a widow sleeping on one side of a double bed, carefully preserving a space that would never again be occupied.

I changed my analogy from widow to widower when the front door of the house was opened by a little man who smelled like the phone booth I'd just used. His gray hair was thick with dandruff and his matching gray glasses were trifocals. He couldn't seem to decide which section of the lenses was right for viewing Owen Keanes. I duplicated his head movements in an effort to keep my eyes on his, and we stood nodding at each other for a moment like a pair of toy mandarins.

When I asked for Kate, the little man gestured toward a staircase. The stairs were steep with shallow treads that encouraged climbing on tiptoe. I could hear music coming from somewhere above me. I didn't recognize the music or even the instruments playing it. One of them might have been a sitar, but I wasn't sure, being decades past my own sitar period.

The stairway ended at a dark, heavy door that was also the source of the music. I knocked and waited and knocked again. In the middle of the third or fourth cycle, Kate opened the door. Her hair was tousled, as usual, but not artfully, and her slender face looked puffy. She wasn't wearing her glasses, and their absence gave her an undressed quality in spite of the oversize work shirt she wore. The impression might have been a flashback to the only other time I'd seen her without her glasses: when she'd been lying naked beside me. Inspired by that memory, I reached out to touch her arm. She stepped away before I could make contact.

"Come in, I guess," she said as she backpedaled. "Get you something?"

Her own pale pink something was sloshing around in a carelessly held wineglass the size of a small fishbowl. Her offer was more of a challenge than a politeness. To avoid an argument, I said, "Okay."

She left me alone in the little parlor, which overlooked the backyard of the house and, in the distance, the casinos. Out in the yard, washing hung on a line. With the glistening casinos as background, the washing seemed so dated that it looked unreal, a prop in some historical theme park. Kate's parlor had the same quality. I'd have guessed that she'd have furniture as modern as her hair, and perhaps as black. Instead, the pieces I could see were old and overstuffed. Somebody's grandparents' furniture. My grandparents' furniture. It had probably come with the apartment, but that didn't explain why Amato had chosen to live with it.

The only modern thing in the room was the stereo, which was still filling the dusty air with unidentifiable music. I looked on the stereo for a CD case but found only two photographs in a single folding frame. They were portraits of the adults from the family shot I'd seen on Kate's desk at the *Post*. Her parents, if I'd guessed right.

The reporter returned, carrying a second goblet. I'd never know what kind of wine Kate was drinking. Mine was a completely new color, a watery yellow.

"Killed the first bottle," she said, tossing down yet another gauntlet that I declined to pick up.

"I met a friend of yours just now," I said. "His last name is Fruscione. I didn't get his first name."

"It's Joe. How'd you two hit it off?"

"Not real well."

She nodded. "Joe's old-fashioned. He thinks he and I are going steady."

"I got that impression."

"Did you come by to complain?"

"I came by because Joe said you were pretty upset about Barbara Lambert."

Kate crossed to the enormous sofa and sat down, tucking her thin legs beneath her. "Joe wouldn't say 'upset about.' He'd say 'fucked up over.'"

I walked to the sofa's opposite end. I tried to sit down lightly on the edge of the cushion, but the old sofa wouldn't hear of it. It pulled me in like an affectionate aunt who turns a peck on the cheek into a bear hug. "He said you thought your article had gotten Barbara Lambert killed."

"The synchronicity is strong. Remember me telling you about synchronicity? It's one piece of chrome on the spiritual junk heap I drive around."

"The theory that unrelated events are actually related somehow?"

"In this case, the events aren't even unrelated. I dig up an unsolved massacre, and, a week or two later, the only survivor is dead."

"Not because of your article."

"Precisely because of it, Owen. Here's the chain. I write the article. It brings Lambert to the *Post.* She meets you. You tell her about the secretive widow Conti. She crosses Conti's street in the middle of the block and dies. Synchronicity."

"Why not go further back? You didn't come up with the idea for that article. You drew the assignment. You might as well blame Tim Gleason for what happened."

"I'm not talking about blame, Owen. That's too medieval. I'm talking about connections, relationships, influences we can't understand. Besides, I wasn't assigned the Lambert story. I came up with it myself. That is, Joe mentioned it to me. He's been interested in the case since he was a little kid. He told me the anniversary was coming up. I looked into it, and it stirred something in me. It was something I had to write about.''

That accounted for Fruscione's eagerness to explain away Barbara's death. He wanted out of the chain of guilty connections Kate was forging. He thought he'd escape by proving the death had been an accident, which suggested that he understood synchronicity even less well than I did.

''What exactly attracted you to the story?'' I asked.

''Barbara Lambert did. That's why I was so jealous of you getting to meet her. She and I should have come together. We seemed to be connected from the start.''

''Kindred spirits?'' I asked. Fruscione had taunted me with a variation—''fucking kindred spirits.'' Now I understood why the concept had bothered him so much.

''Something like that,'' Kate said.

''Because she'd lost her family?''

''Yes.''

''Your parents have divorced, haven't they?''

Kate's glass was empty, but she put it to her lips anyway. Her question came out of it like a voice from a pit. ''Joe tell you that?''

''You told me last night. You said your contemporaries are the children of divorce.''

''I only recently made the grade myself. A year ago, about. Almost on the nineteenth anniversary of the Lambert killings. More synchronicity. Turns out that your parents' divorce is like the chicken pox. Easier to get through when you're little. My brothers have all gone a little nutty over it. They've fired off in all directions like pieces of a bomb. They've left me to feel alone and sorry for myself, the way I imagined Barbara Lambert feeling.''

''She was mostly scared,'' I said.

''Of your Nameless monster? Who wouldn't be?'' She

took another sip of nothing. "You were supposed to save her, Owen. When she showed up and fell in with you, I thought it would work out for her. You'd answer her questions and she'd live happily ever after. I wanted that for her, which, considering how closely we're linked, was pretty selfish."

She set her empty glass down on the floor. "But you didn't save her."

Leaving her kindred spirit without any hope of a vicarious happy ending. "The Nameless wasn't driving that car," I said. "What happened was an accident."

"Keep telling yourself that."

I set my untasted wine down on a coffee table as nicked and scarred as a gym floor. "Guess I'll head out."

"Sorry to disappoint you, Owen. Next time you decide to offer your manly shoulder to a sobbing maiden, you should call ahead to see if she wants it. Save you a drive."

"It was even worse than that," I said from the doorway. "I came by because I feel like sobbing myself. I thought consoling someone else would be a way of getting past it."

"Sounds like the con I tried to work on Barbara Lambert," Kate said. "She had the last laugh."

EIGHTEEN

THE NEXT DAY I had visitors. They arrived by sea, or rather lagoon. I was seated on my dock, going through the motions of a Sunday morning. The Sunday *Post* lay in my lap, its many sections and inserts still in their original order. In my right hand was a cup of strong coffee. Across the water, Fluffy was serenading me. That's how I thought of her yapping that morning, as music. Perfectly normal background music for a perfectly normal day. I hadn't lost a client. I'd never heard of Barbara Lambert or Lake Trevlac or even Kate Amato. If I sat perfectly still and let the yapping fill my head, I could almost make it work.

The horn of Harry Ohlman's boat broke the spell. The boat was still several docks away, chugging down the lagoon at idle speed, but the blast had been loud enough to make me spill my prop coffee on my prop paper. The horn was a good match for the boat, which was also big and loud. It was a cabin cruiser, white with dark red trim, and Harry, who prided himself on his sense of humor, called it the *Velvet Noose*. The *Noose* was twenty-eight feet long and slept six, which meant it had four more beds than Harry's immediate family would ever need.

The other half of that family, Harry's daughter, Amanda, almost nine, stood on the boat's sloping bow, a coil of rope in her hand, her sturdy legs spread wide for balance. She was very tanned, and her hair, which had developed a tendency to darken during the winter, looked now like it would be blond forever. When she waved at me, her smile eclipsed her golden hair.

Harry took the *Noose* past me and turned the boat

around, executing a nautical K-turn in the narrow lagoon. The maneuver ended with the boat's fat plastic fenders kissing the side of my dock. Amanda threw me the bow line and then ran for the stern of the boat. I had no idea how to tie the line, so I passed it around a cleat on the dock and held it there while Amanda secured the stern line. Then she patiently showed me how to tie what she called a hitch, ending her lesson by kissing me lightly on the cheek.

"Hello, Uncle Owen," she said. She asked if she could use my bathroom and then ran off.

The title of uncle was honorary, and Amanda had lately taken to omitting it from time to time, which gave her use of it now a fragile quality. A man who had to be shown how to tie knots couldn't expect to be held in awe, I told myself as I watched her disappear inside the house.

Harry, who seldom held me in awe, climbed down onto the floating dock to inspect Amanda's work. He was a big man, and the dock listed a little under his weight. "Ready to catch some fluke?" he asked me.

"Sure," I said.

Harry had his own coffee cup and a matching Thermos. His cap and tennis shorts also matched, both being a brilliant white. Between them, Harry wore an untucked cotton shirt cut like a maternity dress. For an office worker, he was quite tanned, almost as brown as his daughter.

"How was the trip down?" I asked.

"It was a little rough getting through Barnegat Inlet, but that part of the trip is always like being flushed down a toilet. The ocean part was smoother. You forgot we were coming, didn't you?"

"Yes," I said. "Don't tell Amanda."

Harry laughed lightly. "There isn't much Amanda misses. Where's she gotten off to? She could have used the head on the *Noose*."

"She's visiting her mother, probably," I said. Amanda

never came by without spending a little time with the portrait of Mary Ohlman that hung in my living room. Harry had drawn it himself shortly after his wife's death and at the start of his brief career as an artist. The little pencil sketch, a snapshot of intense love and loss, was the best thing Harry had ever done.

"Do you want to skip this?" he asked. "You already look green, and we're standing on the dock."

"No," I said. "I'd like to go." The outing would fit in perfectly with my plan to lose myself in an ordinary day. Or so I thought.

"Are you working on something?" Harry asked. Amanda got her sharp eye from her father.

"Yes," I said. "I'll tell you about it later."

"Bad?"

"Yes."

Amanda returned, carrying the keys to my house, my sunglasses, and an old baseball cap. "I locked up," she said, handing me the keys. She then passed over the sunglasses and the hat. "These are for the sun. You don't need a lunch—we brought extra."

"What wasn't I supposed to tell her?" Harry whispered.

I boarded the *Noose*, Sunday paper and all, while Amanda cast off the lines. She sat next to me in the stern as Harry slowly negotiated the maze of lagoons that led to the bay. After donning a baseball cap of her own, pushing her blond ponytail through the hole in its back, she read me the *Post's* comics, inventing voices for all the characters.

When she'd finished, I asked her about a mark on her arm, a blue outline in the shape of a dolphin. "Tattoo?"

"It's just a rub-on. I've had it for a while, though. Dad thinks I might be stuck with it."

Without turning his head, Harry said, "She got two hits

in a softball game the day she put it on. She won't wash it off till the season is over."

Yet another spiritual system, I thought.

When we cleared the last lagoon, Harry advanced the throttle and the bow of the boat rose out of the water. Amanda buckled her life jacket and ran forward to enjoy the motion of the *Noose* skipping across the bay swell. Each skip produced a burst of spray that split the sunlight into a misty rainbow. I sat admiring the phenomenon until a gust of wind carried the spray inboard, soaking me. I moved forward to join Harry in the cockpit.

I asked after his father, who had suffered a stroke.

"He still can't walk or do much for himself," Harry said. "He's talking again, but it's just nonsense stuff about a bunch of people I've never heard of. We couldn't make sense of it until his sister came for a visit. She said the names belonged to people who lived on the street where Dad grew up in Boston seventy years ago. Quay Street. I don't know what brought all that back to the surface. Dad talks about this one guy, a fishmonger named Shauncey, like he saw him yesterday. Meanwhile, he's just about forgotten me."

I told Harry I was sorry to hear that.

"It makes me wonder what I'll entertain the nurses with when I'm in a home," Harry said. He gave me a familiar, sidelong glance. I guessed that he was afraid his nursing-home rambling would be about the mysteries we'd chased after when we'd been undergraduates together in Boston.

To comfort him, I said, "You'll talk about Shauncey the fishmonger, too. He's found immortality in the Ohlman subconscious."

Once we were out in Great Bay, Harry set course for the point where the old cannery stood. The haunted cannery, Amanda and I called it, a collection of burned-out buildings that the next hurricane would flatten. We came close enough to the point to identify one pile of rubble as a fallen water tower. Then Harry shut down the engine and let us drift.

I declined Amanda's offer to bait my hook. When she'd finished hers, she deserted us again for her perch on the bow. Harry said, "What have you gotten into now?"

I stalled for the length of time it took me to add a live keely to the sliver of squid already on my hook. At least the keely was alive when I began the operation. By the time I'd finally gotten the hook pushed through it, the little silver fish was dead, perhaps of exasperation over my faint-heartedness. Harry, in contrast, slipped his hook through his victim's gills so resolutely that the keely came through the ordeal with no more than a slightly puzzled expression.

When our lines were in the water, I told Harry the whole story, leaving out only my visit from Kate Amato.

"That's spooky," Harry said. "The Lambert woman's terrified by the idea of a random malevolence, and she's killed crossing the street. Hard to get more random than that."

"It's almost like the random evil she feared so much was correcting its earlier mistake," I said.

"A mindless force that corrects its oversights would be a contradiction in terms, Owen. Or does logic even apply in your cases?"

"I'm always open to a new approach."

Amanda reappeared to show off a sand shark she'd caught. It was two feet long and had glittering golden eyes. She removed the hook under Harry's supervision, freed the shark, and left us again.

"How are you feeling about the accident, Owen? Pretty bad, right? If I know you, you're figuring it was your fault for encouraging her in the first place."

To escape Harry's effortless reading of me, I said, "Ac-

tually, the accident happened because a couple named
Amato got a divorce.''

"You'll have to explain that."

I did, drawing Harry away from my guilty conscience
and into the briars of Kate Amato's philosophy. We ended
where Kate and I had begun, with Generation X. I discovered that Harry wasn't fond of the concept.

"They probably call it Generation X because that's the
only way most of the members can sign their names. What
do they teach these kids in school? It can't be history if
they think they've got it tougher than anyone who came
before them. They can't be studying much literature either.
Didn't Fitzgerald call his bunch the lost generation?''

"It was Hemingway, I think."

"Whoever. I know it was because of the First World
War, a hell on earth this Generation X crew doesn't give a
damn about."

"Neither did we, when we were protesting Vietnam."

Harry grunted. After we'd fished for a while, I said, "Toward the end of his life, your friend Hemingway decided
that every generation is lost one way or another."

Harry allowed himself to be swayed by that authority.
"You've got to feel a little sorry for kids who have to turn
their heads into topiaries to get a rise out of their parents.
All we had to do was let our hair grow over our ears. I
remember Dad's reaction to that. He could have had his
stroke then and there."

Cheering broke out in the bow. Amanda had caught our
first fluke, an ugly, doormat-shaped fish. While her father
dealt with the trophy, she put an arm around my shoulders.
"Who's Kate?"

"You been eavesdropping?" I asked.

"When the wind was right."

"She's a woman I work with."

"Watch out, Owen," Harry said. "Amanda's recently

become a matchmaker. She'll have you engaged in no time.''

"Right, Daddy." Then to me she said, "Well?"

"Well what?"

"Do you like her?"

"Yes."

"Does she like you?"

Recent events made that a difficult question to answer. I hedged. "She said I remind her of Mel Gibson."

Amanda gave my shoulder a pat. "Marry that one, Uncle Owen."

MUCH LATER, sunburned and tired, Harry and I sat in my brittle lawn chairs watching the little edible pieces of the fluke we'd caught cook on a charcoal grill. Amanda stood on the seawall, throwing my stale bread to the lagoon ducks.

"Turning forty was a bitch," Harry said after a long silence.

"I know," I said.

"Going back to the firm when Dad had his stroke was worse."

By the firm, Harry meant Ohlman, Pulsifer, and Hurst, the New York law office that he had briefly escaped to try his hand as a painter.

"But that's only temporary," I said, even though we both knew it probably wasn't.

"Everything's temporary, Owen. Then you die." There was another healthy pause. "Ever think about the old days when you were working for the firm?"

I had thought of them very recently, thanks to Barbara Lambert questioning me about the Carteret case. "Why do you ask?"

"I was just wondering if you've ever thought of coming back."

I looked over at him. He wasn't smiling, and the beer in his hand—the first of the day—was almost full.

"Ms. Kiefner's been asking after you," Harry said, naming the firm's office manager, a woman who had terrified me as few non-nuns could. "Seriously, Owen. I'd like to have a friendly face around. Someone I could talk to."

"I haven't changed, Harry. I still wouldn't fit in."

"The problem is I've changed. I don't fit in anymore myself."

"Besides, I have a job."

"I think we can outbid a newspaper."

"I meant I have a case."

"The girl's death was an accident," Harry said, giving me a very pointed look.

"Right," I said, addressing the fluke. "But I haven't finished what she asked me to do. I can't leave it hanging."

Harry had anticipated that objection. "I could help you there. I thought it over on the way in from the bay. Only one of the old murder suspects isn't known to be dead, the cult leader, Geist. If you're going to learn anything new about those murders, it's going to be from Geist. And," he added, addressing the fluke now himself, "if the Lambert woman's death means that the murderer is back in action…"

"Which it doesn't," I said.

"Right. But if it did, the murderer could only be Geist. To settle it once and for all, we only have to find him."

"How do 'we' do that?"

"Leave it to me. The firm is not without resources. And a little demonstration of them may convince you to come back and keep me company."

NINETEEN

THE *POST* ran Barbara Lambert's obituary on Monday morning. On the subject of her funeral, it said only that the services would be private. The obituary did mention Barbara's connection to the old, unsolved murders, but it stopped short of giving her reason for being in Atlantic City. Even without that detail, the piece conveyed the feeling that a circle of immense circumference had been closed by the accident. I decided that Kate Amato had written it, even though the job was below her station with the paper. Perhaps it had been part of the penance she'd given herself.

I learned a little more about the funeral from Joan Noll when I finally got through to her private number on Monday afternoon. The cousin didn't mention the service with the intention of inviting me. She used the fact of its being held the next day and in Atlantic City rather than Riverton to explain why she had no time to talk to me.

On Tuesday morning I staked out the Pleasantville cemetery where Barbara had told me her family was buried. There could only be one reason for holding her funeral in the city where she'd died rather than the town where she'd lived. And that reason was a reunion.

I got to the cemetery a little before nine, thinking I was playing it safe. It turned out that I'd cut it fairly close. Before my paper cup of coffee had cooled, Barbara's procession rolled in, all four vehicles of it. In addition to the hearse and the matching limousine, there were two cars. I added a third car to the line for the short drive to the Lambert plot, staying far enough back to park by myself.

Four adults got out of the limousine: three women and

a man. One of the women seemed not to belong to the group. She was tall and slender, and the others followed her at a distance. Catherine Lambert, Barbara's guardian, I decided. The others were probably the older cousins Barbara had mentioned, Joan Noll's parents, and Noll herself. The first sedan contained another couple and three children, more cousins perhaps. The man who climbed out of the second sedan carried a Bible.

Barbara had no pallbearers. The drivers of the hearse and the limousine, a man and a woman in matching black suits, transferred the casket from the hearse to a cart and pushed it along a gravel path to the grave. I paralleled the journey at a distance of fifty yards or so, stopping near a tombstone belonging to a Mildred Tucker. The name was vaguely familiar. I worked at remembering where I'd heard it, using that exercise to separate myself further from the service that was about to begin.

The man with the Bible began speaking as soon as the casket was in position above the grave. I couldn't make out his words, but from their singsong rhythm it was clear they were well practiced. I looked down at the tombstone before me. A little wreath of flowers stood next to it, baked brown by the summer heat. Mildred Tucker. The image of a crisp white uniform came into my mind. She'd been a nurse.

A movement in the leftmost corner of my vision distracted me. It was another gate-crasher, a little old man in a raincoat, the coat as wilted looking as Mildred's flowers. The little man looked over at me and nodded solemnly. I tried to place him and came up instead with my connection to Mildred Tucker. She'd been someone I'd met on the Carteret case, a nurse who'd held a critical piece of the mystery. But the woman buried at my feet was a different Mildred Tucker. She'd died in 1980, a year before I'd stumbled across Carteret.

By the time I'd shaken the aftereffects of the coincidence, the graveside service was over. The mourners were passing one by one before the casket. The woman I'd identified as Joan Noll had to be supported by her parents when her turn came. Catherine Lambert, still very erect, stood apart from the others. I looked around for the man in the brown raincoat without spotting him.

Catherine Lambert stayed a long time at the grave. The other mourners were at their cars before she started her walk. I hurried across the crisp grass to intercept her. She spotted me when I was still several graves away and stopped to wait for me.

I noted that her hands were folded together and pressed against her stomach. Their rigidity was at odds with her expression, which was peaceful, almost sleepy. She was younger than I'd expected. Her hair—the same light brown as Barbara's—had less gray in it than mine did, and the skin of her very serene face was taut. During my last few steps toward her, I wondered how old she'd been when the first tragedy of her life had occurred. Surely not much older than the woman she'd just buried.

''Ms. Lambert?'' I asked when I reached the edge of the path.

''Yes?''

''Catherine Lambert?''

''Yes.''

''My name is Owen Keane.''

''The man from the newspaper.'' I waited for a blast of rage to hit me. I'd been waiting for it for two days, but it didn't come. She only said, ''Joanie told me about you.''

''Then you know that Barbara came to us about reopening the investigation into the murder of your brother and his family.''

Her folded hands tugged at each other spasmodically, but her expression remained drowsy. She was brimful of tranquilizers, I finally realized.

"I wanted to tell you how sorry I am," I said.

"You're not to blame, Mr. Keane. No one's to blame. Her obsession was responsible, not you."

"Her obsession with the murders?"

"Yes. I tried everything I could think of to break its hold on her."

I was taking advantage of the drugged woman, I knew, but I pressed on. "So you think there's a connection between the old murders and the accident?"

"Only in that her obsession with the murders caused her to be crossing a certain street at a certain moment. Anything could have been the cause of that. She could have been on her way to a party or going to meet a lover. If her life had been different, it could have been anything. Anything."

She might have gone on forever listing Barbara's unused possibilities if we hadn't been joined by the man I'd guessed to be Noll's father. He was getting along without Valium, judging by the hostile look he shot me.

"We're ready, Catherine," he said.

"You'll have to excuse us," she said to me.

"May I call you sometime?" I asked. "Or come to Riverton to talk with you?"

"If you'd like. I live on Mercer Street, 62 Mercer Street."

She turned and led her escort back to the waiting limo, walking slowly down a row of headstones like a proud gardener touring her prize roses.

I was watching the little procession drive away when a voice said, "Poor woman."

The old man in the raincoat had come up unheard behind me. He reached out and touched my arm. "Sorry. Didn't mean to frighten you, Mr. Keane. Have time for a cup of coffee? You wanted to talk with me, didn't you? I know I'd like to talk with you."

"Who are you?"

"Sorry again. My name's Derry. Patrick Derry."

TWENTY

"SHE DESERVED MORE of a service than that," Derry said.

We were seated on plastic seats in the corner of a fast-food restaurant, a plastic table between us. Behind Derry, on the other side of the restaurant's plate-glass wall, was a playground for younger customers. It was also plastic, each of its tubes and slides and ladders a different unsubtle color. Against that background, the retired cop looked even older than he had at the cemetery. That impression was reinforced by the way he sat. When he'd been standing, his stature had been cut down by a bent back and rounded shoulders. His sitting posture was worse. In addition to bending forward, Derry leaned to his left, resting his weight on his elbow. The resulting pressure pushed his left shoulder up, and his head was inclined a little toward it, giving him the look of a man poised for a nap.

"She deserved more of a life than that," he said.

"You knew her?" I asked.

"No. We never met. Unless you count seeing her twenty years ago when she was a baby. I only meant that nobody deserves to die that young."

He ran a hand beneath his broad, red nose. He had very dark brown eyes with discolored whites, large eyes with wrinkled lids. He wore his iron gray hair extremely short, except in the very front, where the hair stood straight up. The hair of his eyebrows was the longest on his head. The brows curled out and upward like a pair of miniature horns.

"I'm sorry I didn't get back to you after you left that note on my door," he said. "I don't talk to reporters. A reporter from the *Post* came by a few weeks back. A woman. I sent her packing, pronto."

"I'm not a reporter."

Derry raised his head a little. "Johnny said you were. John Ruba. I called him when I found your note. Surprised the hell out of him. I figured you'd been to see him, too. Johnny described you; that's how I was able to pick you out at the cemetery. And he told me you were from the *Post*."

"There was a little misunderstanding about that," I said. "I work for the *Post*, but I was up at Lake Trevlac on my own."

"Johnny said it was because Barbara Lambert wanted the case reopened."

"Right. But the paper wasn't interested. I was poking around on my own time."

"So you weren't after a story?"

"No."

"What then?"

"Answers. Barbara Lambert wanted to know who killed her family. That's not right, exactly. She wanted to know that someone definite had killed them for a definite reason. She was frightened by the idea that it had been a random act."

Derry passed his hand beneath his nose again. "Poor kid. I wish now I'd called you. Maybe I could have given her a little peace of mind."

"How did you happen to be at the cemetery?" I asked.

"How did I hear about the accident? I'm a customer of yours. Of the *Post*'s, I mean. I'm probably your only subscriber west of the Delaware. Comes in the mail a day or two late. It was just yesterday morning I read about the accident. I did some calling around and found out I hadn't missed the funeral. So I drove down. Least I could do."

"Why do you get the *Post*?"

"It's a cheap way to stay in touch with this area. A way of keeping my eye on things. You never know when something might turn up."

"Something to do with the Lambert murders?"

He winked at me. Without an accompanying smile, the wink resembled a nervous tic. "Exactly."

"John Ruba told me you'd solved the murders."

"He should know better than that. We only got half the job done. We knew who did it and why: Russell Conti to bail himself out financially. But that's only half the job for a cop. A cop has to prove who did it. We never managed that.

"Not that we didn't put our souls into trying. Between Johnny and me and the state police, we damn near took that cabin apart looking for physical evidence. We went over that rock-choked forest of a lot like it was a parlor rug. Sent state police divers into the lake. Sent rookie troopers down into that old well they had. Hell, I went down in there myself just to make sure. We never found a thing." He sipped noisily at his coffee. "What else did Johnny tell you?"

"That you couldn't put the Lambert case behind you. That it ended your career."

Derry didn't take offense. "He's more than half right about that. Going into the Lambert case I was a damn good cop. I don't know what I was coming out. A pain in the ass at least. Now I'm a silly old geezer with a bee in his bonnet. A comical character. Except instead of being obsessed with commies or fluoride in the water, I'm all hepped up over a murder case nobody cares about.

"I'd already carried a badge for twenty years when the Lamberts were murdered. My only break had been a stretch in the army. I thought I'd seen it all, and I had seen too damn much. But nothing had hit me like what we found in the Lambert cabin. Not Korea. Not anything. A whole family wiped out. Or almost wiped out. It was a big story for months and months. If the murders happened again tomorrow, it might not even make the front page of the Philly *Inquirer*. That's how much the world has changed, God help us. The Post article pointed that out. But it stopped short of saying what I sometimes think, which is that the world changed because of the Lambert case. Because we didn't solve it, I mean."

"I don't understand."

"Not worth understanding, probably. Just my feeling that our failure to bring the killer to justice opened the door for all the evil that's happened since. I told you I'm a crazy old geezer."

"Sheriff Ruba said you were frustrated by Conti's suicide."

"Did he? That's putting it politely. I was poleaxed. Not by Conti's death. That was okay by me. With the little circumstantial evidence we had, we'd have been lucky to get a conviction. A death sentence, which Conti deserved if any man ever did, would have been way too much to hope for.

"What blasted me was that damn note. The last big lie of the case. If it hadn't been for that, we could have closed the damn thing. I could have closed it. In my gut, I mean. I could have moved on."

"Ruba moved on."

"He was younger. And he had a family to worry about. That might have made the difference; I don't know. I used to think of myself as Russell Conti's last victim, when I was feeling particularly sorry for myself. Now it turns out that the last one was Barbara Lambert."

"What do you mean?"

"Come on, Mr. Keane. Give me some credit for brains. It isn't hard to figure why the girl was in Absecon. On

Bannon Street. I'm not likely to forget that street. She was there to see Grace Conti, wasn't she?''

"Yes."

"Was it a social call or did Lambert have something definite to ask her?''

"It was because of something I'd told her." Catherine Lambert had been in no condition to condemn me for my part in her niece's death, but Derry might provide the service. "Mrs. Conti claimed to have proof that her husband was innocent. She wouldn't tell me what the proof was. She wanted the *Post* to print a story exonerating her husband on the strength of his suicide. Then she'd tell. I mentioned the offer to Barbara on the night she died. I'd intended to talk her into dropping the investigation. Instead, I got her excited about the Conti lead.''

Derry nodded, his yellowed eyes focused on the table. "That's what she was looking at when she stepped into the path of that car. She had her answers in sight." He almost sounded envious. "Of course," he added, "it was a false lead.''

"How do you know?"

"Because it came from Grace Conti. She's as unreliable a source as you could ask for. Always was. A little hysterical by nature and as obsessed as I am in her own way. Only her fixation is her husband's innocence. No martyr ever went to the stake with more conviction than that woman has. She wouldn't believe the evidence of his guilt if you held it under her nose. She wouldn't even recognize it.

"Sometimes I think that might really have happened. She might really have seen the truth and blanked it out. It would have been hard for Conti to hide his guilt from his wife. Impossible almost. He must have given her a thousand little signs. But she suppressed the evidence mentally. And maybe not just mentally.''

"What do you mean?"

Derry shrugged. "One of my crazier theories. When you spend as much time alone as I do, thinking about the same thing year in and year out, you can come up with some pips. One day I thought to myself, suppose the suicide note found with Conti's body wasn't the one he wrote. The one we were handed was typed and unsigned, remember. Suppose it was a ringer."

"Written by Grace Conti?"

"Who else? She found the body. She called the police. She had the opportunity. She could have destroyed her husband's real note, his confession, and substituted the one I've had to live with."

"Why?"

"To protect his name. Her name. So she could live out her life a wronged widow instead of the wife of a monster. Or because she was already so nutty on the subject of his innocence that she couldn't believe his guilt when she held the proof of it in her hands."

"What about this evidence she claims to have clearing her husband?"

"That will turn out to be nothing more than a feeling in her heart that he couldn't have done it. That's a wife's evidence. And it would be true in a way. Because that's the truth she needs."

We sat without speaking for a while, Derry sipping at his neglected coffee. He seemed worn out by his pitch. I wondered if I was the first one he'd ever told it to. I'd proposed equally unlikely solutions myself at the end of other investigations, solutions I'd been just as sure of as Derry seemed to be of his. And I'd been sure for the same reason. It was the reason the old cop had given for Mrs. Conti's faithfulness to her husband's innocence. Each crazy solution had been the truth I'd needed at the time.

I watched the children on the plastic playground behind

Derry. A little boy was seated on the top of a yellow sliding board. A line of children had formed on the ladder behind him and more were gathered at the foot of the slide, all encouraging him to loosen his death grip on the rails. Think it over, I told him telepathically.

"Mind if I ask you a question, Mr. Keane?"

"No."

"How did you get involved in all of this? I know why Miss Lambert came to the *Post*—I read the anniversary article, too. But how did you get custody of her?"

"An editor pointed her my way. He knew I like to solve mysteries."

"For fun?"

"Not for fun."

"Why then?"

On the day I'd toured Lake Trevlac, Patrick Derry's cabin had reminded me of the Pine Barrens shack where I'd first met the storyteller Jim Skiles. Now Derry reminded me of the hermit himself. They weren't much alike physically; Skiles, though older, had been unbent and full of energy. But the bent and tired Derry was showing signs of Skiles's old talent for seeing through me.

"I like to know the answers," I said.

"Like to or need to?" When I didn't answer, he said, "Let me put it this way. Why were you at the funeral this morning? Was it to say good-bye to Miss Lambert? Or to get a crack at questioning her aunt?"

"Or both?" I asked back.

It occurred to me that Derry's sudden resemblance to Skiles might have been a product of my imagination. I might have been projecting Skiles's qualities onto Derry because I missed having someone older and wiser who could listen to my troubles and say the sage, comforting thing. If it was my imagination, it was doing a great job.

"I won't pretend to know what's driving you, Mr.

Keane, because I'm not sharp enough to carry it off. But I do know that you're a driven man. I can see that plainly enough. I've had a certain amount of experience in that line. You're not going to drop this thing. Barbara Lambert has her answers now, God rest her, but you don't. You're going on."

He took out a pen and wrote a phone number on his napkin. "If I can be of any help, even if it's just to listen, call me. If you need someone to cover your back, call me."

"Thanks," I said.

"I want you to do something for me in exchange. I want you to think about these answers you're after. I'm not talking about the Lambert solution now. I'm talking about *your* answers. Ask yourself if they're things you're ever likely to know. If they're not, you may want to consider another way of spending your free time. Otherwise, you could end up like me, an eaten-out husk of a man who's no damn use to anyone."

He'd given me his napkin, so he wiped his mouth with the back of his hand before standing up. "It's good advice."

"It always has been," I said to his empty chair.

TWENTY-ONE

ONCE AGAIN, the trail led to Grace Conti. And, once again, it proved to be a dead end. I drove to Bannon Street in Absecon and found only the weeping willows at home. After wearing myself out on the brass door knocker, I paced the flagstone porch for a while because there was no one to shoo me along. I could see no signs of a hasty departure, apart from the rolled-up newspaper that still lay where Joe Fruscione's toe had left it on Saturday. Something wasn't right about the place, though. To pass the time, I worked at figuring out what that something was.

Just as my mind was being lured off the subject by the sounds of traffic on Bannon Street, I realized that the wrong something was the single newspaper. There should have been three more deliveries since my last visit. Mrs. Conti could have called to stop delivery. I picked up the paper to check a second hypothesis. Sure enough, Saturday's *Post* had become Tuesday's. That could only mean that someone was collecting them—Mrs. Conti herself, emerging from some hiding place in the house, or someone else.

I walked back to the street to check the mailbox. The old black box stood on the Bannon Street side of the willows. It was unprotected, in other words, exposed to the dirty, noisy world from which Grace Conti had hidden, the world that had claimed Barbara Lambert. As a result, the box was less well preserved than the widow who owned it. The black paint was flaking away, revealing patches of the galvanized steel beneath. The box was dented, and its little red flag hung by a piece of string. The box was also empty.

I'd had one successful stakeout already that day, so I

decided to try for another. First I checked two neighboring mailboxes to verify that the day's delivery hadn't come. Then I moved the Chevy to Mrs. Conti's side of Bannon, but a few doors west, parking in a shady spot. I left it there and walked the half block to the corner of Bannon Street and the shore highway. Across the highway was an affront to local property values, a combination gas station and convenience mart. There I gathered the kind of supplies real detectives used: bags of chips and cookies and a hoagie wrapped in enough plastic to keep it edible, according to its freshness date, until the following Thursday. My own estimate was a year from Thursday. As an afterthought, I bought a magazine, an expensive one whose narrow focus was wooden boats.

As it turned out, the magazine was the only purchase I really needed. When the mail truck came at two o'clock, most of my junk food was still uneaten. The truck extended my wait by depositing something in Mrs. Conti's box. I wasn't as happy about that as I should have been. I'd become very conscious of my proximity to the spot where Barbara had died. Earlier in the day, I'd gotten through her brief, impersonal funeral by studying headstones. I found a safer hiding place now in the glossy pages of my magazine.

I read about incredibly expensive and labor-intensive wooden yachts, envying their owners not for their disposable incomes but for the distraction their money provided. When I ran out of articles, I imagined owning a boat like that myself, mentally trying out Patrick Derry's advice about a change of hobby. My boat would be bigger than Harry Ohlman's *Velvet Noose*, but it would have the same kind of unfunny joke name. The *Blind Eye*, perhaps. The *Noose* was Harry's remedy for his failure as an artist, but he only used it sparingly. I would apply my anesthetic liberally. I'd sail out onto the ocean and not come back. All

I had to do first was rob a bank and find a cure for sea-sickness.

A little after three, a dark red Buick station wagon pulled into my previous parking spot across from the Conti house. A young black man—dressed as I had for Barbara's funeral in dark suit pants, a short-sleeved white shirt, and a neck-tie—got out of the wagon, crossed the street carefully, and disappeared behind the willow screen. A minute later, he was back, rolled-up newspaper in hand, to collect Mrs. Conti's mail.

I started the Cavalier. The junior bagman used a break in the Bannon traffic to pull into a driveway on my side of the road. He backed out and drove off the way he'd come. I followed, thinking, So far so good, and we made the right at the Route 9 light one behind the other.

I didn't stay three cars back or try any of the other tech-niques I'd read about in detective novels for remaining in-conspicuous in traffic. I drove a Chevrolet after all, a car that included "unremarkable" on its list of standard fea-tures. Unfortunately, another item on that list was a four-cylinder engine. The Buick was better equipped, and I had to floor my gas pedal after every light to match the wagon's acceleration.

My target made a left onto Highway 30 and headed east. Before the coming of the expressway, 30 had been the main route into Atlantic City. Now it was the locals' route, nar-row and badly paved but relatively free of gambler-laden tour buses. Today it even had decent scenery. To our left as we crossed the tidal flats was Absecon Bay. Some qual-ity of the brown water near the edge of the bay had at-tracted seagulls. Hundreds of them rode the little waves in tightly packed groups that were as bright as new snow in the afternoon sun.

The bay air or the feeling that I was accomplishing some-thing for a change revived my appetite. I found my bag of chips and tried to open it. I was still trying when the Buick arrived at the Brigantine Boulevard light. The light turned yellow, and the wagon's brake lights came on. I slowed too, happy enough for a chance to regroup. Then, without warning, the Buick accelerated, shooting through the intersection on the first few seconds of the red light.

The move could have been impulsive or the driver could have spotted me. Either way, he'd done a very complete job of leaving me behind. When the light finally turned green, there was no sign of the burgundy Buick and no way to tell if it had gone north when 30 ended, toward Gardner's Basin, or southeast, toward the boardwalk casinos. I chose southeast. I cruised behind the big hotels, every entrance to a parking garage or surface lot making my search seem more hopeless.

I ended up a few blocks from the *Post* building, an accident that made going there seem like a logical move. I parked the Chevy in the employee lot, checking the rows for the Buick wagon. It wasn't there.

"Where is synchronicity when you need it?" I asked the lot attendant. He had no opinion on the subject.

Suzie, my editor, was in her seat of honor in the slot. She asked how my vacation was going and whether it was ever likely to end. Before I could answer, she picked up a phone, saving herself an earful. I sat down at an empty desk and used its phone to call the Atlantic County prosecutor's office.

"Joseph Fruscione, please," I said to the woman who answered. I ended up saying it several more times to several different voices. The last in the series told me to hold; the investigator was on another line. I passed the time by watching one of the television monitors that hung on the newsroom walls. In theory, they were there to inform us of breaking stories, one medium's concession to another's strength. In practice, they were used to watch ball games

and the current fare, soap operas. Two beautiful, dangerously thin people were locked in an embrace, their heads
thrown back so they could continue to deliver their lines. I
couldn't hear what they were saying above the newsroom
clatter. That made my enjoyment of the scene complete.

"Fruscione." The word jarred me awake.

"Keane," I said. "Just checking in."

"What am I now, your parole officer?" It wasn't a
friendly question, but Fruscione asked it in a friendly way.
Our last conversation had started friendly and gone down-
hill, so I didn't get my hopes up.

"Have you found out anything about Barbara Lambert's
death?" I asked.

"I found out that something you told me was bullshit,"
Fruscione said. "Lambert never went to the Atlantic City
police for help. There's no record of it."

"Would there be a record? A woman off the street with
a crazy request?"

"Maybe not. But somebody would remember something
that oddball. Nobody does. I used to be an Atlantic City
cop. I know the layout. I've talked with everyone over there
but the guy who cleans the cans. No one interviewed Lambert. You can take my word for it or screw yourself."

Either alternative seemed to be fine with the investigator.
To give myself time to think them over, I said, "How about
Mrs. Conti?"

"She's not answering her phone. That's all I know."

"I think she's hiding somewhere. Someone's picking up
her mail and newspapers."

"How do you know that? Been playing detective
again?"

"I happened to be passing Bannon Street when today's
pickup was made. I was on my way to buy a yacht."

"Sure you were. I suppose you accidently tailed this
party."

"I tried to. I lost him."

"Perfect," Fruscione said happily.

"He was heading for Atlantic City. A young guy driving a big maroon station wagon. A Buick."

"License number?"

I read off the number from the corner of glossy paper I'd torn from my boat magazine. "I think the car will be registered to one of the casino hotels. I think Grace is hiding out in one of them."

"And they're sending a bellhop to collect her mail? She must be one great tipper."

"Or she has the right kind of connections. Frank Botticelli's niece might get that kind of service."

"The only things Smiling Frank is connected to these days are tree roots."

"I was thinking of his friends."

"If he'd had any of those, his Cadillac wouldn't have blown up. But I'll check it out."

"Thanks."

"Don't thank me. I want to talk to Mrs. Conti as much as you do."

"So you can convince Kate that Barbara's death was an accident," I said to show off my memory.

"Not anymore. We're treating the Lambert death as something more serious than a hit-and-run. A new witness has come forward."

"Who?"

"A surprise witness. I'll be in touch."

I hung up the phone quietly and glanced back at the television monitor. A commercial for fabric softener had taken the place of the emaciated lovers. While I watched a teddy bear free-fall onto a stack of folded towels, I wondered what Fruscione's new evidence could be. I wondered, too, why he'd leaned so hard on his parting "surprise witness." Surprise to whom? Me, presumably. Did that mean it was someone I'd never heard of? Or someone I knew but wouldn't expect? Who did I know who could have seen anything that night? Joan Noll had already told Fruscione her story. Was it Mrs. Conti? If Fruscione had already spoken to her, why would he pretend to be interested in my station wagon tip? And why was he so damn happy?

I'd guessed wrong about the investigator's sunny mood being a feint. He'd ended our chat on its opening note of cheerful contempt. I no longer bothered him, and I felt as let down by that as I was by the revelation that the case had gotten away from me. Fruscione's mood had turned sour on our first meeting because he'd been jealous of my dealings with Kate Amato. He no longer was, which suggested that he knew how things stood between me and Kate. So they'd talked since Saturday. That was fine with me. Then, a second later, it wasn't fine.

I waved good-bye to Suzie and walked into the end of the newsroom where the reporters lived. Kate was at her desk, looking very much like she had when I'd first talked with her. She was wearing her safari outfit again and pounding her keyboard as if it were the back of a choking victim.

Kate's return to her old self was an act. When she spotted me, she bolted from her desk. I zigzagged through the newsroom clutter and followed her down the hallway that led to the candy machines. As I entered the hallway, I saw Kate leave it via the stairwell door. The stairs led up to Kate's private smoking room on the roof, but I didn't believe she'd head for that dead end. I took the stairs down, toward the noise and heat of the pressroom.

The paper kept its ancient presses in the basement. And the subbasement, each press being two stories tall. I circled the upper pressroom, its floor made into a rectangular balcony by the huge holes cut for the presses. The presses were running, and the racing paper sliced through the light escaping from the subbasement, creating moving shadows on the ceiling that resembled a nightscape seen from a speeding train. The noise of the presses added to the illusion. When I descended a steel staircase into the subbasement, I had the uncomfortable feeling that the old building was swaying beneath my feet.

A burly pressman I didn't know came forward to confront me at the foot of the stairs. Before he could shout his challenge, an alarm sounded and the presses shut down.

"Shit," the pressman said, the word sounding enormous in the sudden silence.

He hurried off down the row of dead machines. I followed at a distance, scanning the now stationary shadows for Kate. I found her in an alcove the size of a small apartment, standing between the huge rolls of newsprint and the forklift used to move them around. If she had crouched behind the nearest roll, I would have missed her. But that indignity had been too much for her. She'd also balked at fleeing through the alcove's back door, whose red exit sign lit a dim corner. She was standing her ground, with her hands in the pouches of her khaki vest and her head high, looking so much like the bait for a trap that I almost glanced around for the net.

"Lose something in there?" I asked from across a roll of paper.

It was a natural opening for an insult. Marilyn would have said "respect for you" or "interest in men" or something sharper-edged.

The best Kate could do was "Leave me alone."

"You can't be afraid of me, Kate. I'm no threat to anyone."

Her ear for a straight line finally kicked in. "No use to anyone either."

"No. I'm not a practical guy like Joe Fruscione. I hear you two have patched things up."

Kate reordered her stylish hair with an indecipherable movement of her head.

"His old-fashioned attitude doesn't bother you anymore?" I asked.

"No. It feels good. He deals in facts, not monsters."

I might have asked her next what had happened to the "spiritual junk heap" that she'd driven lately, her grab bag of beliefs and superstitions. But I already knew: It had thrown a rod. That same thing had happened to me at critical moments in the past. And I'd tried the same solution Fruscione offered Kate. I'd hidden in the knowable, buried myself in safe facts and figures that could be checked and double-checked and used to fill an empty space inside me. Or almost fill it. I silently wished her better luck.

"Joe tells me he has new evidence," I said. "A surprise witness has come forward. He wouldn't tell me who the witness is."

"And I'm supposed to?" Kate asked. "What makes you think I know?"

"I think you know because you're the surprise witness." That was the unsettling idea that had come to me back on the rim. Unsettling because it wasn't possible, even though I believed it completely.

Kate stated the objection: "I was with you when Barbara Lambert died."

"When you left me, did you go straight to the paper or did you stop in Absecon? You'd promised me you'd talk to Mrs. Conti."

"I drove straight to the paper," she said with perfect assurance. I recognized the emotion on her face. It was the relief of a person prepared to lie who is handed a chance to tell the truth. She hadn't spotted the snare in my question.

"If you didn't see anything after you left me, it had to be before. There wasn't anything in my house to interest

Fruscione, present company excepted. You told me when you came in that you'd gotten there in time to see Barbara leave. What else did you see?''

"Your monster." Her relief had given way to resignation. "I would have told you about it that night when I called, but it didn't mean anything to me then. I didn't know the make and model of the car then.''

"The murder car?''

"Yes. Lambert's cousin didn't identify it until Saturday morning. I didn't hear about it until after you came by. Joe showed up right after you left. He might have followed you. After he'd calmed down, he told me. Lambert was killed by a blue Lincoln Town Car. Electric blue.''

"I know.''

"That's what I saw on Lake Champlain Drive. The car. You and Lambert were standing in your doorway when I drove up. So I parked my car and waited. Lambert got into a little Japanese thing and drove away. A second later, headlights came on behind me. This big boat of a car came gliding by. A big blue Town Car. The only thing I thought at the time was that it was too rich for your neighborhood. I didn't spot that it was tailing Lambert. I didn't even know then that the woman was Barbara Lambert.''

"Did you see the Lincoln's driver?''

"No, the windows were tinted." She drew in her shoulders. "If they hadn't been, would there have been anything to see?''

"Our friend Joe would have something colorful to say to that.''

She almost smiled. I reached across the roll of paper. "Thanks for telling me.''

Her fingers brushed mine. Then she headed for the exit.

TWENTY-TWO

I GOT BACK to my house in Mystic Island just after six. Harry was probably still at his desk in New York City, but I didn't try him there. I might have accidently gotten my old nemesis, Ms. Kiefner. I filled an hour with dinner—reheated fluke—and a drive down to the bay. I didn't make it all the way to the water. Within sight of the little community beach, I was waylaid by a block of solid concrete as big as my house.

Before the First World War, before the developers who conceived Mystic Island's lagoons were themselves conceived, a German company built a transatlantic radio transmitter on the edge of Great Bay. The state-of-the-art technology then was long-wave radio, which required colossal, crackling towers, symbolically correct for the expanse of water to be crossed.

When America entered the war, the German company lost its transmitter. A few years later, the tower itself was gone, made obsolete by short-wave radio and sold for scrap. All that remained were the huge concrete pads on which the tower had stood. I'd driven past one of these, known locally as the south pedestal, many times without stopping. On this particular evening, the ugly brown block seemed a better place for meditating than the bay, more in tune with my current mood. I didn't want to be distracted by mindless natural forces. I wanted to contemplate a man-made enigma. So I parked on an open stretch of sand and weeds and walked to the artifact.

The block looked to be a perfect cube. It reminded me of the puzzles that had been so popular a few years back, puzzles I'd never been able to work. The difference was that the German cube had no seams where smaller pieces joined. Its surface was discolored, but that was all that eighty years of weather had done to it. They'd known how to build gigantic concrete blocks in those days.

In addition to the weathering, there was some man-made discoloration: graffiti sprayed around the base of the cube by local kids. It was a halfhearted job, the names and designs nowhere near as creative or crammed together as they were on the parkway underpasses. There was no challenge to defacing the cube and no point: The people the vandalism would have offended had been dead for decades. The graffiti certainly didn't offend me. The illegible scribbling added to the block's appeal, making it seem even more like an archaeological find, a monument from a civilization whose language was now indecipherable.

I pictured some future archaeologists discovering the cube, still intact after the little homes around it had all turned to dust. The scientists would try to understand their discovery. Was it the tomb of a king? Did it have some religious significance? Was it used for human sacrifices or to identify the winter solstice or as a landing platform for ancient astronauts? Could it sharpen razor blades? Was it the source of some energy force whose secret had been lost over time?

To test this last idea, I placed my hands against the rough concrete. It was surprisingly cool after a long day in the summer sun. As I leaned against the cube, the coolness traveled through my shoulders and down my spine. I became aware of another sensation. I closed my eyes and concentrated and the answer came to me. The feeling was the one Barbara Lambert had described during our last meeting, the one she'd felt in the cemetery. It was the feeling of not being alone, of being watched.

I looked around. No one was stirring in the yards of the

tract homes that circled the cube. Cars were passing on the road, but my waiting Cavalier was the only one parked nearby. I shook the feeling off, telling myself that anyone who fondled concrete blocks in search of psychic energy had good reason to feel self-conscious.

I'd wasted enough time, in any case. I drove back to Lake Champlain Drive, checking my rearview mirror involuntarily for electric blue Lincolns. When I was safely inside my house, I called Harry's home number.

Amanda answered with "Ohlman residence."

"Exactly what part of the residence is speaking?" I asked.

"The laundry room," Amanda said. "I get all the dirty jobs. How's Kate?"

"Not so good."

"How are you and Kate?"

"Worse. I'm on the rebound."

"Again," Amanda said. But she was young and resilient. "This could be good. I've been thinking about you and Marilyn. She works in New York, doesn't she? If you came to work for Dad, you and Marilyn could get back together. You would be bumping into each other all the time."

Only if the other million and a half bumpees were willing to give up their turns. "Could be," I said.

"Are you going to take the job?"

"I don't know yet, kiddo."

"I wish you would. Dad's real lonely."

Amanda was too young to know how widespread that condition was. I wasn't about to enlighten her, so I said, "Is the gentleman of the house around?"

"He's taking a shower. Can he call you back?"

I agreed to the plan, and we said our good-byes. Amanda ended hers with a bit of advice that brought her dead mother to mind: "Don't lose hope."

I took Amanda's counsel so seriously that I didn't hang

up the phone. I waited for the dial tone and then tapped in Marilyn's number. She might have been taking a shower, too. It took her that long to answer, and she put that much negative energy into her hello.

"It's me," I said.

The handset cooled noticeably. "Thank God," Marilyn said. "If it had been another solicitation from a long-distance company, I was going to jump out a window. You just saved a life."

Getting me back to even for the month, I thought.

"I'm glad you called, Keane. I feel bad about the way I left things. I was sticking you with baggage that doesn't belong to you. That was weak of me."

Once upon a time, an apology from Marilyn had been a rare and valuable object. Over the past year or so, though, she'd flooded the market, apologizing to me as much as I habitually did to her. I hadn't figured the change out, but I knew it wasn't a positive one.

"Make it up to me," I said.

"How?"

"Take me to lunch. I'm on the rebound."

I expected some echo of Amanda's "again" but Marilyn said, "You have been as long as I've known you."

I was afraid she might apologize again, so I said, "Pick a day and I'll come in to New York. A company there wants to interview me for a job."

"Get them to take you to lunch. And hold out for an office with a window."

"I'd like to talk with you about something I've been working on." The line hummed in my ear. "A mystery."

"A serious one?" Marilyn asked.

"Life and death."

"I'm free on Thursday. Noon Thursday."

"By an odd coincidence, so am I."

Marilyn gave me the address of a restaurant she wanted

to try. Then she hung up to lie in wait for phone company solicitors.

I opened a book by a Spanish philosopher named Miguel de Unamuno. I'd been attracted to him by a quote the *Post* had printed in the "thoughts for the day" box that ran opposite the index on the front page of every issue. Unamuno's contribution had been "Life is doubt, and faith without doubt is nothing but death."

That teaser had been enough to send me to the library, where I'd gotten to know the Spaniard through a long-neglected book. I'd found that his philosophy was less a logical system than a statement of need: the desire to survive beyond the grave. His only real proof that he would was the force of his desire, but I didn't hold that shortcoming against him.

Unamuno figured in my current dilemma. He'd tipped me to the Tennyson poem in which the Nameless had been mentioned, the poem that had inspired the headline that had in turn brought Barbara Lambert to the *Post*. So it was possible to build another chain of coincidence and circumstance that made Unamuno, dead fifty years, the prime mover in Barbara's death. It wasn't the kind of immortality the philosopher had longed for, and blaming Unamuno wasn't an out for me. So I absolved him of guilt, being a generous guy.

I was dozing over the yellowed pages when Harry finally called. "Sorry, Owen. Amanda spaced the message. Remembering just now woke her up."

"It wasn't worth that," I said.

"It was if you called to accept the job."

"Let's say I'm willing to go ahead with an interview."

"I don't need to interview you, Owen."

"I know. I'm going to interview you. Thursday at ten. Wear a nice suit."

Harry's long exhalation came over the line like the crash of distant surf. "Why did you really call?"

"To find out if you'd gotten a line on Gary Geist."

"Why the rush? I thought you believed that the Lambert woman's death was an accident."

He was asking for payment, so I forked it over. "I've had second thoughts."

"What are the odds of that?"

"Did you find him?"

"I've set the wheels in motion," Harry replied grandly. "I should know something by Thursday if you're serious about coming in. Make it eleven. Wear a suit. It doesn't have to be a nice one."

"Good night," I said.

TWENTY-THREE

IT TURNED OUT to be a short night. Like Amanda, I was awakened by the idea that I'd left something undone. That was far from an unusual feeling for me, especially since I'd taken up the Lambert investigation. Two sins of omission came to mind as soon as I opened my eyes in the humid darkness. I hadn't learned Mrs. Conti's secret and I hadn't found Gary Geist. But those were old failures. I'd been sleeping in spite of them for days. Some third thing was eating at me. Thanks to Kate, I knew that Barbara Lambert hadn't been the victim of an accident or a slow-moving curse. She'd been killed very deliberately by someone very human. That was the unfinished business that woke me. I had to find a living, human murderer.

Samuel Calvert certainly didn't meet the "living" requirement, and I couldn't see his adoring daughter, Rebecca Topley, carrying on the family feud. The killer had to be connected with one of the other two members of the trinity: Geist the survivor or Conti the survived.

I told myself that I had those bases covered. Joe Fruscione was canvassing the casinos for Conti's phantom widow and Harry's mysterious operatives were searching for Geist. But my reassurances didn't lull me back to sleep. I rolled around for a while, trying to find a cool stretch of mattress. Then I got up and started the coffeemaker.

I'd been trying to wean myself from caffeine by diluting the coffee I shoveled into the paper filter every morning. First one scoop of decaf for two scoops of regular, then two decafs for every one of the good stuff. This time I left the decaf on the shelf. If I was stuck with insomnia, I was going to enjoy it.

Inspired by the coffee dribbling through the limed-up machine, I tried to force thoughts through my limed-up brain. Specifically, I looked for a premise I could build on. I started with a fact more certain than my next breath: Barbara Lambert was dead. She'd been murdered. She'd been murdered because she'd wanted the old case reopened. That meant that the killer had somehow found out what she was up to. How? If the murderer was someone connected to Mrs. Conti, the leak was easy enough to identify. I'd told Mrs. Conti about Barbara Lambert myself. But I hadn't told Geist, having failed to find him. The closest I'd come was a cul-de-sac named Bruce Somers.

"Somers," I said to my empty kitchen. The coffeemaker was only halfway through its cycle, but I poured a cup anyway, the coffee as black as old motor oil. I carried the cup over to the sliding glass doors. By a movie-grade coincidence, dawn was breaking in the eastern sky.

I'd talked to only one member of the old cult: Bruce Somers. He'd denied knowing Geist's whereabouts, and I'd believed him. I'd let his monogrammed cuff link and Rotary Club appointment convince me. I'd let appearances convince me. I'd told Somers about Barbara and he had told Geist and Geist had killed her. It was another chain, perhaps at last a useful one.

Before the sun was much higher in the sky, I was dressed and on my way to Easton, Pennsylvania. I took the most direct route, which happened to be a familiar one. Northeast through the Pine Barrens to my hometown of Trenton. Then north out of Trenton on 31. There could have been an Owen Keane historical marker every few miles, each describing a different failure from my past. I ignored the associations and their implicit warning.

I left 31 when it intersected with Interstate 78 north of

Allerton. Then it was a straight shot west to Easton as fast as the Chevy could manage. That was too fast, as it turned out. When I arrived at the little building with INSURANCE chiseled over its door, the blinds were still closed and the door was locked. I moved the Cavalier to the end of the block and waited.

Somers kept better hours than any bank president. It was almost ten o'clock before he showed up, sans icy receptionist. He drove by me in a golden Acura sports coupe and pulled into an alley beside his building. A few minutes later, the office's front blinds opened in a slow, ceremonial way. Before the ritual had ended, I was knocking on the still-locked front door.

Somers smiled in greeting. "Mr. Keane. Win another lottery?"

"I think I may have."

He didn't step out of the doorway. "I hope you won't mind if I ask you to take your winnings somewhere else. I'm expecting clients. Serious investors. Very diversified portfolio."

"I wonder if they'd be interested in hearing about your personal portfolio, Somers." I dredged his cult name out of the pool of drying coffee in my head. "Or should I say Stone? You're diversified in ways they'd never guess."

He laughed at me. "This particular couple would take it in stride, I suspect. Their claim to fame around the country club is having attended Woodstock."

"How many murders have they attended?"

Somers lost his salesman's gleam, but he didn't move. "I may have exaggerated my vulnerability to gossip when I talked with you last week. I'd prefer that details about my past didn't come out, but I'm not going to let myself be pushed around to prevent it. I sure as hell won't be blackmailed over some ancient murders I had nothing to do with. So get the hell out of here before I call a cop."

"The murder I'm here to discuss isn't ancient. It happened last Friday night. The victim was the last of the Lamberts. The one who was still alive when I came by here last week. We're going to talk about that. If you'd like a policeman to sit in while we do it, that's fine with me. I know one in Atlantic County who'd pay for the privilege."

Sweat had begun to dull the shine on Somers's waxy scalp. "I don't think…" he began.

He stopped speaking when I stepped into the doorway. He backed into the waiting room, and I followed, closing the door behind me.

"I do," I said. "I think you're an accessory before the fact, Somers. I think you tipped off Gary Geist that Lambert was reopening the case. I think he killed her."

"I don't know where Geist is. I couldn't have told him if I'd wanted to, which I didn't. I wouldn't give that con man the time of day."

"That's last week's story. Today I'm wondering about old loyalties and old debts."

He backed up until he hit the receptionist's empty desk. "I don't owe Geist anything. And I've never been loyal to him. When he asked me to back up his alibi twenty years ago, I wouldn't do it."

"Did you tell the cops he'd asked you to lie for him? They would have been very interested."

"No, I didn't rat on the guy. Betty wouldn't have liked that."

"Let's talk about Betty. You were fanning that old torch with both hands last week. Did you call her for old times' sake?"

"No," Somers said, mad now. "I mean, I did think about that, I really did. But I never got past the thinking stage. I wouldn't know how to find her. And I'm married."

The order in which he'd given me his two reasons for not calling Betty was unflattering enough to ring true.

Through vents in the ceiling, I could hear the laboring of an air conditioner as it struggled to undo the night's buildup of heat. Every puff of cool air that entered the waiting room seemed to be tilting the balance Somers's way. He was no longer sweating, literally or figuratively.

"How about one of the other cult members?" I asked. "Maybe you bumped into one of them at your Rotary meeting."

"Or on the moon," Somers added. I was grasping now and he knew it. "I told you last week—I don't even remember their names. Their real names, I mean. Their cult names, the ones Geist gave them, have been coming back to me. I told you that Betty was Sunrise. I think that was because Geist liked waking up to the sight of her. You know I was Stone. We had a Bamboo, a girl so thin her joints looked swollen, and a Snowman, a guy who was too shy to speak. And we had flowers, too, a Daisy and a Rose. They were the two women who alibied Geist. Rose had red hair, but that wasn't the inspiration for her name."

He paused to give me a chance to guess the true inspiration, never dreaming that I'd guess correctly. "She wore a tattoo of a rose," I said. I pointed to my left arm. "About there."

A little of Somers's panic returned. "Right," he said, "she did."

When I turned for the door, Somers took a swipe at the sleeve of my shirt. "No cops, okay? I didn't hand the Lambert girl over to Geist, I swear."

"I know you didn't," I said. I'd done it myself.

TWENTY-FOUR

I DROVE FROM Easton to Scranton on a succession of week-day-morning interstates, which is to say almost empty ones. I broke every speed limit I came to and broke them with an easy mind. My circle was closing, just as Barbara Lambert's had. Nothing would stop me now, not state troopers or road construction or even the nagging feeling that I wasn't alone. When my hundredth rearview mirror check convinced me that I wasn't being tailed, I played with the idea that Barbara Lambert was haunting me. Patrick Derry had said that Barbara had her answers, but I thought she still might need my help. The possibility didn't intimidate me. I was sure that Barbara and I would both have our answers soon.

I made it all the way to Lake Trevlac without consulting a map, and from the lake to Camp Paupack. I stopped under the front gate's stone arch and listened for the happy screaming of the Philadelphia refugees. There wasn't so much as an echo.

I parked near the combination lake and swimming pool, in the same shady spot I'd used on my previous visit. The lake was empty today and as still and brown in the midday sun as a cup of tea. The water was surrounded by little frame buildings that looked to be the cabins where the campers slept. Two buildings on my side of the lake didn't match this pattern: a bungalow-type house too small for its massive stone chimney and a large shed, as big around as a barn but only one story tall.

I tried the little house first. I could see what looked like an office through the screened front windows, but no one answered my knock. The large sliding doors of the shed stood open. As I passed through them, I smelled hot grease and other, subtler cooking odors. I crossed the dark main room, using an aisle that divided two files of tables. My passing stirred up a few of the fat, black flies that were napping on the plastic tablecloths.

The dining room ended in a wall broken up by two pass-throughs, one on either side of a screen door. Through these openings I could see a kitchen and, in its bright fluorescent light, the woman I was after: Beverly Simzack.

I stopped on the dining room side of the door. Simzack was standing at a long gas range with her back to me. She was browning ground beef in a skillet, the skillet as big around as the toy spare tire in my Chevy's trunk and just as black. It was the source of the greasy odor that had grown from a faint smell back at the shed door into a physical presence that gave the overheated air the feel of used dishwater. Beside the skillet were three battered aluminum cauldrons, each nearly full with a foamy liquid.

I'd had hours of driving in which to plan my approach to Simzack. I'd analyzed my near failure with Somers and decided that I'd played my best card—the news that Barbara Lambert was dead—too early in the game. I reminded myself to hold that back now. It was possible, just possible, that Simzack was more than Geist's informant, that she was his accomplice. If so, I might be able to maneuver her into a slip. Stranger things had happened.

I knocked on the door and opened it. Simzack looked over her shoulder, smiled, and set the giant skillet on a cold burner. The job took two hands, but she was equipped for it. She wore gray oven mitts as long as a debutante's gloves and a full-length apron, not quite gray but getting there. Her red hair was drawn up under a redder bandanna. Her face was also red, from the heat, and wet with perspiration and secondhand grease. Her foggy glasses had slipped down to the end of her nose.

"Mr...." she began and stopped. "Sorry, I've forgotten your name."

"It's Keane, Rose. What's for dinner?"

"Chili. Don't say it's too hot for chili—I know it is. The kids like it. And if there's any left, we can make..." She stopped again. "What did you call me?"

"Rose. Heard that lately? It's the name Gary Geist gave you back when you were cooking for him. Was he a big chili guy?"

She didn't answer, so I rambled on. "I'd guess he was, from what I've heard of him. No point in laying off the spicy food when the world is about to end."

Simzack had frozen in the act of drawing off one of her gauntlets. I waited for her to rap me in the teeth with it. Instead, she said, "How did you figure that out?"

"Simple math, Rose. It's the only kind I ever use. Two-plus-two stuff."

"Don't call me Rose," she said. And then, "Please."

"Okay. If you prefer, I'll use the name you gave yourself. You dreamed up Beverly Simzack, didn't you?"

That was more two-plus-two. Beverly Simzack had to be an alias because the name hadn't appeared on Kate's list of the cult members.

"It's my mother's maiden name," Simzack said. "She'd sue me for using it if she knew, but she's dead, so there's no problem. I thought of it as a joke once. Taking her name. I told myself that it was my inheritance."

"Any special reason you needed an alias?"

Simzack finished removing her gloves and used a bare pink hand to push her thick, blue glasses back into place. "Your math really is limited," she said. "I needed a new name so I could come back here and run this camp. I wasn't worried about being recognized. Not twenty years older and sixty pounds heavier. But if the right someone had heard my real name, someone who remembered the murders, I'd have been out of business before I started.''

I thought about asking why she hadn't just picked another derelict camp in another part of the state, but I didn't want my math skills insulted again. The story she'd told me about picking up the camp at a sheriff's sale had to be as bogus as her name. ''How did you really come by this place?''

''It was part of my divorce settlement,'' Simzack said. She fumbled with the strings of her apron for a while, trying to free herself. Then, after a last angry tug, she gave up. ''I should say the camp *was* the settlement.''

''When did you and Geist marry?''

''Just after the Lambert thing cooled down. After Earth folded for good. Earth,'' she repeated, a little amazed. ''Gary was kind of stunned by that whole scene. Shrunken by it. His stock in trade had always been an indifference to the source of his next meal. That con worked with us kids every time. We'd shower whatever we had on him, like the women who fussed over Jesus in the Bible. But it was a very conscious pose, like Gary's whole act.''

She tugged at her apron again, drawing the greasy cloth so tight against her broad stomach that I could make out the depression of her navel. ''After the murders, Gary couldn't concentrate hard enough to keep up the act. He became very anxious about that next meal and the roof over his head and the robes on his back. So he looked around for someone to take care of him. And he picked me.''

''Why you?''

''I could tell you it was because I was the best-looking woman in his harem, but you probably wouldn't believe me. I know I was the youngest. And the most ignorant. But my real selling point was my rich family down in Philly.''

"You told me you came from the wrong part of Philadelphia."

"I used to think I had. I mean, I used to think that coming from a well-to-do neighborhood was some kind of sin against humanity. I really rubbed my parents' noses in that, especially my mother's. She was a traitor, I thought then, a Polish girl from a blue-collar family who'd married a WASP goof and spent the rest of her life pretending she knew how to spell Bryn Mawr. I hated her for every advantage she tried to give me. No wonder she ended up disowning me."

"Over Geist?"

"Over a thousand things, the last one being Gary. Do you mind if we go outside? I'm dying in here."

She turned down the heat under her cauldrons and led me out through a side door. Once outside, she headed for the little lake, working at the knot in her apron strings as she walked. When she finally figured it out, she pulled the apron up and off, losing her bandanna in the process. I stooped to pick it up and, when Simzack deposited the apron on a dying lilac bush, I hung the bandanna beside it.

My guide didn't stop when she reached the lake. She kicked off her thongs without breaking stride and waded in until the water was almost to the bottom of her cutoffs.

"Damn, that feels good," she said.

I was tempted to find out for myself. "Where are the kids?"

"Field trip to an old gristmill over near Hartsdale. Not much of a trip, but it will give us fresh material for tonight's campfire story. 'The Haunted Mill.'"

She was facing me with her fists on her hips, but looking beyond me at the camp. "We do good work here. It would be a sin to screw it up because I was once married to a jerk."

"How long were you married?"

"Nineteen months. That's how long it took my folks to convince Gary that they'd really cut me off. We wouldn't have lasted much longer anyway. I did more growing up in those nineteen months than I had in the previous nineteen years. Gary was an accelerated course in human behavior. A certain bizarre type of human behavior.

"But I'd be lying if I said I dumped him. He dumped me and unloaded this camp at the same time. He was afraid to show his face around here after the police cut him loose."

"You had a lot to do with the police letting him go, didn't you? You were half of his alibi."

"Yes," Simzack said, "but the two halves didn't make a whole anything. That alibi business was another of Gary's cons. He came to me right after the murders and asked me to lie for him. Begged me to. He told me he'd been with one of the other women on the afternoon in question. Denise Dailey."

"Alias Daisy?"

Simzack wasn't impressed with my inside information. "Her name was Denise. Gary said he was afraid the police wouldn't be satisfied with one witness. So I promised to back up Denise's story. That bastard knew Denise and I hated each other, that we were each jealous of the time he spent with the other. He knew we wouldn't compare stories."

Simzack's indignation was traveling out from her across the surface of the pond in the form of tiny ripples. They died just short of my bank.

"Years later, after the divorce, I met Denise again. I was working my way through a Philadelphia community college. As part of a behavioral science course, I was interning at a drug rehab center. Denise was there, too. As a patient.

"If you'd seen our reunion, you would have thought we'd been sorority sisters. We were, in a way—the 'I sur-

vived Gary Geist' sorority. Of course, we talked a lot about
Earth and the murders. And I found out that Gary had told
her the same story he'd used on me.''

"He told her he'd been with you on the afternoon of the
murders?''

"Yes. She'd lied to the police, too, thinking she was
backing up my story.''

"Where is she now?''

"She died in eighty-six. Hepatitis.''

"So Geist didn't have an alibi for the afternoon of the
murders. He could have been the killer.''

"Yes, he didn't have an alibi. But no, he couldn't have
done it. My conscience is clear on that. I saw every inch
of the underside of the Gary Geist rock. Hell, he was almost
all underside. But he wasn't a killer. He was strictly a
dreamer. His dreams hurt people, but *he* couldn't. He was
too squeamish to cut up a supermarket chicken. He never
could have hurt those kids.

"The cops that came sniffing around after the murders
scared all of us, but they terrified Gary. He couldn't sleep
after that. Couldn't eat. Couldn't get it up, even, which he'd
been better at maybe than dreaming. As soon as the cops
let him, he got away from here. He would have sold the
place right then if there'd been any offers. Instead, I got it
as my one-lump alimony. I couldn't tell which of us Gary
was happier to unload.''

"That was the last you saw of him?''

Simzack considered the question at length. "I haven't
seen Gary since the divorce,'' she said.

I admired her careful phrasing. "In other words, you've
only heard from him.''

There was another pause while she weighed the chances
of an outright lie. "Yes. He's called me a couple of times
a year since the divorce.''

"Why?''

"At first, it was just to talk. Usually in the middle of the night. He may call a dozen different women on some regular rotation, but I don't think so. I think I'm the only one he's kept in touch with. I wasn't the great love of his life, but we were married. That little fragment of a normal life is important to Gary."

"You've done your best to convince me you hate the guy," I said. "Now you tell me you're phone pals."

"He calls me, I don't call him. So what if I listen? You can hate something and still find it fascinating."

"You've called him at least once, Rose," I said, underlining her cult name. "Just after I came by last week. Don't waste my time saying no."

She didn't say anything. She stood there radiating anger. Literally radiating it, the concentric ripples she'd been sending out across the pond having grown into little waves. I could hear them kissing the grass at my feet.

"You called to tell him I'd been here and that I'd reopened the case at Barbara Lambert's request."

"How could you know that?"

"First tell me why you went out of your way to warn a man you hate."

"I didn't warn him," Simzack said. "I called to rub his nose in it. I told you just now that he only called to talk. That's the way it started, but lately it's turned nasty. Gary's had a couple of good years and gotten full of himself again. When he called the last time he really lorded it over me. He knows what a struggle I've had with this camp. He used that to get to me. He did his best to make me feel small-time.

"You gave me a way of hitting back at him. He's still haunted by those old murders. So I called him in the dead of night and told him that the Lambert girl was stirring it all up again. That got Gary squirming."

It had done more than that. "Tell me where I can find Geist. I'll finish the job you started."

"This camp is more important to me than getting back at Gary, Mr. Keane. I would have told you where to find him a week ago if I could have trusted you to keep me out of it. I'll tell you now if you'll promise there won't be any fallout for me."

It wasn't a promise I could give. If I found Geist and proved he'd murdered Barbara, Simzack would be up to her neck in fallout. The police would question her about the information she'd given Geist, and every secret she had would come out.

Instead of lying, I stalled. "Why did you hang on to this place? Why didn't you sell it or let it go for taxes?"

"I'm not sure why I kept it at the start. I was just being stubborn, I guess. The camp was all I had to show for all I'd given up. It was a symbol, maybe, for how stupid I'd been. I worked my tail off to pay the taxes on it and put myself through school. Sometime around graduation, I started to dream about reopening this place. I dreamt about it through all the years I worked as a school counselor. But I could never save enough money.

"After my mother died, my dad looked me up. My goofy WASP dad. We had a long talk, and I told him about this place. He ended up lending me the money to open it. He wanted to give me the money, but I wasn't comfortable with that. So he became my silent partner. It was his idea for me to use my mother's name. He said he'd always liked it.

"I don't want to lose this place, Mr. Keane. I can't hand Gary over to you. I can't risk the publicity."

"You asked me how I knew you'd called Geist. Something happened since I was here last week. Barbara Lambert was killed in a hit-and-run. It wasn't an accident. The car that did it had been following her around."

Simzack descended, very slowly, into the lake. She ended up sitting on the bottom, the brown water soaking the ends of her thick, red hair.

"He lives in Jersey," she said, gasping for air between each word. "In Camden. He's got another con going, a business he calls Lifeforce. He's using the name Anthony West."

"Don't call to tell him I'm onto him. I'll do my best to keep you out of it."

"You don't have to lie to me," Simzack said. "I'll never call him again."

TWENTY-FIVE

LIKE SO MUCH of New Jersey, Camden got more shade than was good for it. In Camden's case, it was courtesy of Philadelphia, whose shadow, while not as wide as the one New York threw across the northeast corner of the state, still stunted what it touched. Philly's shadow made up in density what it lacked in breadth, the city having once been second only to Boston in the category of inflated self-image. That illusion was passing away, but Camden remained the poor relation, permanently on the wrong side of the tracks, or rather the Delaware. The boarded-up warehouses and factories I saw when I crossed the Ben Franklin Bridge were humbler versions of the ones collecting pigeons back on the Philadelphia side. The Camden pigeons were probably humbler, too.

I'd gotten the address of Lifeforce—One Pomona Plaza—from Information during a turnpike gas stop, but I didn't know Camden well enough to find the place unaided. I drove around the downtown area, asking for directions and occasionally getting them. At one point, I wandered past Walt Whitman's house, which seemed to me a good omen. The long-dead poet and I had once worked together successfully on a case. I could have used his company now.

I thought more than once about turning Geist's new name and address over to Detective Fruscione and running home to Mystic Island. The persona I'd worn so far that day— the avenging detective—was cracking. Playing the part for Somers and Simzack hadn't been very hard. I'd seen them, first one and then the other, as Geist's pipeline to Barbara Lambert, but I'd never really believed that either the in-

vestment counselor or the camp counselor had taken a hand
in her murder. I couldn't pretend that Geist was innocent
or harmless. But I also couldn't let the thing go. So I wandered on, becoming more my old, uneasy self with each
wrong turn.

My wandering finally brought me to Pomona Plaza. It
was an old office building of shiny brown brick, and it was
big by Camden's standards. It had recently been renovated
as part of a neighborhood renewal, probably at the expense
of taxpayers as far away as Paramus. The city's involvement in the project was proclaimed by a large sign that
blocked the sidewalk in front of the building. The sign also
stated that prime office space was still available to renters
who acted quickly. The urgency of the message was undercut by the sign's paint, which was peeling away in long
strips. I pulled one of these off as I passed and carried it
with me into the underlit lobby.

The largely blank building directory told me that the
Lifeforce offices were on the third floor. I rode up to them
in an elevator as big and solid underfoot as a bank vault.
And nearly as quiet. For what seemed like the dozenth time
since I'd met Barbara Lambert, I was reminded of the Carteret investigation. One lead had taken me to an office
building near the New York City Medical Center, a building with an elevator as silent as Pomona Plaza's. The whole
building had been tomblike, which had exaggerated my
nervousness. I'd been there to interview a doctor I thought
might be the evil genius behind the mystery, a Dr. Schiel.
In place of an elegant stock villain, I'd found a big, jolly
man, a Santa Claus lacking only a white beard.

The memory of that happy twist didn't console me now.
I took more comfort from the sound of typing that greeted
me when the elevator doors slowly opened. It was com-
puter-age typing, a rhythmic plastic tapping that contained
no answering echo of ink striking paper. It came from a

glass-fronted office a few steps from the elevator. Beyond the glass, a young woman sat, profile toward me, her attention on her computer screen. On the wall behind her the word *Lifeforce* was painted in large, sweeping letters like the masthead of a comic book. The color of the paint was electric blue.

I opened the suite's glass door, setting off a little chime. The notes lingered on the air, reminding me of the bells I'd rung as an altar boy whenever the priest elevated the Host. Then the receptionist looked up, and I forgot I'd ever been an altar boy. She had enormous brown eyes surrounded by lashes that looked like they'd been individually curled and painted. Her skin and hair were lighter shades of brown, the skin as flawless as her eyes and the hair as carefully worked as her lashes, a mass of long, corkscrew curls highlighted here and there by a thread of silver. I decided these highlights were phony, that they were yet another example of youthful self-expression through hair dye. I liked them anyway; they gave us something in common.

She was wearing a mauve blouse, a satin blouse whose peaks and valleys shimmered as she pointed to my hand. "What's that?" she asked.

I looked down and saw the strip of paint I'd pulled from the plaza's sign. It had rolled up like a tiny window shade.

"It's a scroll," I said. "Ancient papyrus, I think."

"Remarkably well preserved," the receptionist said, looking from the curled strip to me.

"Thanks," I said. "I found it in Peru. It's written in hieroglyphics. Aztec hieroglyphics."

My audience didn't bat a single faultless lash. "The Aztecs lived in Mexico," she said. "The Incas lived in Peru."

The steady gaze of those giant eyes was making me light-headed. "That's what I used to think, too," I said.

"What does the papyrus say?"

"It's a prophecy about the end of the world. I thought Mr. West would be interested."

"You did?"

"Yes. The apocalypse used to be a hobby of his."

She seemed to find that harder to buy than Aztecs in Peru. She raised her perfect eyebrows and then the handset of her phone.

"A gentleman to see you." She hesitated and looked up and at me.

I thought she was giving me a chance to improve my story. I waved the paint papyrus encouragingly.

"Your name," she whispered.

"Oh," I said, and then, "Omega."

That got a smile out of her. "A Mr. Omega. He's found an ancient prophecy about the end of the world. He wants to show it to you. He says it used to be a hobby of yours."

She held the handset away from her ear, anticipating the storm of indignation that would wash me out into the street. What she actually heard made her smile again and blink, the blink a brief solar eclipse.

"Mr. West will see you," she said. She indicated a wooden door just beyond her desk. A very heavy wooden door. Beyond it was an office lit by a wall of windows. An empty office.

I had stepped into the meeting end of the room. A semicircle of comfortable-looking chairs upholstered in blue were grouped around a low table. They faced a wall that was all but covered by a white display board on which three words were written in blue marker: *Unlock hidden realities.*

"Check," I said.

The office end of the room was to my left. More overstuffed chairs, a modern wooden desk far too wide for its narrow depth, a half-wall of bookcases. Geist wasn't behind the desk, but he was well represented on the bookshelves. They held copy after copy of the same book, the copies arranged to display their glossy covers. Each cover was a portrait of Geist, although the subject was identified with his current alias, Anthony West. The upper portion of each cover bore the title *Lifeforce* in the same dramatic lettering that decorated the reception area.

A copy of the book lay on the desk. I picked it up and carried it to the light of the nearest window. If I'd seen the book on a newsstand, I wouldn't have connected West and Geist. Too many of Geist's messiah touches were gone. The long, straight, center-parted hair was now cut short and brushed upward in the latest spiky style. The New Testament beard was also gone, and that was the biggest difference. It changed the geometry of the face, shifting attention upward from the very ordinary chin and the mouth of perfect teeth to the prominent brow. That outcropping of bone was the feature no makeover could disguise. It had once given Geist's eyes a flattering depth. Now they looked sunken and small.

When I looked up from the book, Anthony West was standing behind the desk. I wanted to examine the bookcase behind him for its hidden door, but I couldn't take my eyes from his. The pale blue eyes were impressive in person, small certainly—tiny compared to the pair I'd just admired in the waiting room—but very commanding—twin collapsing stars from which light could barely escape. He broke eye contact to examine my tired suit, freeing me to return the compliment. He was wearing a silken, pearl gray number that had surely cost more than my first car. The suit tapered gracefully from well-padded shoulders, emphasizing West's height, six feet five at least, and his extreme thinness.

"Mr. Omega?" he asked, his voice steady and slow. "Won't you have a seat? You've something for me, I believe."

I did have something, a tiny roll of dried paint. I could

have called the gag off, but it had gotten me this far. I crossed to the desk, handed my precious artifact to West, and sat as he did.

He broke an inch or so off the scroll trying to unroll it. "Sorry," he said.

I waved airily.

On his careful second attempt, he managed to get the thing unwound. "It's blank, Mr. Omega."

"Invisible," I said. "The writing, I mean. You have to be psychic to read it."

West let the scroll rewind. Then he held it to his forehead, closed his eyes, and said, "The bearer's name is Owen Keane, reporter for the *Atlantic City Post*."

He opened his tiny eyes, pleased with his performance and very pleased with my reaction. "Calm down, Mr. Keane. Do parlor tricks always frighten you?"

"No," I said. That West had guessed my name didn't even surprise me. He'd probably been on the lookout for me since Simzack's taunting call. "Synchronicity frightens me."

West's stage business, the laying of the scroll on his forehead, was a common enough, television-inspired thing to do. But it was also another echo of my visit to Dr. Schiel. The jolly doctor had taken my letter of instruction from Robert Carteret, a letter he should have known nothing about, laid it on his forehead, and read it word for word.

"Synchronicity," West said in his church-organ voice. He intertwined his bony fingers, holding his hands slightly above the polished desktop. "That's an old one. Had a vogue back in the seventies."

"Didn't we all," I said.

"It's a Carl Jung toss-off. The idea of a connection between casually unrelated events. I think that's how he defined it. The idea that some coincidences are too meaningful to be coincidences. It twists acausality, the absence of a relation between two events, into some kind of proof of a connection, not unlike the way Kennedy assassination fanatics twist an absence of evidence into proof of a conspiracy. Have you been encountering a lot of synchronicity lately?''

"Heaps," I said.

"Did you read about the theory of synchronicity recently? Or did someone mention it to you?''

Kate Amato had mentioned it repeatedly, the first time when she'd discussed the odd coincidence of Samuel Calvert's son dying in an accident just days before the Lambert murders. "Yes," I said.

"I thought so," West said. "Hearing about synchronicity or talking about it seems to increase the instances of it. It makes us hypersensitive to the little coincidences that are always around us. It's like when a friend tells you about a new car he's bought. A Mercedes, say.''

"Or a Lincoln," I said.

"All right, a Lincoln. And suddenly you're seeing Lincolns everywhere you go. The Lincolns were always there, just like the little coincidences are always happening. You've just had no reason to notice them.''

"So there's nothing to worry about, doc?''

"Well, each case should be considered individually. What did I do, remind you of someone?''

"Yes. A backwoods mystic named Gary Geist.''

There was a silence, during which West's pale eyes seemed to recede even more. Then he broke my roll of paint into little pieces and swept them, backhanded, off the desk.

"Let's get this over with, Mr. Keane. My real name is Geist. I changed it quite legally to West for professional reasons. I know you're poking around in my past because the Lambert girl wants to know who killed her family. I can understand her obsession with that. She should be able to understand my refusal to be persecuted again.''

"You'll have a hard time getting that across to her.''

"Then I'll have to get it across to you. Or to your editor. If I can't do it, my lawyers will. I'm not the unworldly, spiritual person I was twenty years ago. I'm not going to be pushed around by the legal system again.''

"Is that what happened twenty years ago? You were the victim of the legal system?''

"I'm not going to discuss anything related to that time.''

I'd had a hard time lying to Beverly Simzack. With West it came easily. "Think of this as off the record.''

"Nothing's 'off the record' in this life, Mr. Keane. Nothing we do, no word we speak, ever really goes away. I've tried to start fresh. I've made a success of myself.'' He pointed at me like a recruiting poster. "And here's my record back again, scratching at my door.''

"Tell me about your success. What is Lifeforce?''

"Something you're sworn as a journalist to mock. A spiritual solution.''

"I don't scoff as well as I used to. Run it past me.''

West shrugged, the gesture dampened by his padded, pearl gray shoulders. "It's based on a geological model, the theory called continental drift. You'll say the relationship is just an example of pseudoscience trying to borrow credibility from real science, but to me the parallel is clear and inescapable. I was reading an article in a scientific journal when the insight came to me. The article presented the idea that our current continents were once combined in a supercontinent. Some authorities called this original landmass Pangaea. I prefer to think of it as Atlantis.''

I started to say "How appropriate,'' but it came out "I'm with you so far.''

"The supercontinent fragmented and the continents as we know them today began to drift apart. They're still drifting, in fact. When I heard that, it struck me as a perfect model for the spiritual fragmentation of our times. My thinking evolved into that." He pointed to the book I'd examined at the window. "Lifeforce.

"I feel it's possible to identify 'belief plates' moving away from what was once a single 'spiritual continent.' These drifting plates sometimes meet, grinding together along psychic fault lines, generating tensions that result in spiritual upheavals, sometimes on a global scale. Our only chance for happiness, our only chance for survival, is to identify these lines of tension and guide the energy into constructive channels."

"How?" I asked, genuinely curious.

West smiled. "I don't give the answer away, Mr. Keane. I sell it."

"I should buy the book?"

"That would be too easy. I sell the book, of course, but it's mainly a sales tool, a better-documented version of what I just told you. The answers come from within each individual. Finding them requires personal exploration and reflection. Supervised exploration."

I turned in my chair to read the display board behind me. "To unlock hidden realities?"

"Exactly." West stood and crossed to the meeting end of the room, his movements practiced, easy. "I started with personal counseling, but that was…inefficient." When he reached the board he turned to face the half-circle of empty chairs and, coincidentally, me. "I now deal only with groups. Corporate groups, church groups, college groups. I'm extending my reach every day."

I stood up. "I can understand why you would want Gary Geist to stay buried."

"You think I'm a charlatan, don't you? You think I'd change creeds again tomorrow if there was a dollar in it."

As an exercise in mind reading, it buried his earlier work

with the Aztec scroll. "I think it's a long way from 'the world ends tomorrow' to 'harness psychic earthquakes.'"

"Perhaps. But twenty years is a long time. And something important happened since I was Gary Geist."

"What was that?"

"The world didn't end, Mr. Keane. That's the central disappointment for our generation, the self-absorbed children of the sixties. The world didn't end when our youth did. What Gary Geist taught was wrong, but it was appropriate to the times. Lifeforce is appropriate to these times. I'm helping a generation grope toward a substitute for the fading illusion that the universe revolves around them. That's all I've ever been: a servant and guide to my generation."

"Any customers in Generation X?"

"You're thinking of Barbara Lambert."

Actually, I'd been thinking of Kate Amato, wondering if West might be the guru she'd taken me for. But his guess was more to the point, so I nodded.

"Barbara Lambert," he said again, intoning the name in his lowest register. "I've often wondered what became of her."

"She ended up living ten miles north of here in Riverton. Odd that you two should have been so close."

"More synchronicity, Mr. Keane. In any case, I meant that I've often wondered how being spared like that affected her. There would be two ways to react, as far as I can see. You could think of yourself as an unfinished piece of business in some kind of family curse. You'd go through your life timidly then, jumping at the fall of every leaf."

"What's the other way to think about it?"

"My way. I'd explore the spiritual ramifications of it, the spiritual legacy the experience had left me."

"In other words, you'd milk it."

West was too relaxed now to take offense. "Consider

Ms. Lambert's options. She could combine the thought that she'd been spared by a higher force for some great future work with the idea that she'd been blessed with second sight because she'd been at the center of a psychic upheaval."

"Her crib straddled a spiritual fault line, you mean."

"If you like. Or she could discover some enduring bond with her dead family, a connection so strong that she has one foot on the spiritual plane and one on earth. I could write any number of books if I had Ms. Lambert's history."

"Some people have all the luck," I said.

"So which way did Barbara turn out? Is she a timid doe or a seer?"

"A little bit of both." I started across the room to West, my movements anything but relaxed and easy. "When I first met her, she was scared to death. Of the unknown mostly. Then, late in our relationship, she told me she was sensing a presence. Something watching her."

"Late in your relationship? Has it come to an end, Mr. Keane?"

I arrived at West's little classroom. We stood facing each other at opposite ends of the white display board. "Yes. She's joined her family on the spiritual plane."

The ongoing process that was Anthony West came to a halt. The breakdown occurred within the span of a single one of the plastic keystrokes I could hear through the heavy office door. West's arrogant smile had been caught by the change and frozen in place. I hated the sight of it.

I picked up a blue marker from the display board's ledge, struck out West's slogan, and wrote below it the thought I'd woken with that morning: *Find the murderer.*

By the time I'd finished, West was up and running again, his smile gone. I put the marker back where I'd found it. "That's our goal for today. The murderer I'm looking for is Barbara's, of course. She was killed in a hit-and-run last week, a day or two after your ex-wife's call. I'd tell you more, but the police will probably prefer you unrehearsed. Any comments? Off the record, of course."

"Get out," West said.

I walked to the door. The effort of not hurrying or looking back over my shoulder nearly finished me.

TWENTY-SIX

THE BEAUTIFUL receptionist flashed me the high beams as I passed her desk, but I didn't pause to bask in their warmth. I took the stairs down to the lobby, metal stairs that rang reassuringly with the arrhythmic jangle of my steps. Before I could impose some pattern on the noise, I was on the first floor and out into the cool, dark lobby.

One other person was in the lobby, a security guard old enough to tell me stories of the city's heyday. I asked him for a more specific bit of information: Did the building's tenants have their own parking facility?

"The rental office is on Two," the pensioner said.

"I just came from there," I said. "But I forgot to ask about parking."

"You thinking of renting an office?"

"Right."

"What's your line?"

"I'm a detective." The lie was my reward to myself for getting back down to the lobby alive.

The guard considered me critically, perhaps concerned for the tone of his building. I would have ruined his day with spiritual plates and psychic fault lines, but I didn't have the time. "Is there free parking?"

"There's a garage behind the building. On Widener Street. Used to be the Camden Savings and Loan. I mean, that's where the bank used to stand. Now it's standing on the corner of Dead and Buried."

I left him on that up note, hurrying to the Chevy's parking space in front of the plaza. I circled the block, first finding Widener Street and then the parking garage. No legal parking spaces were available within sight of the garage, so I parked illegally beneath a little sign that held a pictogram of a car being towed away. I was no more worried now about being towed than I had been earlier in the day about getting a speeding ticket. I knew no policeman would find me because I wanted one to. I'd paid part of my debt to Barbara Lambert and perhaps an older debt to myself. I'd found Gary Geist and faced him. Now I would have happily passed West to Fruscione or Patrick Derry or John Ruba or anyone who happened to be dressed in blue.

But a policeman had to find me; I couldn't go in search of one. West had been jumpier at the end of our interview than I'd been at the beginning. He wouldn't sit behind his wide-screen desk waiting for the legal system to drag him in again. He'd move, and someone had to move with him.

No volunteers stepped forward before West himself appeared in the exit of the parking garage, driving a black Cadillac. I'd been on the lookout for a damaged blue Lincoln, but luckily I'd kept an open mind. I would have spotted West if he'd been driving an ice cream truck. The way he checked and double-checked the empty street for traffic was one giveaway. Two better ones were his eyes, pinpoints of frightened blue in the car's dark interior.

I'd already taken off my suit coat. Before pulling onto Widener behind the Caddy, I removed my tie and rolled up the sleeves of my shirt. There wasn't much disguise material in the Chevy, only the same sunglasses and ball cap Amanda had selected for our fishing trip. I considered putting the cap on backward, but that would have been overreaching.

West and I took Mount Ephraim Road out of the city. It was one long stretch of traffic lights, which forced me to stay closer to the Cadillac than I wanted to, my recent failure in Atlantic City a very tender wound. Fortunately, we became part of a rigid formation of cars and trucks that stayed steady light after light. That happy situation lasted until Mount Ephraim met Interstate 76. Most of my cover took the interstate ramp, but West stayed on the surface road. I stayed, too, pulling my ball cap down until the brim touched my sunglasses.

Mount Ephraim turned into the Black Horse Pike shortly after we passed under the interstate. The road didn't live up to its romantic name. It was lined with strip malls and fast-food restaurants, with an occasional used-car lot thrown in for flavor. The name Black Horse Pike suggested that the road was a survivor from colonial times. I fell into imagining what it must have been like then. I pictured a dirt track through the woods, with only an occasional inn or cabin to light the darkness. The road may have been worked by highwaymen, perhaps one in particular. One who rode a black horse.

I came out of my reverie in time to see the Cadillac slip into the left-turn lane just as it arrived at a light. I tried to follow, but my way was blocked by an aggressive tow truck. I was through the intersection before I could change lanes, passing West as he made his left. The sign on the cross street read Audubon Park Road.

I made a U-turn just past the light, misjudging it enough to run two wheels onto the far curb. I steadied the car and turned right onto Audubon Park. The road was winding, giving me no clear view ahead. The short stretch I could see contained no black Cadillacs. A block from the pike, the zoning changed from commercial to residential. Very nice residential. I scanned the drives of old stone and brick homes for West's car, at the same time bending the twenty-five-mile-an-hour speed limit nearly double.

Then the road straightened and began to rise gently. I could see miles of it, not one of which contained the black car. I turned around in the crescent drive of a demi-mansion and retraced my route at something below the speed limit.

Within sight of the Black Horse light, I saw a commercial property set well back from the road. Its sign was less discreet, a large plastic padlock bearing the words CAR-MINI'S U-LOCK SELF STORAGE. The place was surrounded by a high, chain-link fence topped with a spiral of razor wire, but the front gate stood open and the blockhouse office was empty. I determined the latter by cruising slowly past the office's grimy picture window. Beyond the gate were six narrow buildings, each made up of a dozen one-car garages joined at the hip. They didn't offer much cover, so I left the Chevy behind the office and went in on foot.

The six buildings sat parallel to the access road, which divided them into two groups of three. The end of each building bore a number tall enough to be read back in Camden. Between buildings one and two, I found the Cadillac. I didn't find West. A garbage container stood between his car and my corner of Building Two. I made my way down the side of the building and crouched behind the big, white box, feeling the sun-heated metal and, worse, smelling it—an oily, stale sweetness.

Before I'd gotten used to the aroma, the garage door closest to the Cadillac opened noisily. West stepped out into the sunlight, his face the same shiny gray color as his suit. He closed the overhead door quickly, but not before I'd seen what was inside the bay: a blue Lincoln Town Car.

West was in his Cadillac and gone and still I knelt by the trash container, the top of my cap pressed against its side. Then someone said, "Hey," in a nonthreatening nineties way.

I looked up. A young man stood behind me, a safe ten yards behind me. He wore a T-shirt, baggy shorts, and basketball shoes, and his legs were spread well apart to support a nascent beer belly. I noted that his baseball cap was on backward, but it was too late to adjust mine.

"Are you okay?" he asked.

"Fine," I said.

"You can't be here. What are you doing?"

"Meditating."

The kid looked from me to the trash bin and back again, perhaps establishing some mental link between us. I decided it was time to update my wardrobe.

Whatever the kid was actually thinking, it made him less polite. "If you give me any shit," he said, "I'll call the cops."

"Permit me," I said.

TWENTY-SEVEN

SOLVING A MYSTERY is usually a positive experience, at least for a time. There's a definite high that comes from knowing what no one else knows and holding on to that knowledge. The subsequent release, the slow passing on of the solution in logical, connected bits, can also be intoxicating. This is especially true if, as often happens, the person I'm enlightening is one who previously doubted that I could tie my own shoes.

I couldn't hold on to West's secrets for any length of time, but that didn't make my phone call to Investigator Joseph Fruscione any less pleasurable. Fruscione didn't break out in admiration for me—he had too many calls of his own to make—but I got the satisfying impression that I had ruined his day.

I kept watch on Carmini's U-Lock Self Storage from a safe distance until relief arrived. It was Fruscione himself, in the company of other plainclothesmen and local uniformed police. I slipped modestly away before the last patrol car door had slammed. I knew the police would want the rest of my story, including the part I'd promised Beverly Simzack to protect. And I knew I'd tell them. The best I could do for Simzack was put the moment off.

I had other calls to make, anyway. The first was to Kate Amato. I had to settle for her voice mail, a technical innovation I disliked. I appreciated any opportunity to talk to another human being, even the wrong human being. Thanks to the march of science, I now got to talk to the right human being's electronic echo. I told it that there'd been a break in the hit-and-run and that Joe Fruscione was the man to see for details.

Then I called Patrick Derry. That is, I started calling him. I tried once on my way back to Mystic Island and half a dozen more times after I got there. Finally, just after dinner, he answered.

"Mr. Keane," he said. "Been trying to get me, you say? I hope it wasn't anything important. I took my own advice about free time. Been fishing. You ever try that?"

"Yes," I said. "The last time I went I was skunked by a nine-year-old."

"Oh. Well, maybe something else would serve better."

Before he could suggest something, horseshoes, perhaps, or whittling, I said, "I found out who killed Barbara Lambert."

I gave Derry a more detailed account than I'd shared with Fruscione because I expected a more satisfying return: the old cop's approval. I didn't get it.

"It doesn't add up, Mr. Keane. Geist was never more than the patsy Conti tried to frame. You've still got some work ahead of you."

I tried not to let the obsessed man's denial get me down. By the next morning, though, a reaction had set in. That would have happened without Derry's help. Mystery solving is never more than a temporary fix for me. As I'd explained to Barbara Lambert, sooner or later I always realize that the answers I've found aren't the ones I really want, that the facts somehow don't add up to the truth. That realization came quickly now, helped along by the memory of Barbara's death. No amount of phony self-congratulation would make that go away.

The next day I set out early for New York City before Fruscione could come and squeeze me dry. Early, but not too early. I waited around for the morning *Post* to arrive, hoping to read the text of West's confession. I was disap-

pointed. Kate's story told me only that the police were
questioning West in connection with Barbara Lambert's
death. The rest of the article was a summary of West's
previous incarnation as Gary Geist.

About the only thing I gained by hanging around to read
the paper was lighter traffic on my drive north, first on the
Garden State Parkway and then the New Jersey Turnpike.
The traffic didn't really begin to collect until I reached the
feeder highway for the Lincoln Tunnel. Then it collected
with a vengeance. By the time I reached the long, curving
descent to the tunnel's tollbooths, traffic was bumper to
bumper and creeping along. I selected the rightmost tube
of the tunnel, knowing that changing lanes at the far end
to make my exit would require a cabbie's nerve. The right
I had to make was the entrance to the Port Authority parking garage, which was only a few hundred yards from the
tunnel's mouth. I turned in and climbed on steel and concrete ramps narrow enough to make the Cavalier seem ex-
pansive until I reached the quiet of the garage roof.

I left the Chevy to bake in the sun and descended to
Forty-second Street. It took me a block or two of being
bounced around to relearn the rhythm of the foot traffic,
whose rapid, impersonal currents and riptides were as powerful as anything Harry and Amanda had encountered at
Barnegat Inlet. Once I was comfortably in the flow, I
gawked away at the buildings and the people like the small-
town tourist I was.

Harry's offices were in the Johnson Tyre building, on
Forty-second just east of Madison. It was a stuffy old tower
whose tiny lobby was all marble and hardwood and brass.
The building had once seemed to me the physical manifes-
tation of the atmosphere of Ohlman, Pulsifer, and Hurst.
That had been during the reign of Harry's father. I wondered as I ascended the familiar stairs if Harry would alter
the firm's tone or if it would drop his an octave. I was on

the lookout for clues to that mystery as I entered the firm's cluttered offices.

Two changes greeted me immediately: a new receptionist—a young man with an unsettled complexion—and the office he identified as Harry's. It was Harold Ohlman, Senior's old office. That Harry had taken it over made me uneasy for some reason. Maybe I was just worried about my reunion with Ms. Kiefner. I needn't have been, as it turned out; her carefully arranged desk was vacant. She was lurking somewhere nearby, though. A fresh rosebud—her trademark—stood in a crystal vase on the corner of her desk. I'd once stolen Ms. Kiefner's rose at a particularly desperate moment. I thought of doing it again now and presenting the trophy to Marilyn at lunch, but it was only a fleeting impulse. The passage of years had made life more precious to me.

Harry was at his father's desk, reading. His head was bent slightly forward, allowing me to note the progress of his hair loss. I was always careful to do that, hairline integrity being the only category in which I had an edge over him. He knew it, too. When he finally looked up from his reading, he raised a hand to smooth his remaining hairs self-consciously.

"Owen," he said. "Good. How does the old place look to you?"

"New," I said, referring to Mr. Ohlman's office. I'd never been allowed inside the room when I'd worked for the firm. It was smaller than I'd always imagined but very nice. Where the walls weren't old dark wood, they were paneled in something even more expensive: shelf after shelf of books, huge ones in long matching sets. There were six shelves of burgundy, five of forest green, three each of gray and tan and black, all embossed in old gold. On the walls between the shelves were paintings, some of ships under sail and others of Mr. Ohlman's native Boston. Harry's old office had had Boston paintings, too, ones he'd done himself as an undergraduate. None of these were currently on display. A double frame stood on the desktop, its back to me. I knew the frame would contain photos of Mary and Amanda, Harry's own private photos.

"What did you think of the receptionist?" he asked.

"He needs a new blade in his razor."

Harry chuckled. "Ms. Kiefner's latest innovation. She's determined to drag us into the nineties. Have a seat. I have some information here for you." He pushed a single sheet of paper across the desktop to me, a move that might have sprinkled me with déjà vu if I hadn't already been drowning in the stuff. "I think you'll find that interesting. It's a report on Gary Geist."

I was tempted to reprise Geist's mind-reading routine, but I didn't want to have even that much in common with him. So I left the paper untouched. Harry was spilling the goods anyway.

"Geist's deed on that camp of his was on file with the clerk of Mason County, Pennsylvania. In the same file was a Notice of Federal Tax Lien form and the subsequent release. It seems Geist forgot to pay his income taxes the year before the Lamberts were murdered. Both the lien and the release carried Geist's Social Security number. That's what we needed. With that, we were able to obtain his current address. We also found that he'd had his name legally changed."

"To Anthony West?" I asked. It was a lousy way of saying thank you, but Harry and I had a relationship that transcended etiquette.

"How the hell do you know that?"

"I bumped into him yesterday. In Camden. Running a company called Lifeforce."

"I know all that," Harry snapped.

"Sorry," I said, insincerely.

"I suppose you also know what kind of car he drives."

"Yes," I said. "I even know where it's parked. At least I know where it was. The police have probably towed it by now."

"Damn," my benefactor said.

"I don't know, Harry," I said. "Maybe you should come to work for me."

"Very funny. Consider the job offer withdrawn."

Now I was sincerely sorry that I'd cheered myself up at Harry's expense. "As long as we're on the subject, what were my duties going to be?"

"Same as before. You were going to be in charge of building little innocent research projects into something out of Raymond Chandler's wastepaper basket. My hope was that you'd get us sued out of business so I could go back to doing something worthwhile, like mowing lawns."

"I never got you sued."

"You had the potential," Harry said. "You just wouldn't apply yourself. How about buying me lunch? You can tell me how you tracked down Geist."

"Next time," I said. "I have a date today."

"Marilyn? Amanda's prayers have been answered. I wasn't kidding last Sunday when I said she's turned into a matchmaker. She doesn't think adult males can survive in the wild."

He had the look of a man with more to unload. I stood up before he could, not wanting to hear about any matchmaking Amanda had done on his behalf.

Harry waved me back into my chair. "There's something else about Geist, Owen. My operative got Geist's address from a company called Modern Research. There are similar setups around the country, but Modern Research is the big one in the Northeast. They provide last-known-address information, among other tidbits, for law firms, private investigators, collection agencies. All they require is a Social Security number and a fee."

"I'll have to owe it to you," I said.

"It's not that. Our contact at Modern Research was pretty sure that someone else had submitted an inquiry about Geist. Sometime in the last couple of weeks."

"Someone named Kate Amato?"

"He didn't give a name. It may be they won't give that kind of information out. He just mentioned it in passing."

"Could you find out who it was?"

"I thought you had this case all figured out."

"I have. But I'm curious."

"There's a news flash. Okay, I'll see what I can do."

"Thanks."

"And I'm unwithdrawing that job offer."

"Okay," I said. "Maybe I'll unresign. Start calculating my back pay."

TWENTY-EIGHT

MARILYN WAS already at the restaurant, the Bou Afra, when I walked in. I was hoping I'd be the first to arrive, as I was sweating from my ten-block march through the city's lunchtime crowds. I was a decade too late to make a good first impression on Marilyn, but I kept trying, piling up in the process enough bad impressions to turn off a whole sorority house. In spite of them, Marilyn had agreed to meet me. And in spite of my general dampness, she smiled as I sat down at her table. It was almost enough to make me believe in the efficacy of Amanda's prayers.

Marilyn had dressed for the Bou Afra. It was a Moroccan restaurant, and the interior looked like a set from the old Bogart movie *Casablanca:* white walls of textured plaster, solemn ceiling fans, scattered oriental rugs, arched doorways, all inadequately lit. Marilyn was wearing a white linen jacket over a white blouse, the color choice accentuating the deep tan of her broad face. The fans even lent a little life to her decimated hair. Its curls moved languidly in the hot desert wind of the place.

"Sorry I'm late," I said. "I couldn't find my pith helmet."

"It does sound like the sun's gotten to you," Marilyn said. "How did the job interview go?"

"Fine. I start at first base for the Yankees on Monday. What's Moroccan for cold beer?"

Our waiter, who happened to be passing, demonstrated his grasp of English by reciting a list of imported beers. I selected an Italian one.

"Our special today is lamb," the waiter said by way of an exit line.

"No lamb for you, Keane," Marilyn said. "It's too close to cannibalism."

After that remark, ordering the special was almost obligatory. I struck the blow for my manhood and then sipped my beer, which, to judge by its temperature, had come from southern Italy. Marilyn launched into a long complaint about a co-worker, a man she'd been paired with for a special project. The story had a punch line that I saw coming a long way off.

"We made a tug-of-war out of the whole assignment. Then, when it was over, he asked me out."

"Huh."

"And I ended up having a good time."

"Huh."

"You've used 'huh,' Keane. Try 'no kidding' or 'you don't say.'"

"How about 'son of a bitch'?"

"Out of character," Marilyn said.

It was, too, but it was also how I felt about her announcement. Luring her to lunch had been step one in my master plan to win her back. Now I felt as cheated as Harry had been when I'd yanked the Anthony West rug out from under him.

"It's nothing serious, Keane. I think that's why I'm enjoying it."

"You walked out on me for not being serious enough."

"No," Marilyn said. "It was for being afraid."

It would have been a great line to have ended a book chapter on. Or an act of a play. The Owen Keane character could have thrown his napkin down and stalked out. Or, more probably, the Marilyn character would have, her honest head held high.

Neither of us took advantage of the opportunity. I had

too much warm beer left, for one thing. For another, I'd gotten used to Marilyn's habit of saying whatever she happened to believe. And I knew that, on this particular point, what she believed happened to be true.

The arrival of our salads doubled as the curtain going up on a new act. "I've been thinking a lot about the Carteret case lately," I said. "Do you remember that?"

"I remember the trouble you got into," Marilyn said. "And how I let you down."

"You didn't in the end."

She brushed some bread crumbs from the table. "It's only natural for you to be thinking of that business since you're back in New York for the day."

"It started way earlier. With a crazy nightmare I had. Ever since, I've felt a little haunted by Carteret and company."

"I'm surprised you'd notice an extra ghost or two. Tell me about your new case. Your life-and-death case."

I did. Even with the romantic interludes omitted, the telling took us past the salad course and through the long wait for our entrées. I was on my way to Camden when the apologetic waiter finally came through for us. My lamb, a dark, lumpy stew, had been served on a bed of something I didn't recognize. Tiny golden brown kernels of something, like dissected rice. I explored them with my fork.

"It's couscous, Keane. Moroccan pasta. Eat it, for God's sake; it won't hurt you. So you tracked Gary Geist to Camden."

"He was Anthony West by then."

"Okay, West. What happened next?"

"I went to see him, alone and unarmed. And afraid," I added, unnecessarily.

"That was a stupid thing to do. You might have gotten run over yourself."

There was no pleasing some people. "It turned out West

scares easier than I do. After our interview, he made a beeline for the garage where he'd hidden his car. I followed him and called the police."

"So why did he kill Barbara Lambert?"

"He never admitted doing it. But it had to be because she was reopening the case."

"Why? He'd been cleared by the police twenty years ago. Why would he be afraid enough of Barbara Lambert to kill her? And why kill her when he did and where he did? If she was right about being watched, he was tailing her most of that day, at least. Why did he wait to kill her till then?"

Because it had gotten dark, I thought, and she had stepped out into the street. Maybe West hadn't been planning to hurt her. Maybe the idea came to him when he turned the corner and saw her in his headlights. But that wasn't the answer Marilyn was prodding me toward. She wanted one explanation for two whys: Why had West killed Barbara and why had he chosen to do it on Bannon Street?

I chewed my miniature pasta and thought about it. "West wasn't cleared twenty years ago. The police lost interest in him because they were fixating on Russell Conti. Even Conti's suicide note didn't convince them they were wrong. But if something convinced them now, some new evidence, West would become suspect number one. Mrs. Conti claimed to have the evidence. Barbara Lambert was on Bannon Street to get it. That's why she was killed there."

It was the assumption that had guided my roundabout pursuit of West. Marilyn saw it from the outside and found it wanting.

"But how did West know about Mrs. Conti's information? He couldn't even be expected to know where she lived. How could he know that she'd been holding on to some secret for twenty years? She only told you on the morning of the day Barbara Lambert was killed. The girl was already being tailed by then or shortly afterward, if she was really being watched at the cemetery. Could Mrs. Conti have somehow found out Geist's new name? Could she have called him herself?''

I countered with a why or two of my own. ''To threaten him? Or blackmail him? The only thing she wants is to clear her husband's name. She can't have expected to bully West into a confession. Besides, she practically swore to me that she hadn't told anyone else her secret.''

''That settles that,'' Marilyn said. ''Nobody's ever lied to you.''

''Right,'' I said.

''Right. Her whole story about having new evidence is probably a lie. Or a truth she made up to get her through the last twenty years.''

I recognized a rephrasing of Patrick Derry's theory. I'd half believed it when he'd run it by me in the fast-food restaurant. Now, in this slow-food restaurant, I had a change of heart.

''Mrs. Conti can't be lying,'' I said. ''She must have something valuable to tell. If she didn't, Barbara would still be alive. West would have had no reason to stop her from crossing that street.''

Marilyn pushed her plate away. ''That assumes that West not only knows Mrs. Conti has a secret, but also that he knows what the secret is, or at least how dangerous it is to him. Which brings us back to the 'how could he know?' question. Who could have told him?''

I buried some lamb in couscous, intending to dig it up during the cold months ahead. ''Maybe nobody had to. Maybe West has firsthand knowledge of the secret. Maybe there's some connection between West and Conti that everyone missed twenty years ago. Maybe that's the widow's secret.''

"Where did you come up with that insight?" Marilyn asked.

"It's the old 'when you've eliminated the impossible, whatever remains, however improbable, must be true' gambit."

"Too logical for you, Keane. Your motto is, 'When you've run out of facts, dream things up.'"

It lacked a certain elegance of phrasing. Otherwise, I had no quarrel with it.

"You have to find Mrs. Conti, Keane. You have to get the secret out of her."

"I know," I said.

The storytelling hour that had preceded the main course didn't leave Marilyn any time for sampling the Moroccan desserts. Or perhaps my story had put her out of the mood. We parted company on the sidewalk in front of the Bou Afra. The emotional potential of the moment was lost when Marilyn spotted a cab unloading passengers a door away. When she'd reeled it in, she turned her attention back to me.

"You're not right, Keane," she said with one hand on the cab's door handle.

I thought she was echoing Patrick Derry again, so I said, "It had to be West."

"I don't mean your solution's not right. You're not right yourself. I know you. This girl's murder should have laid you out flat."

"It did," I said. Something was making me nervous, perhaps the traffic backing up behind the waiting cab.

"It will," Marilyn said, getting into the cab at last. She leaned her head through the open window. "When it does, you can call me."

The cab pulled away before I could say thanks. I waved instead.

TWENTY-NINE

THE ATLANTIC COUNTY prosecutor's offices were in Mays Landing, the county seat, a little town far enough inland from Atlantic City to be safe from passing hurricanes. It was well within the high-water mark of the casino prosperity, though, to judge from the shiny new municipal building. The little palace was built of red brick and prefab limestone panels and it had a gable roof of corrugated metal painted lime green. The busy architectural style was a reaction to the glass-and-steel boxes of the fifties and sixties, but for me the net effect of the extraneous porticos and unmotivated cupolas was a feeling of nostalgia for the honest shoe boxes of old.

The offices of the Major Crimes Unit had the air of an upscale detective bureau. That is to say, there were cops—whatever their titles might actually be—and the attendant atmosphere of a cop's workplace, a quality that combined the impersonal bureaucracy of a license branch with the intimacy of a locker room. What lifted these offices above the average police station was the absence of criminals. At least until I walked in. It was going on dinnertime, but the place was still bustling. The young men and women hurrying about all looked at me like they were sure they could find me guilty of something if they put their minds to it. I shared the belief, so I lost no time tracking down Fruscione.

The investigator was not hurrying about. He was seated in a little office looking out a heavily tinted window. He was wearing his standard gray slacks, this time with a black silk shirt. The shirt was only slightly darker than the five-clock shadow I noted on his sagging chin when he swiveled around to face me. His half-closed eyes were bloodshot, and I wondered if he'd been up all night or drinking. Both, I decided after his opening line, which he delivered at the end of a lengthy deliberation.

"It's funny how on a garbagey old suit like that the jacket and pants no longer seem to match."

It wasn't a greeting that lifted my spirits. "Don't tell me West escaped," I said.

Fruscione read his reply from a sheet of paper, one of the fifty or so scattered randomly about his desk. "'Gary Geist, a.k.a. Anthony West, was picked up for questioning by the Camden police at eight p.m. yesterday evening.'" He looked up from his reading. "Following a telephone tip received from a hoodoo amateur detective named Keane."

"So what's the problem?"

Fruscione read to me again. "'Mr. West was released at six forty-five this morning.'"

"Why?"

"He didn't do it. He had an alibi, one of the great ones of all time, which he finally shared with us after his lawyers and his lawyers' lawyers had all shown up. It seems that Mr. West was pitching his Lifeforce crap to a bunch of deep thinkers at a church up in Bordentown at the moment Ms. Lambert was struck down. An audience of thirty-two. We've spoken with twelve so far, including the pastor and his wife. West was their guest of honor, no doubt about it."

"Then he had an accomplice."

"And he gave the accomplice the keys to a car registered to Anthony West? That was bright of him. Or was it that one fatal slip the murderer always makes?"

I started to sit down in one of Fruscione's spare chairs. Something in his red eyes told me it would be a better idea to stay on my feet.

"West's car is a blue Lincoln," I said. "Barbara was killed by a blue Lincoln. That can't have been a coincidence."

"It wasn't. West's Lincoln was the murder car, all right. The lab report hasn't come in yet, but when it does, it'll back you up. The car has a damaged front end complete with traces of blood and some bits of thread." He tugged at the collar of his shirt. "Black thread. If it wasn't West's car that killed Lambert, I'll sleep with you."

"So West has to be behind the hit-and-run," I said. "If he was stupid enough to use his own car, it's no reason to let him off."

During our previous encounter, I'd noted the tendency of Fruscione's face to settle. Now his whole body was in on the act, inching steadily downward in his chair as he glared at me.

"How's this for a reason?" he asked. "Mr. West reported his car as stolen last Friday morning, approximately twelve hours before Barbara Lambert's death. Claimed it had disappeared from his condo parking spot the night before. The investigating officer incorrectly identified the car as a Continental on his report. That kept it from turning up on the check of stolen Lincoln Town Cars we did as a matter of routine earlier this week."

"If the car was stolen, how did West get it back? And why did he hide it?"

"It came back all by itself, sometime late Friday night," Fruscione said, using small arm movements for emphasis, boneless movements that were a half-second off the beat of his words. "Mr. West figured that some kids had taken the car for a joy ride, an all too common occurrence in the Garden State. Kids don't usually return their stolen rides, but they frequently bang them up, which explained the front-end damage to Mr. West's satisfaction. He didn't notice the blood traces or the fiber evidence. Not then.

"As for him hiding the car, the one-word explanation for that is insurance. Mr. West's lawyers gave it a self-righteous twist, something about their client being afraid the car could never be put right after the vandalism and worried that he'd end up victimized again if he reported the car's return, screwed over this time by his insurance company. What it all boils down to is this: When the Lincoln turned up, West saw a chance to make a quick buck by collecting his insurance money and then disposing of the car. Probably to a chop shop. It's just the kind of angle you'd expect a nickel-and-dime grifter like West to work."

"West isn't nickel-and-dime. He's made a killing with this new company."

"He tried that bluff on us, too, but somehow, limited though we are, we sat through it. West's business success is mostly an act. He's got enough dough to pay for lawyers, but not much else. The up-front money for his performance in Bordentown was a fast six hundred and forty bucks. Not exactly what Donald Trump pulls down for a personal appearance.

"In fact, his cash-flow situation is the reason we caught him. He would have been long gone if he hadn't had to root around for some traveling money."

"How did he explain his decision to run?"

"You could just about write that scenario yourself." Fruscione pushed himself back into an upright position and immediately began sliding down again. "Innocent victim of previous murder investigation who has painstakingly rebuilt his life after twenty long years is visited by a vindictive reporter whose unscrupulous newspaper is using the old murders to build circulation. The innocent party learns from the evil reporter that there's been a new murder, a hit-and-run. He makes the connection to his damaged car, hurries to investigate, and discovers what might be blood traces. He realizes that he's being framed again, just as he was twenty years ago. Fearing that no one will believe his story, our hero panics and tries to escape. Etcetera, etcetera.''

My insides joined Fruscione's steady slide toward the floor. West's story fit perfectly with what I'd observed of his reaction at the storage garage.

"Who does he think tried to frame him?" I asked. "The other two suspects are dead.''

"Mr. West, not unreasonably, considers that to be a question for us to work out. He was reasonableness itself, in fact, once he realized that he had an alibi for the time of the murders. At least he was reasonable with the various law-enforcement agencies that had conspired against him. He's planning to take a harder line with the *Post*.''

"Over the article they ran this morning?" I asked.

"Kate's article," Fruscione said. "Inspired by a tip from none other than that enemy of mental health and a good night's sleep, Owen Keane. For that reason alone, I should flatten your fucking nose. I told you Kate was worked up over the idea her original article had gotten Lambert killed. So what do you do but give her proof it happened just that way. I ought to toss you out my fucking window, which, incidentally, doesn't open.''

The weary detective's threats didn't worry me, as they required that he first get up out of his chair. "Pretending Kate had nothing to do with the hit-and-run isn't going to get her past it," I said. "I thought that giving her a chance to help expose West might do it. You must feel the same way. You told her why West was being questioned.''

"Like I had a choice," Fruscione said. "Like I've ever been able to tell her no. Maybe now that she'll be looking for work I'll have more pull with her.''

"Kate's been fired?"

"Not yet. Not that I've heard. But I gathered that it was one of Mr. West's goals.''

It should have been another reason for Fruscione to hit me, perhaps the decisive one. Instead, it seemed to have gone a long way toward healing the rift between us. The investigator had already told me why.

"You'd love for Kate to be fired," I said. "You're hoping that will improve your chances with her."

"It isn't every day a guy can dump two rivals at once," Fruscione said. "You *and* the goddamn *Post*. Now, if you don't mind, I'm thinking of crawling home. When the time comes to comfort Kate, I want to be up to the job."

Our interview was ending, and I hadn't even asked the question that had brought me down from New York. "Have you found Mrs. Conti?"

"No. I can only handle one goose chase at a time."

"Finding her is the key to the whole mystery. It has to be. It wasn't an accident or a coincidence that Barbara was killed on Bannon Street. She was killed to keep her from talking to Mrs. Conti."

"Sounds like somebody's been coaching you, Keane. Or did your 'positive thinking' class meet today? Who killed Lambert to keep her from talking to Conti? As you pointed out just now, we're running short of suspects. Or have you started to believe this Nameless crap? I'll be believing it myself if I keep wasting time with you."

He leaned forward with an effort, resting his elbows on his papered desktop. His shoulders sagged inward like the back of a cartoon horse. "To give you an example of how you're affecting my thinking, I went to the trouble today of verifying that the stiff they found in Russell Conti's study back in 1973 really was Conti. Luckily, somebody had thought to check the body's prints. So we're back to no suspects, not even dead ones."

"How about the mob?" I asked, improvising to keep the interview going. "We've been thinking all along that the

Mafia have been helping Mrs. Conti, but maybe they've been working against her.''

"'We've been thinking'?" Fruscione repeated, his indignation rousing him slightly.

"The Mafia would have the resources to track West down and the expertise to steal his car."

"Spoken like a real suburbanite. I had that much expertise when I was twelve. How would the mob even know to frame West?"

"Because they remember Gary Geist. Because they've been involved all along. That may be the secret Mrs. Conti wants to pass on."

Fruscione shook his head so violently that the movement carried down into his sagging shoulders. "Think before you say this stuff, goddamn it. The last thing Mrs. Conti would want to tell the *Post* is that her beloved husband conspired with the mob to kill the Lamberts."

"Suppose Russell Conti wasn't working with the mob. Not willingly. Suppose they used him to get to the Lamberts."

"I'd ask what the Mafia was supposed to have against the Lambert kids, but I wouldn't want you to break stride. How did Mrs. Conti find out about all this? And don't say her uncle, Smiling Frank, told her on his deathbed, because he didn't have one."

"Neither did her husband," I said. A genuine idea glimmered behind the reply, but I couldn't bring it into focus.

Fruscione was having the same problem. "Meaning what?"

"Conti might have told his wife the truth just before he killed himself. In his suicide note. Patrick Derry thinks the note the police found with the body was a fake supplied by the widow."

"Patrick Derry? One of the original investigators from Pennsy? Is he still kicking around?"

"Yes. And he's still obsessed with the Lambert murders."

"He'd have to be to have come up with this suicide-note idea. If the original note had cleared Conti, his wife wouldn't have suppressed it. She'd have published it."

"Maybe it damaged her uncle. He paid her bills after Russell's death. Maybe Uncle Frank did it because Grace was holding the original note."

"Maybe maybe maybe. Keane, you drive me nuts. I don't know how you sleep at night with all those goddamn maybes bouncing around in your head. I don't know how I'm going to sleep myself after this bull session, and I was halfway to la-la land when you walked in."

"Find Mrs. Conti, and we'll both sleep better."

"I tried; it didn't pan out. I called in a favor from an old buddy on the AC force. The burgundy Buick was a courtesy car from the Royal Palm Casino. But the Royal Palm management denies sending anyone to Mrs. Conti's house. And they claim not to know which of their sizable staff was using the car you saw on the afternoon you saw it. The pickup could have been a private arrangement worked out with one of their people, but that doesn't get us very far. No one's stopped by the Conti house since you blew that tail. The mail and the papers have been piling up. Needless to say, the Royal Palm has no Grace Conti registered."

"So she's registered under another name."

"So she is, so what? What are the cops supposed to do, search every room in the place?"

It sounded like a great plan to me, and I wondered why Fruscione's police pals felt differently. Unfortunately, I speculated aloud. "Patrick Derry thought somebody on the Atlantic City end protected Russell Conti twenty years ago because he was married to Frank Botticelli's niece."

Fruscione rose very slowly from his seat. Given his rubbery fatigue, the ascension was as dramatic as Beverly Simzack's descent into the water of her private lake had been.

"If you're saying what I think you're saying, Keane, I am going to flatten you. And don't think you can get away with it by quoting Derry. You're saying the Atlantic City police—my old department—ran interference for the Mafia twenty years ago and are up to the same trick again. Or maybe it's this office. Maybe it's me this time. Is that what you're saying?"

"I'm saying that the only woman who knows why Barbara Lambert was killed is sitting in Atlantic City right now, ordering room service. And nobody but me seems very interested in finding her."

"Get out of here," Fruscione said. "Go check in at the Post. Something tells me they'd rather find you than Grace Conti."

THIRTY

NO ORDINARY OFFICE grapevine can compare with a newspaper's. The reason isn't the staff's overdeveloped verbal skills or its special training in the dissemination of information. It's the unique pressure that journalists are under, the pressure of always knowing more than they can officially tell. The release valve for this is unofficial telling, gossip as therapy and, occasionally, art.

The *Post*'s grapevine had done some of its best work on me, judging by the general nonreaction to my return. I had the feeling that I could have crossed the newsroom by swinging Tarzan-style from the fluorescent lights and not drawn a decent stare. My regular desk on the rim was unusually neat. No long-term projects were piling up. No junk mail even. Only a single yellow note on which was written: "See Tim Gleason."

That was easier said than done, or so I thought. The serial meeting that was Gleason's workday was still going strong when I reached his office. The current installment featured a couple of front-office types whose names I didn't know. To my surprise, when Gleason looked up and spotted me outside his office door, he shut the open folder on his desk and said something to the man and woman seated opposite him. The gist of his message must have been "Beat it." They closed their own folders and vacated their seats, looking straight through me as they passed.

Gleason waved me in, his google-eyed examination a relief after my bout of invisibility. "Owen. We've been trying to get hold of you most of the day."

"I was in New York," I said. For no particular reason, I added, "For lunch."

"Oh," Gleason said. "Have a good one?"

"Okay."

"I didn't get lunch today myself. I could use something to eat. Actually, what I could really use is a drink." He pulled open the file drawer of his desk. "If I were an old-time newspaper editor, I'd have a bottle in here. As it is, I've got the gym stuff I wore in the city marathon last May. Pretty crusty, too."

He shut the drawer firmly. "Let's go find a drink. How does that sound?"

"Fine," I said.

We got as far as the *Post*'s security guard before Gleason had his next thought. "The PT will probably be crowded."

PT was short for Post Time, the name of a bar down the block. As the name suggested, the PT was the official watering hole of the paper. So the crowd Gleason was referring to would be my co-workers. My soon-to-be former co-workers. He was offering me a chance to avoid their company.

"It probably will be crowded," I said.

"How about Junior's or Stan's?"

"How about a casino bar?"

"Ouch," Gleason said, one of his nervous hands making an involuntary check of his wallet. "A little rich, I mean."

"I'll buy."

"Forget that." For a moment, I thought he would scrap the whole plan and give me the bad news right there on the steps of the building. "What the hell," he finally said. "Which one? The Claridge is the closest."

It would have given the occasion a certain symmetry. I had been working at the Claridge when Gleason had rediscovered me. But I had other ideas.

"The Royal Palm," I said. He waited for an explanation, so I gave him one: "Playing a long shot."

We drove the few blocks to the casino separately, which eliminated the challenge of making small talk. The editor was waiting when I arrived at the entrance. Against the Palm's glittering golden façade, Gleason, in his denim shirt and rumpled, khaki pants, almost looked like one of the boardwalk's homeless. He also looked small, standing as he was beside the casino's trademark, a giant palm tree made of brown concrete and green aluminum.

Gleason knew the casino better than I did. He suggested a secluded mezzanine lounge that had a view of the ocean. I insisted on a big, public bar on the first floor that had a view of the maroon-and-gray lobby. And perhaps, if I was lucky, Mrs. Conti.

The bar was also maroon and gray, as were the waitresses' outfits, which looked like a drum major's uniform coat worn without the trousers. Gleason's large eyes got even larger when our waitress showed up, a reaction I initially misread. It turned out to be because she was carrying a bowl of popcorn.

I asked her for a scotch. Gleason ordered a liqueur on the rocks, one that combined Irish whiskey and cream. When the waitress had gone, he said, "I need something from you, Owen."

"Salt?" I asked.

"Your resignation."

To cover my surprise at not being fired outright, I said, "Did Kate give you hers without a fight?"

"No. I mean, we haven't asked her for one. We're not going to, either."

"I thought that was one of Mr. West's demands."

"Who told you that?" Gleason asked, one hand in front of his full mouth.

"An anonymous source."

The lobby traffic beyond Gleason's shoulder was heavy and contained a high percentage of little gray-haired ladies. None was Mrs. Conti, however.

Our drinks arrived. Gleason's first sip gave him a little milky moustache, which he daubed away with a gray napkin. My first sip gave me a little glow of recognition. It was my first taste of hard liquor in months.

"Your mystery source is correct as far as what Geist or West or whatever he's calling himself today wants," Gleason said. "But he isn't going to get it. The paper's going to stand behind Kate. Everything she said in her story was true. The police did question Geist in connection with Barbara Lambert's death. He was a suspect in the original Lambert murders. If the story had the unfortunate side effect of exploding this new identity Geist created for himself, that's too bad. He'll never prove malice on the *Post*'s part, and without malice, he hasn't got a case.

"Besides, firing Kate would be like an admission of guilt. No paper would do that, even if the reporter had screwed up. So don't worry about Ms. Amato. Her halo may be tarnished, but her job is safe."

"Glad to hear it." If for no other reason than that it spoiled Fruscione's plans.

"You're another story, Owen. Did you tell West that you're a reporter for the *Post*?"

"Not West," I said.

"But others, right? One of whom told West. We have what is probably an incomplete list. The paper put together a damage-control team today to backstop Kate on this morning's article and on the original Lambert anniversary piece. Several of the people they talked to on the phone mentioned a second Post reporter named Keane. A couple of them even saw his press card. Who the hell gave you a press card?"

"You did," I said.

"Oh. Then it's only right that I should take it back. I specifically told you when you took this Lambert business up that you weren't representing the *Post*."

"I remember."

"Now you do, you mean. Why didn't you remember before?"

Because I'd wanted some legitimacy for once, some justification for asking my questions, so I'd borrowed the *Post*'s authority. Gleason knew that already, so I didn't bore him with it. He also knew why I'd thought I'd get away with the act: I hadn't expected anything to come of Barbara Lambert's request. I hadn't expected her to die.

Gleason finished his drink. The ice cubes in his glass looked unclean in their dairy coating. In contrast, the ice in my empty glass shone like very cubic zirconia. The waitress brought us another round, the gold braid of her epaulets swaying in rhythm with her hair as she bent to retrieve our empties.

"Let me ask you one," I said. "Why didn't you just can me back at the office in a nice loud voice?"

"Not my style," Gleason said. "I hate firing people. I bitch about having to deal with a union, but I secretly thank God for it. I can only tell people they're incompetent if I know it isn't going to affect their careers."

"I'm not in the union," I said.

"Neither am I. That's why I'd rather not fire you."

"I still don't get it."

"My ass is hanging out in the breeze over this, Owen. Is that image clear enough for you? I'm the one who brought you and Barbara Lambert together. Your whole under-the-table investigation was something I cooked up so I wouldn't have to deal with her. I've got to do the decent thing by you and let you resign. If you get mad and blow the whistle, I'm out the door, too."

It was a clever enough plan, or would have been if Gleason had kept it to himself. The way he'd laid it all out for me made me suspicious. The suspicion or the scotch had me wondering whether he was asking me to let him off or prodding me to take him down.

"You're not responsible for what happened to Barbara Lambert," I said.

"What makes you think I'm feeling bad over that?"

"There's a lot of it going around right now."

"I'm immune to that bug," Gleason said. "I'm a journalist. Death and suffering is the material of my medium, like stone for a sculptor or eggs for a short-order cook."

He sucked on his latest set of milky ice cubes.

"Right," I said. "I forgot."

I'd barely touched my second drink. The first one had made me sentimental enough. I took out my press card. The card wouldn't make it into my tin dispatch box of souvenirs, which bothered me as much as losing my job. On the back of the card, I wrote a two-word resignation. Then I signed and dated it.

Harry had been right about my capacity for getting other people sued. I was thinking of his plan for early retirement as I handed Gleason the press card. "Your job is safe as far as I'm concerned. You won't have to go back to cutting lawns."

Gleason unbuttoned his shirt pocket and tucked the card away. "I had a paper route," he said. "Newsprint's in my blood."

I stayed on after Gleason left, my untouched drink serving as a lease on my chair. As the evening wore on, the lobby traffic became progressively younger. Mrs. Conti would have stood out nicely if she'd put in an appearance. She didn't oblige. I racked my mental store of paperback and movie plots for a ruse that would give me her room number. I couldn't think of a plan that didn't depend on first having the name she'd registered under.

The waitress came by every few minutes to see if my drink had evaporated. I decided to improve her tip prospects by moving on.

"Good luck out there," she said, referring, I guessed, to the casino.

Thinking back on my paperback heroes had put me in the mood for some detective talk. "Never heard of the stuff, sister," I said.

THIRTY-ONE

I SPENT THE NEXT DAY licking my wounds. It was a day made for wound licking—quiet and hot and still. The only interruption was the arrival of the personal stuff from my desk at the Post. It came by messenger, a Jimmy Olsen-grade reporter who knocked on my front door and then ran off before I could get there. Tim Gleason had probably warned him that my career had died of something contagious. Or maybe Kate had. In addition to the odds and ends I'd left at the paper, the box I found on my front step contained a final paycheck, one that was unusually large. More penance on Gleason's part, I thought, and the best kind. Negotiable penance.

I stayed inside all day. I didn't want to miss the call that would break the case wide open. There had to be a call. Otherwise, the investigation would wither and die for lack of an inspiration on my part. That would leave the Lambert story without an ending, an outcome so inconceivable to me that it made a case-breaking phone call seem like a sure bet.

I was still within arm's reach of the phone when the sun went down. I was sitting there in the dark two hours later when someone began knocking on my front door. The soft tapping barely qualified as a knock. Its timidity had me hoping that Mrs. Conti had come in person to hand-deliver her secret. I didn't bother to verify this wishful thinking before I opened the door, but I did switch on the outside light. Its yellow bulb illuminated a shrunken, frightened Anthony West.

"Turn out that light," he snapped at me.

"Thanks anyway," I said, shrinking a little myself.

"Let me inside then." He held up his hands to show that they were empty. They were also trembling, which was more persuasive. In spite of his trendy haircut and designer clothes, he looked like an old man. I stepped aside and he rushed past me, saying "No more lights, okay?" in a tequila-scented voice.

He sat down in the darkest corner of the living room. I sat near the picture window and the patch of yellow front-porch light beneath it, feeling like one of Beverly Simzack's campers. In that analogy, West was one of the threatening, wild things crouched just beyond the campfire's light. It was how I'd once seen West, as the dangerous unknown. Now the only dangerous thing about him seemed to be his lawyers. Or so I told myself.

"Is darkness part of your standard act?" I asked.

West blinked and didn't answer. I was working on another ice breaker when he said, "No. I've never liked the dark. I came about your job. To say I was sorry."

"A card would have been enough. Or flowers." My voice had a giddy quality. To slow it down, I asked, "How did you find me?"

"The cops mentioned this burg when they were grilling me. I was supposed to have stalked Barbara Lambert here. I didn't kill her, Keane."

"Fine. Who did?"

West was watching the picture window intently. I wanted to check it, too, but that would have meant taking my eyes off my guest.

"And I didn't have anything to do with the Lambert murders," West said. "I couldn't have."

"Yes, you could have. You faked your alibi twenty years ago. Your ex-wife told me all about it."

"I mean I had no reason to kill those people. My whole

setup, the whole Earth business, was a con. You don't kill people over a con.''

"Unless you start to believe the con yourself," I said. "One of your former disciples, Bruce Somers, spotted that trap."

"There's never been the slightest danger of me believing in me," West said, his deep voice hollow. "You'll have to come up with something else."

"How about your plan to expand your commune? George Lambert stood in the way of that."

"So what? A lot of those hicks did. As far as I know, the rest of them are still alive. George Lambert would still be alive if I had anything to say about it. I never met the guy, but I'd give anything to bring him back. No lie, Keane. If I could raise one person from the dead, it wouldn't be Kennedy or King or my own mother. It'd be George Lambert. He could tell the world that I had nothing to do with his death. That I was the original innocent bystander."

"Tell me about the day the Lamberts were killed."

"It isn't much of a story. I spent most of the day in Scranton. That's pretty pitiful, isn't it? The most important day of my life in a lot of ways, and I spent it in Scranton, PA."

"Doing what?"

"Something I don't want to read about in tomorrow's Post."

"I don't even get home delivery anymore."

"I was buying grass. Marijuana. It was the most important ingredient in my system, and we went through a bale of it a month. Pot made Earth possible. Hell, it made Gary Geist possible. I miss it a lot these days when I'm talking to a room full of JCPenney suits, trying to sound like I believe every word I'm saying. I find myself wishing I had a little stash to pass around to make things easier.

"Everything was easier in the old days. The world made

more sense. It hung together, you know what I mean? After those murders, it all came apart. Now even a good-sized piece is rare.''

It was West's theory of continental drift with the pseudoscience replaced by heartfelt conviction. I recognized the true inspiration for Lifeforce: the Lambert murders.

West's lament reminded me of something else. ''I spoke with an old friend of yours who thinks that the world has gone to hell because the killings at Lake Trevlac were never solved.''

''What old friend? Somers again?''

''No. Patrick Derry.''

West pushed himself farther back into the dark corner. ''That bastard. I still have nightmares about him. When the angel of the Lord comes to cut me down, I expect him to look like Derry. Mr. Law and Order, the other cops called him. Whenever they said that, I always thought, Mr. Right and Wrong. Derry couldn't see things any other way. You were one of the righteous or you were on the other side. And God help you then. Who's that fanatical cop from the old French novel they turned into a play?''

''Javert from *Les Misérables?*''

''Right, Javert. That was Derry. With any other cop I might have tried to hint around about my real alibi. Not with Derry. If he'd known I'd been off buying grass on the day of the murders, he would have had me charged as an accessory before the fact. He would have done the same thing if I'd told him I'd jaywalked that day. I couldn't admit to doing any evil thing on that day of ultimate evil. Not if I wanted to get away from him.''

''You're wrong about Derry. He never saw you as anything more than the man Russell Conti tried to frame. When I called to tell him I thought you'd run down Barbara Lambert, he told me I'd gotten it wrong.''

''Who does Derry think is trying to frame me now?''

"He didn't say."

"No," West said. "He couldn't say it out loud, could he? It's almost enough to make me feel sorry for the old pig. He's a Javert whose quarry had made the ultimate getaway. How do you track down a guy who's slipped across the big border by blowing a hole in his head? How do you track down a dead murderer, Keane? And how do you get away from one who's trying to frame you?"

Oddly, it wasn't a rhetorical question. "Russell Conti didn't use your car to kill Barbara Lambert," I said.

"Who did then? Samuel Calvert? Same problem, Keane. The guy's dead. Conti and Calvert are both dead, and I'm being framed and…"

"And what?"

"You told me that before Barbara Lambert died she had the feeling she was being watched. Was that on the level?"

"Yes."

"I have the same feeling now. Someone's watching me."

"The bunco squad, probably."

"No. Someone else."

"Who?"

"Someone out there," West said, his eyes fixed on the window beside me.

This time I turned to look out the window. I saw my Chevrolet and, beyond it, the dark street. West didn't take advantage of the opportunity to rush me. I would have preferred an attack to dealing with West's crazy fear of a dead murderer. It didn't help that I'd felt someone's eyes myself on and off since Barbara's death.

"It's my old friend from Lake Trevlac, Keane. I know his work. Twenty years ago he tried to nail me to a bloody cross. Now he's used my car to kill the last Lambert. Who else but the Trevlac murderer would want to hurt her? Who else would want to get back at me for slipping off the hook twenty years ago?''

The Mafia, I'd told Fruscione. I was too tired to explain that leap to West, so I took a simpler line. "If the Trevlac murderer stole your car, then Derry missed somebody twenty years ago. A fourth suspect. Someone who's still alive and frightened.''

Over in his corner, West shook his head. "Tell yourself that if it helps you sleep tonight. You know it isn't true.'' He hit his chest with a balled hand. "We know it. We just don't know why we know it.''

He started to stir in his chair like a man waking up from a nap, running a hand through his spiky hair, pulling first at his chin and then at the cuffs of his shirt, looking at his watch. The mannerisms all said it was time to leave, but West couldn't seem to bring himself to take the first step. I wasn't that anxious to lose his company myself.

"Why did you come here tonight?'' I asked.

West had gotten as far as sitting upright in his chair with his hands on his knees. "I wanted somebody to know that I'm being watched. And that I'm innocent. In case something happens.''

"In case what happens?''

"Nothing. I'm going to make myself scarce. That's all I meant.''

I almost asked him where he thought he could hide from a ghost, but striking out at West no longer seemed very important.

He wasn't feeling as chummy. "You may not have been the one to tell, Keane.''

"Why not?''

"You're too exposed yourself right now.''

He stood up and crossed the part of the room lit by the window so quickly that it scared me out of my seat. He was past me and at the door before I got my left up.

"Watch your back," he said as he flipped off the porch light. Then he was out the door and shutting it soundlessly behind him.

As soon as the front door closed, I ran for the back door. The sliding-glass part of the door was already open. I slid the matching screen panel out of the way and stepped into the hot night. In two long strides, I reached the corner of the house. I checked the alleyway formed by the house and the neighbor's fence and then made my way down it in a crouch, my head below the saw-toothed top of the fence.

From the dark street came the sound of West's car door shutting and his engine turning over. I reached the edge of the fence in time to see the familiar black Cadillac pull away. Then I waited. None of the other cars wedged along Lake Champlain's curbs came to life to follow West. If any dead murderers had tailed him to my street, they had decided to stay.

I told myself that the only thing West had brought me was a bad case of the willies. But recognizing the willies never made them go away. When I got tired enough of swatting mosquitoes to retreat up the alleyway, I still kept my head down.

THIRTY-TWO

As soon as I got back inside the house, my phone began to ring. I'd been listening for the sound all day, but when the ringing started—magnified by the stillness of the night—it made me jump. I whispered my hello.

"Owen? It's Kate. I can barely hear you."

I tapped the handset lightly on the edge of the kitchen table and then spoke in a normal voice. "Is that any better?"

"Lots. Are you okay?"

"For the moment," I said. "Anthony West was just here."

"Did he want to gloat?"

"No. He wanted to warn me. He thinks he's being watched. He's afraid the Trevlac murderer may be after him. Or me." I tried to sound amused by the possibility, but I didn't carry it off.

"You're fading out again, Owen. What are you going to do?"

"I don't know."

"Get out of there, for starters. West may still be hanging around. He may be playing some kind of sick game with you. Throw some stuff in a bag and get out. Stay somewhere else tonight."

"Where?"

"How about the Royal Palm Casino? I've got some information about that place that'll interest you."

"You found Grace Conti?"

"I'm not going to tell you over the phone. Not when

you should be moving. Meet me in front of Cleo's as soon as you can make it.''

Even working in the dark it didn't take me long to fill an overnight bag. I'd have to wait till the next morning to find out what I'd filled it with. I broke off the process several times to check Lake Champlain Drive and never saw so much as a stray dog. The street was even emptier when I moved from the house to the Chevy. As I turned the ignition key, I thought, too late, of Smiling Frank Botticelli and his exploding limo. The oversight didn't cost me. The car settled into its normal rattle, and I slammed it into reverse.

I didn't see any taillights in my rearview mirror until I was out of my neighborhood and onto Mystic Island's main street. The pair I spotted then followed me all the way to the Garden State Parkway, but not onto the highway, as far as I could tell. I had plenty of new headlights to watch in their place. Some of the new lights exited with me onto Highway 30, the road on which the Royal Palm driver had lost me. I tried to repeat his trick of being the last car through a yellow light and finally pulled it off at Baltic Avenue. I made the next right and wound my way around to Duck Town.

I hadn't expected to see Kate again. When I spotted her pacing Cleo's corner, wearing a tie-dyed T-shirt as long as a nightgown, her arms wrapped tightly around her chest as though it were December, I was happier than I should have been. She and I had said our good-byes in the *Post*'s press-room. My one attempt at an epilogue, the tip on West I'd left on her voice mail, had been a disaster for both of us. So this last meeting was pointless at best. I told myself that I was there for the secret of the Royal Palm and nothing else, but, as usual, I wasn't listening.

"Finally," she said when I joined her on the corner. "I've been propositioned three times in the last five minutes. Shows what working for the *Post* has done for my personality when everyone takes me for a prostitute.''

Her pale skin had taken on the blue tint of Cleo's neon sign, giving false support to my earlier idea that she was cold.

''Your personality's fine,'' I said. ''This corner's isn't. Let's go inside.''

''Get your bag,'' Kate said. ''We're going to my place.''

''Joe Fruscione wouldn't like that.''

''He'd hate it. But Joe's no longer a player.''

''And I am?''

''You're a friend who needs a sofa. I've got one.''

''What about the Royal Palm?''

''It's too late to go knocking on doors tonight. And you don't even know which door to knock on. If you don't let me help you, you're never going to know. Now come on. A marked man like you shouldn't be standing around on street corners.''

The sidewalk that led to Kate's house had been made narrow and winding by piles of trash set out for the next day's collection. As we made our way through the maze, I said, ''The *Post* wouldn't approve of your taking me in, either.''

''The jury's still out on me and the paper,'' Kate said. ''It's not the fearless bastion of truth I thought it was. I'm not sure anyone at the *Post* would recognize the truth if they accidently printed some. I'm not sure I would either. Not anymore.''

''Is that why you're not going after Mrs. Conti yourself?''

''One of the reasons.''

The first floor of the solitary house was dark. Kate got us inside using a brass key that looked huge in her hand. Then we climbed the steep stairs with the treads that encouraged tiptoeing. I didn't need the encouragement.

When we were inside the apartment, I started to relax for the first time since West had knocked on my door. Kate picked up on that and smiled. "You're safe here, Owen."

Over the past week or so, I'd tripped over some reminder of the Carteret case wherever I'd gone. The current parallel was easy to spot. Late in that investigation I'd shown up on Marilyn's Brooklyn doorstep, beaten down and tired. She'd taken me in and even tried to comfort me, after a fashion. Now I'd been granted sanctuary again by a woman who should have known better. Sanctuary, but not the amenities.

"Sorry I can't offer you a drink, Owen. I eliminated the middlewoman this evening and poured the last of my wine cellar straight into the toilet. Hope you don't mind."

I wasn't about to admit that I did. "What brought that on?"

"Almost getting fired. And receiving a proposal of marriage. And realizing that I wasn't exactly sure how I'd gotten into either fix."

"Fruscione proposed?"

"Tonight. I think he wanted to get me on the rebound." I knew he did, but I kept it to myself. "So?"

"So I said no. It just shows you how close great timing is to rotten timing. Joe came within a hair of being the new leaf I turned over. Instead, he ended up standing for the old, nasty leaf."

She was smiling as she said it. Then she blinked once behind her windowpane glasses and started to cry. She joined me on the bottomless sofa, and we sat for a long time with our arms around one another, survivors of different shipwrecks who had washed up on the same beach.

Somewhere on the floor below us, a clock struck midnight. Kate said, "Grace Conti is in Room 1221 of the Royal Palm."

"How did you find her?"

"I didn't. It was Joe. He told me tonight after I turned him down. He said he didn't want to tell you, but he didn't care if I did."

Like hell he didn't. "What name is she registered under?"

"Joe didn't know that. But she is being looked after by some old friends of her Uncle Frank. Joe wanted me to be sure to tell you that. He thought it might make you change your mind about talking to her. Will it?"

"No. Has Joe talked to her?"

"Not yet. He's going over in the morning. Ten o'clock."

Old Joe was getting very sporting late in the game. I couldn't decide whether the clear field he'd offered me through Kate was a grudging favor or a subtle trap. I was still wondering about it when Kate kissed me and stood up.

"You'll solve this for Barbara yet, Owen." It was the rest of Kate's reason for not going after Grace Conti herself. She wanted to give me one last chance to come through for her dead alter ego.

"It's too late to do Barbara any good," I said.

She kissed me again, this time on my fevered brow. "We can't know that for sure."

THIRTY-THREE

I CROSSED THE Royal Palm's lobby at nine o'clock sharp to the accompaniment of a dozen vacuum cleaners. The janitors herding them around took no notice of me. Nor did the maroon suits behind the hotel's front desk. Not that I'd been worried about getting past the Royal Palm's personnel. I was on the lookout for Grace Conti's private staff, the bodyguards provided by her late uncle's friends. No black hats rode up in the elevator with me and none waited in the little vestibule on Twelve where the elevator dropped me. Their absence didn't settle me down. Even the empty hallway that led me to room 1221 seemed at best a mixed sign.

It wasn't until Mrs. Conti answered her door herself that I realized I'd been running a gauntlet of my own imagining. It was her bathrobe that did it. The robe was fuzzy and turquoise and it made her yellow skin look even yellower.

"Mr. Keane," she said. "I thought you were the person come for my breakfast tray." She didn't seem put out by the substitution. "Come in, won't you? I can't offer you coffee. I only have the one cup. Would you like me to call down for another?"

"No, thank you," I said, a little confused by her welcome. For the second time in our brief relationship, Mrs. Conti was giving me the impression she'd been expecting me.

I'd pictured her installed in a suite of rooms, perhaps one normally reserved for visiting businessmen from Sicily. Room 1221 was actually so small that there was scarcely space to step around the breakfast tray that sat on the floor near the door.

"Can I put the tray in the hall for you?" I asked.

"They'll knock. It gives me a chance to say hello."

A table and two chairs were wedged in beside the bed, the table so small that the top barely accommodated an unfinished game of solitaire. Mrs. Conti raked in the cards as she sat down. Each one had a hole in its center.

"Casino cards," she said. "They hardly use a deck before they have to get rid of it. They drill a hole through the old decks so nobody can slip them back in."

I sat down opposite my hostess, my knees touching hers until she pulled away. She'd tried to brighten up her little room. Fresh flowers stood on the dresser next to a framed picture of Russell Conti I remembered from her house. A statue of the Blessed Virgin shared the tiny nightstand with an industrial-size clock radio.

"You're here to tell me why the police let that horrible Gary Geist go free, I hope," Mrs. Conti said. "I can't understand it. I've been following it in your newspaper. I order a copy every morning with my breakfast. My own paper stopped coming. And my mail. I haven't been able to find out why. All I get when I ask are rude answers.

"When I read in the *Post* that the police were questioning Geist, I thought my nightmare was finally going to end. I started packing my bag to go home, Mr. Keane. I really did. Russell always said that Geist was the person the police should have been after. It made him close to crazy when they let Geist go the first time. Now they've done it again. Why?"

"He had an alibi. He couldn't have killed Barbara Lambert." Before she could cite her husband again, I asked, "Why are you hiding here?"

"I'm frightened for my life, Mr. Keane. I heard that poor girl get hit. I actually heard it. That is, I heard the sirens afterward. Daughter of George Lambert and all, she didn't deserve that. No one deserves to die like that, unless it's Gary Geist.''

"How did you know it was Barbara Lambert who'd been killed?''

"I didn't at first. I was standing at the edge of the street with some of my neighbors, watching the ambulance people. And saying a prayer," she added to improve the picture a little. "There was another girl in the street. She was close to hysterics. I heard her tell a policeman that the girl who'd been hit was Barbara Lambert and that she'd been coming to see *me*.

"That was all I had to hear. I locked up the house and walked to a phone. I haven't been so frightened since the night I found Russell. I don't think I was as frightened then.''

"Why didn't you call the police?''

"The police," she repeated, making it sound like I'd suggested calling a plumber.

"Who did you call?''

"Old friends of the family. They helped me at first. Now all they'll say is that I should go home. How can I go home with that murderer out there somewhere?''

It was a problem the widow and I shared. I saw a way out for her. "You have to tell your story, Mrs. Conti. Barbara Lambert was killed to keep her from talking to you. If you're in any danger, it's because you know something that no one else knows. Tell the police what you know and the danger will go away.''

"Why the police? What good have the police ever done me? They're not going to clear Russell's name. I depended on you for that, and you let me down. Is that why you're here? Has your paper had a change of heart?''

It would have to grow one first, I thought. After Barbara's death, I'd made up my mind to lie Mrs. Conti's secrets out of her. My big chance had arrived, but I couldn't do it.

"I don't work for the *Post* anymore," I said. "I lost my job. The people at the paper aren't interested in your story. Your only chance to clear your husband is to help me find the real murderer."

Mrs. Conti gave me a short refresher course on how it feels to be without credentials, even borrowed credentials. Her big black eyes narrowed and her drawstring mouth tightened. Then she asked me the question I'd expected at the start. "How did you find me?"

"I got a tip from a cop. I don't know how he found you. My guess is that one of your uncle's old friends is getting tired of baby-sitting."

"I'll have to ask you to leave, Mr. Keane."

"First tell me what proof you have that your husband was innocent."

"No. I told you before that I'd only break faith with Russell if I could be sure of clearing his name. You can't help me do that and you can't frighten me into telling you. Nothing would be worse than bringing more shame on Russell for no good reason."

I did a little of my single-digit math. Mrs. Conti's secret was damaging to her husband. It proved him innocent of murder but guilty of something as bad or worse. It was Anthony West's story all over again, the alibi that was a confession to another crime. The coincidence made me dizzy, so I pushed it aside for a moment.

"Where was your husband on the day of the murders, Mrs. Conti?"

She stood up and started for the door, kicking the breakfast tray on her second step. Before the cymbal crash had died away, she'd opened the door wide. "Please leave," she said, "or I'll make some calls."

"There's no one left to call, Grace. You're alone on this one."

"I'll yell then. Get out or I'll start screaming. See if that doesn't bring someone."

I stood up. I had only one play left—Patrick Derry's crazy hunch—and only the short walk to the door in which to use it. "Why did you destroy your husband's real suicide note?"

By the time I'd finished asking the question, I was certain that the old cop had come through for me.

Mrs. Conti's mouth had formed a lowercase o. "How could you know?"

I reached past her and shut the door. She slipped away from me, coming to rest on the edge of the bed, her outstretched right arm holding her upright. She used her left arm and hand to express her shock. The conventional gesture would have been a hand to her heart. Mrs. Conti used her hand to press her left ear against her head with enough force to make her whole body tremble.

I didn't give her a time-out. "Your husband's note was a confession to the Lambert murders. You destroyed it and substituted a note that maintained his innocence. You took away your husband's last chance to confess his sin."

"No," the widow said in a voice I had to lean down to hear. "I destroyed his note but not his confession. His sin was against me and God and we both knew the truth. No one else had to know. The police would never have understood what he wrote. They would have seen it as proof that Russell had killed the Lamberts when it was really proof he hadn't. So I wrote a new note that made his innocence clear."

"What did your husband's note say?"

She squinted at an invisible page suspended in the air between us. "'A great evil has poisoned my life. I can't go on living.'"

"The murders were a great evil, Grace. How can you be sure they weren't what your husband meant?"

"Because if he'd meant the murders he would have just said so. He would have written, 'I killed them.' There wasn't any reason not to. Everyone knew about the murders. They weren't a secret. Don't you see? The great evil had to be something Russell couldn't bring himself to name, something he didn't want me to know about even after he was dead."

Grace made a tiny fist and struck at the bed. "The thing is, I already knew. Uncle Frank told me all about it. He came to my house one afternoon, weeks before the murders. He sat me down and told me, 'Your Russell is cheating on you.' Just like that. One of his associates had found out by accident. Uncle Frank asked me if I wanted him to talk to Russell or if I wanted him to have Russell watched. I told him no, that I would handle it. But I didn't. I never could bring myself to mention it to Russell. I tried a hundred times.

"Then the murders happened. They gave me an excuse not to mention the other woman. Why should I have added to his worries? And besides, Uncle Frank told me that Russell had stopped seeing her."

"Before the murders?"

"No, just after. The police investigation put the fear of God in Russell. Being accused of a crime like that would make any man straighten himself out. I thought I'd been right to keep silent. I thought everything would get back to normal.

"But those awful police kept hounding my husband. They let Gary Geist go and chased after Russell because he couldn't account for his movements that afternoon. They broke his spirit. And all the time they were persecuting him, he had an alibi and couldn't use it. He'd been with *her* that day, I'm sure of it. With his mistress. He couldn't tell the police that without ruining the woman's reputation and damaging our marriage. So he let his own reputation be ruined.''

I took Conti's photograph off the dresser. The photo's two dimensions probably made the face more angular and the eyes emptier than they'd been in life. Even conceding that, it was hard to see it as the face of a man so sensitive that he would kill himself to protect a woman's reputation or to spare his wife's feelings. Anthony West's tale of pot buying in Scranton had been easy to believe in comparison, in part because it hadn't forced me to reevaluate West. Mrs. Conti's story stood the portrait I'd built up of Russell Conti on its head.

His widow took his photograph from me and pressed it to her chest. "I blame myself," she said. "If I'd only let him know that I'd heard about the other woman, it would have been easier for him to make a clean breast of it.

"I blame her, too," she added with considerably more feeling. "She could have stepped forward and told her story to the police. She had to know what Russell was going through. Her lily white reputation was worth more to her than his sanity.''

"Whose reputation? Who was your husband's mistress?"

She looked away. "I never knew her name. Uncle Frank never told me.''

"You're lying now, Grace. When you talk about this woman, you're describing a person you know.''

"Stop calling me Grace. And stop trying to confuse me. You've tricked me into telling you enough.''

"Give me a name, and I'll help you get your husband's alibi.''

"She'll never admit to anything. Not that one. She wasn't fit to wipe his shoes. She doesn't deserve to have her name mentioned in the same breath with his. Ever.''

I sat down on the edge of the dresser, nearly upsetting the vase of flowers. A minor revelation had knocked me backward. Mrs. Conti would never tell me the name of her rival because she was still jealous of her. She wouldn't share her husband, or the littlest part of her status as his widow. That was the real reason she'd held her secret all these years.

"You'll have to leave now," she said. "I'm very serious. You've bullied me enough."

I checked my watch. It was almost time for Fruscione's turn at bat anyway. I stood up, trying to word a final question that would win me Mrs. Conti's last secret. I hadn't worked it out by the time I reached the door. She stopped me there with a question of her own.

"How did you know that I wrote another note?"

"The police have always suspected that the note they found was a phony. Your note was typed and unsigned."

"Shows what geniuses your police friends are," Mrs. Conti said. "Russell's note was typed and unsigned, too."

FRUSCIONE WASN'T haunting the Royal Palm lobby. I had time to make a clean getaway, but I lingered near the portals of the casino's vast room of slot machines. I was feeling lucky for a change. I'd played a long shot with the suicide-note hunch, and it had paid off. I briefly considered trying to extend my streak at one of the slot machines. I decided instead to try the hotel desk.

I was convinced that Mrs. Conti knew the name of the other woman. More than knew it. I didn't believe that Grace had gone a day in all the years since her husband's suicide without thinking of his mistress, without secretly saying her name. Fruscione hadn't passed along the name Grace Conti had registered under at the Royal Palm, because, according to Kate, he didn't know himself. The widow's "old family friends" might have given her an

alias. She might have been sentimental like Beverly Simzack and taken her mother's maiden name. Or she might
have just picked one. Why not the name that was always
in her mind? Why not turn the tables on a rival who could
very well have registered as Mrs. Conti any number of
times?

A cocktail waitress passed by, overdressed for the early
hour and underutilized. I asked her for one of the little
paper napkins with the casino's palm tree logo. On it I
wrote the name of a dead woman who was never far from
my thoughts and the number 1221. Then I took a twenty
from its hiding place in my wallet and folded it in half.

Several clerks were on duty behind the registration desk.
I selected a young man who was typing on a computer. He
typed the way I did, using his index fingers to tap out the
letters and his thumbs to space. He gave me a new hire's
cheery "May I help you?"

"I hope so," I said. "I'm having trouble locating a
woman I met last night. She's staying here. We were supposed to meet for breakfast this morning." I laid the cocktail napkin on the counter, the folded bill almost entirely
beneath it.

The kid pulled the napkin to his side of the counter,
squinting at my writing and palming my twenty at the same
time. "Mary Ohlman," he read. He tapped away at his
terminal with a grim look on his face. "Sorry, buddy. No
Mary Ohlman is registered here."

I was surprised at how sad that inevitable news made
me. I shook off the feeling and pointed to the napkin. "She
might have used a made-up name. But I'm sure that's her
room number: 1221."

More tapping. "Right. She handed you a line. Your
friend in Room 1221 is named Lambert. Catherine Lambert."

THIRTY-FOUR

I TOOK THE expressway out of Atlantic City, driving west toward the blue gray of an approaching storm. In comparison, the sunny, summer-morning sky over the city seemed to me something the chamber of commerce had slapped together to fool the tourists, like a bright mural painted on a gutted building. I spent as much time watching the sunny road behind me as I did the dark road ahead. It was mostly from force of habit. I didn't expect to spot Anthony West or any bogeyman passed on to me by West. Occasionally though, I caught a glimpse of someone else in the rearview mirror. He looked like me except for an unfamiliar narrowing of the eyes. The day was quickly becoming too overcast for sunglasses, but my reflection appeared to need them. He was squinting as though at a painful light.

The light's name was Catherine Lambert. She'd been part of the story from the start, but only in a succession of bit parts. George Lambert's sister. Barbara's overprotective guardian. The spaced-out mourner I'd accosted in the cemetery. Now the sister/guardian/mourner was back in a larger but less likely role: Russell Conti's lover. She was also his unused alibi, if the faithful Grace Conti was right. I saw another possibility in the widow's story. Catherine Lambert could have been Russell Conti's accomplice. If Patrick Derry was right about Conti being the Lake Trevlac murderer, there had to be an accomplice. Not for the original killings, but for the final one, Barbara Lambert's. I didn't believe that Conti had struck out at her from his grave. Some living person had finished his work. And I thought I knew where to find her.

At Winslow, I traded the expressway for Highway 73, thinking that a quiet country road might settle me down. It worked for a while, until 73 double-crossed me and turned into a four-lane near Tansboro. The traffic grew heavier the closer I got to the Delaware and the Tacony Palmyra Bridge. Just shy of the bridge, I jogged north and then west at the sign for Riverton.

It was a stretch of riverfront that might easily have contained a rotting dockyard or a rusting refinery. There was probably one of each not far away, but Riverton's little niche was prime real estate. I detoured around a golf course that stood guard on some hilly land outside of town. The flags on its green battlements were standing straight out in the steady west wind. Below the club, near the river, were a few tree-lined streets of homes from various periods in various styles. The only thing the houses had in common was an obsession with privacy. Windows were curtained or protected by small trees or large shrubs. Hedges or walls or iron fences guarded almost every lawn. The whole town resembled Mrs. Conti's little compound, right down to the gates that blocked all but the most modest driveways.

Catherine Lambert had given me her address, 62 Mercer Street, when she'd been under the influence of something, sedatives probably. I was hoping her supply hadn't run out. The Lambert house was smaller than its neighbors, but still impressive: an English cottage done in stucco and brick with a steep slate roof and plenty of ivy. The stucco had a yellow tint, but that might have been a side effect of the arriving storm, which had given the day a theatrical light. The front steps lacked a porch roof or any kind of overhang. The first fat drops of rain hit me as I rang the bell. The sky over the river was now completely black. As I watched, a shaft of lightning landed somewhere in northeast Philadelphia. I rang the bell again, just as the bolt was drawn back.

Catherine Lambert was still a contender for lifetime achievement in posture. She towered over me from the elevated threshold of the arched front door, every button buttoned and every hair in place, but the skin of her unsmiling face oddly slack. Something about her studied elegance bothered me. It might have been the contrast between this erect, regal woman and my memory of Barbara, stooped and frightened. Or maybe it was the image of a younger, Barbara-like Catherine in the arms of Russell Conti. It might just have been that the lady of the manor was keeping me standing in the rain.

''Yes?'' she said when it couldn't be put off any longer.

I introduced myself and reminded her that I was there at her invitation to discuss her niece. That didn't get me out of the rain, so I said, ''We met at the cemetery.'' When you were stoned, I didn't say.

I didn't have to. ''Oh, of course,'' Lambert said. ''Won't you come in?''

A little of the breaking storm blew in with me, scattering raindrops across the entryway's dark, parqueted floor. She led me into a living room right out of an issue of *House Beautiful*. A very old issue, one with loose staples and brittle pages. The room had a high ceiling crossed by black wooden beams. The same dark wood showed up in the bookcases on either side of a brick fireplace whose hearth was cleaner than my kitchen floor. To my left as I entered were a pair of French doors that rattled when the wind gusted. The furniture was upholstered in faded velvet, except for one sofa whose brocaded fabric featured hunting dogs and horses.

I was reminded of Kate Amato's rented room. Catherine Lambert also seemed to have acquired some older person's furniture. Unlike Kate, Ms. Lambert had grown into it. We were roughly the same age, but as we sat down I was having flashbacks to interviews in the principal's office.

She came to rest on the edge of the hunt-club sofa, still ramrod stiff and still trying to explain away the fact that she'd forgotten me.

"I expected you sooner, Mr. Keane. The day after the funeral or the day after that."

"Haven't you really been expecting me for twenty years, Ms. Lambert?"

"I don't understand."

"Ever since your brother and his family were murdered at Lake Trevlac, you've been waiting for someone to come and ask you about it. I'm that someone."

She played dumb. "Barbara often asked me about it, Mr. Keane. I couldn't tell her anything from firsthand knowledge, and I refused to discuss the little I'd learned from the newspapers and the police. Do you think I was wrong to hold it back from her?"

"I think you're wrong on both counts, Ms. Lambert. You were wrong to hold out on your niece and you're wrong about not having any firsthand knowledge of the murders."

That didn't shake her composure. Even a thunderclap directly over the house that made my heart miss a beat failed to phase her. I would have guessed she was drugged again, except that she was friendlier when she was drugged.

"You're the one who's wrong," she said.

"I just came from an interview with Grace Conti. Do you remember her? She remembers you. You two must have met in the old days."

Outside, it had gone from noon to early evening. Lambert turned on a table lamp next to her. Its base looked like a Greek column done in brass. "We did meet once, at my brother's house."

"Is that where you met Russell Conti?"

"What did Grace tell you?"

"That her husband had had an affair around the time of the murders. Grace thinks her husband was with his lover on the day your brother and his family died. That's why he didn't have an alibi. His lover could have cleared him, but she didn't. Grace believes her husband killed himself so the lady in question would never have to sully her reputation."

"That's funny," Lambert said, looking like she had never found anything funny in her life. "Russell wanted me to give him an alibi. He wanted me to tell the police he'd been with me that day. He begged me to."

"Why didn't you?"

"Why do you suppose, Mr. Keane?"

"Because Russell Conti didn't spend that day with you. He was at Lake Trevlac, murdering your brother and his family."

"Yes, he was. Not that I have any proof. I've never had any proof beyond what I found in his eyes."

A flash of lightning nearly coincided with a boom of thunder. The lamp near the sofa went out, leaving us in twilight. Lambert gave the lamp her best patrician stare, but that didn't bring it back to life.

"We used to have a live-in maid when I was little," she said. "Whenever the power went out in a storm, she would light holy candles."

"So did my mother," I said.

"Oh," Lambert said, mildly embarrassed. "Where were we?"

"You were finding guilt in Russell Conti's eyes."

"Yes. I think he used me from the start. It was easy for him. I'd never even dated very seriously before he swept me off my feet. He wasn't a romantic man, but he had a certain directness that was very hard to resist. Before I knew what I was doing, we were meeting at motels and at the apartments of friends of his. Apartments his friends used for their own affairs, I guessed, because they were always so impersonal. All the time, he was promising to leave his wife and asking me questions about my brother.''

''What questions?''

''Too many to remember. I do remember one answer, though. One evening, I told him that George was planning to dissolve their partnership. I told Russell so I could see how he would react, to see if it would make any difference for the two of us.''

''How did he react?''

''He killed five people.''

We sat through another gap in the dialogue while the storm moved off to the east. When the rain became too soft to hear, I said, ''Did Conti ever ask you about a zoning controversy your brother had gotten into up at Lake Trevlac?''

''He may have. I don't remember. He was very curious about the lake and the cabin. About the neighborhood and the family's routine.''

''Why didn't you tell all this to the police twenty years ago?''

''Because I was afraid that they'd think what you're thinking now, Mr. Keane. That I was Russell Conti's accomplice. That is what you're thinking, isn't it?''

''Yes.''

''Why would I have taken any part in that horror? For love of Russell Conti? For my brother's estate? We had to borrow money to pay for his funeral.''

''He had an insurance policy that Russell Conti collected.''

''Do you think I would have helped to murder my own niece and nephews for money?''

''People have murdered their own children for money. Or to stop them from crying. That kind of horror is all around us. I don't know why you were involved in the original murders, but I know you were involved. If you had just been Russell Conti's innocent dupe, you wouldn't have had a reason to kill Barbara.''

Lambert bent forward slightly at the waist. "Barbara?"

"She was run down to keep her from talking to Mrs. Conti by someone who has a secret to protect. You have a secret: your involvement with a murderer. You know that Conti tried to frame Geist for the original murders. Your home is only a few minutes from Camden, where Geist has been living under a new name. The agency that found Geist for a lawyer friend of mine said that someone else had been looking for him. I think it was you. You stole Geist's car and used it to follow Barbara to Atlantic City. You knew that she was staying with Joan Noll. You knew why she'd gone to Bannon Street. When she stepped from the curb, you ran her down.''

As my solutions went, it was ironclad. Lambert should have cracked under the weight of its logic, started sobbing, come at me with the brass lamp, or admitted to it all in her calm, crazy voice. Instead she said, "Would you please see if the phone is working?''

She nodded toward a little table standing by itself against the wallpaper. On the table was a black rotary phone of a type I hadn't seen for years. I stood up and crossed to the phone, without turning my back on my hostess. The metal handset was as heavy as a beginner's dumbbell.

"It's working," I said.

"There's a number written on a card beside the phone. Please dial it.''

The number began with an Atlantic County prefix. The rest of the number was also familiar, but I didn't place it before the other party answered.

"Fruscione.''

"It's Keane," I said. "Hold on." I looked to Lambert for instructions. She rattled off a question, and I repeated it. "Where was Catherine Lambert on the evening her niece was killed?"

"She went into Philly with some people to see a play. Society Hill Playhouse. She was the first one we checked."

"Why?"

"Standard procedure for us nonmystics. She's the victim's next of kin. What got you thinking about her?"

"I'll tell you later."

"Wait a minute. Did you talk to Grace Conti? She was gone when I got to the Royal Palm. Left her stuff and walked out."

"Check her house," I said and hung up.

As I sat down again opposite Lambert, I told her I was sorry.

"Don't be," she said. "You were keeping faith with Barbara. I'm grateful to you for that. And you'll believe me now when I say I was afraid to go to the police twenty years ago. They would have been as quick to accuse me as you were."

"When did you know that Conti was the murderer?"

"I knew it in my heart right away, but I wouldn't admit it to myself. Then, when I told Russell that I wouldn't lie to the police for him, he threatened me. He promised to name me as his accomplice if I spoke out against him. When he said that, I was sure of what he'd done. As sure as if I'd been at the cabin when he shot Irene down in the doorway. When he rushed in and murdered George and Jerry. When he killed little Ruth in the closet where she'd hidden and left Paul for dead beside her. I might as well have been there. I've lived through it all a thousand times."

Another long silence followed. It lasted until the power came back on. Lambert switched off the Grecian lamp, breaking into my vision of Conti standing by Barbara's crib.

I asked, "Why did he spare Barbara?"

"I don't know. Maybe because he was sick by then of killing and he knew she couldn't identify him. The other children could have. Even little Ruthie knew Uncle Russell. That's what the children called him. If he had divorced his wife and married me, he really would have been their uncle."

She sobbed once and caught herself. "I don't think he spared Barbara to tie my hands—he wasn't that clever—but that was the effect it had. Because he let Barbara live, I could never denounce him."

"Why not?"

"As frightened as I was of the police, I would have turned Russell in and taken my chances if it hadn't been for Barbara. Someone had to take care of her."

"The Nolls could have taken her in."

"No, it had to be me. I gave Russell the information he used to plan the murders. I had to be the one to take care of Barbara, to atone for what I'd done. That's really why I kept silent. Even if by some miracle I could have convinced everyone that I wasn't Russell's accomplice, the damage would have been done. I would have never been given custody of Barbara. I would have been judged unfit. I *was* unfit.

"I tried to make up for it. I dedicated my life to raising Barbara. I gave up everything to protect her. I still failed."

I knew now why Lambert had been slow to condemn me for Barbara's death: She hadn't had any condemnation to spare.

"When I found out that Barbara had gone up to Lake Trevlac, to that awful place, I was furious with her. I thought it was the most dangerous place in the world for her. It turned out she wasn't safe anywhere."

"When did Barbara go to Lake Trevlac?"

"Right after her cousin sent her a copy of the Post article on the murders. Barbara went up to see that old policeman, Patrick Derry."

THIRTY-FIVE

TREVLAC HILLS was enjoying a late afternoon siesta. My Chevy was the only car squeezing rainwater out of the neighborhood's gravel roads. I had no joggers or hikers to steer around, not even a wandering squirrel. I could sympathize with the universal decision to be somewhere else. I was only in Trevlac Hills myself because I had nowhere else to go.

If Jim Skiles had still been alive, I would have driven to his Pine Barrens shack and paraded my troubles before him. I would have admitted that I'd failed, that I was tired, that I wanted to give up. He would have enjoyed the diversion and, in exchange, he would have given me something I needed badly: the encouragement to go on.

Skiles was dead, so I'd driven into the Poconos to see the man I'd drafted as his successor, Patrick Derry. Derry could provide the affirmation I needed, at least as far as the Lambert case was concerned. He was sure to pat me on the back when I told him he'd been right about Russell Conti's suicide note and probably about Conti's guilt. When he heard Catherine Lambert's testimony, Derry might finally be able to put the old case behind him. In return for that blessing, maybe he would help me spot what I'd missed, the second secret hidden in the Widow Conti's story, the one that explained why Barbara Lambert had been killed. At the very least, I'd get Derry to explain why he'd lied to me about meeting Barbara.

The lie didn't disqualify Derry for the job of replacing Skiles as my confidant. Skiles himself had lied to me more than once. I said earlier that Skiles had marooned me in his haunted corner of the Pine Barrens because I'd lied to him, but it had really happened because I'd caught him in a lie and lorded it over him. He'd left me in the forest to teach me to be less judgmental. I'd learned the lesson so well that I felt no righteous indignation now toward Derry. Only tired curiosity.

Derry was at home at his prefabricated cabin. The boxy Plymouth he'd driven to Barbara's funeral was sitting in the crescent track in front of the house. As I stepped from my car, the man himself appeared in the cabin's doorway, just as Skiles had often done. Derry was dressed in olive green fatigues and held a fishing reel. Nobody had been surprised to see me that day, and the old detective fell into the pattern.

"Come by for a fishing lesson?" he asked.

"You might say that."

He led me into his dining room, which was small and furnished in unmatched discount pieces. A plastic tackle box sat on the table. Beside it were some hand tools and lures and a spool of green fishing line.

"Got my reel fouled up this morning," Derry said. "Didn't have the drag on tight enough. Instead of a fish, I landed a lap full of knotted line. That was before the storm chased me off the lake. Did you have rain down your way? We must have had two inches. Care for a beer?"

"Sure," I said.

He shuffled off and came back after a time with two green bottles of Rolling Rock. Mine was so cold it hurt to hold it.

"Only way to drink beer," Derry said. "Ice cold."

A beer only had to be wet for me, but I agreed politely.

"What's on your mind, Owen? Something is. Let's get right to it."

"On the day they buried Barbara Lambert, you told me

you hadn't seen her in twenty years. That wasn't true. You met her recently, just before she came to the *Post*."

"Who told you that?"

"Barbara was the first. She said she'd been to see the police about reopening the case and been turned down. Your old partner, John Ruba, denies talking to her. So do the Atlantic City cops. I didn't think of a third possibility—a retired policeman—until Catherine Lambert told me her niece had come here to talk to you."

Derry smiled. "It's not very comfortable being on the receiving end of an interrogation. I have to tip my hat to you, though. You found me out. Barbara Lambert did come up here to visit me. She got my address from the DA's office, same as that female reporter from your paper. I did try to talk her out of reopening the case."

"Why?"

"For the same reason I tried to get you to think about your own questioning. Because I know firsthand what happens to a person who wants to know things that can't be known. Your life's half over already, Owen, and it still breaks my heart to see you walking my path. It damn near killed me to see that same fate hanging over Barbara Lambert, a woman that young and unmarked."

"She wasn't unmarked."

"No, I guess she wasn't. The old murders had seen to that. But I thought she might still turn her life around. That was my reason for trying to discourage her. I didn't spot the danger she was in, the physical danger. The only thing I feared for her was that she'd end up like me."

"Why did you lie to me about meeting her?"

"I hated to do that, Owen, but I didn't have a choice. Miss Lambert made me swear I wouldn't tell anyone. Made me cross my heart and hope to die. She was afraid her aunt would find out. Sounds like the aunt did anyway."

"Yes," I said.

"We on the same side again? Good. Now what else do you have to tell me? You didn't drive all the way up here to chew me out."

"I spoke with Grace Conti this morning. You were right about Conti's suicide note being switched. Grace destroyed the original and substituted her own."

"I knew it," Derry said. "I *knew* she was the one. God damn that woman. Did she say why she did it? It was because the truth was too much for her, wasn't it?"

"Not exactly. She still doesn't believe that Conti committed the murders."

"Damn her," Derry said, banging the tabletop with his fist. "How could she be so stubborn? My career ruined, her own miserable life stunted, Barbara Lambert's life stolen away, all because of her blindness. I told you. I said it, didn't I?" He hit the table again. "She couldn't see the truth when it was laid out in black and white in front of her."

"She saw it, but she misread it." I'd expected the news that he'd been right about the note to please Derry. Instead, it had nearly maddened him. I rushed through my explanation. "Around the time of the murders, Mrs. Conti found out that her husband was having an affair. When she read his suicide note, she thought he was confessing to his infidelity. She was afraid the police would misinterpret the note, so she destroyed it."

"She destroyed herself with it. She destroyed me." Veins were standing out in lightning forks across Derry's temples. He pressed the heels of his hands against them. "All these years wasted. And why? Because Russell Conti was sleeping around. How could she think he'd kill himself over that? How could anyone? How could she see that as the great evil that had poisoned his life?"

Derry froze in the act of lifting his hands from his temples. I froze, too, trying so hard not to react that my stillness was like a signal flare. I had a vision of the moment that was as vivid as a drug-induced hallucination: Derry sitting cockeyed in his chair, his fingers extended upward in a parody of his bristly hair, his black eyes on me; the green bottle at his elbow, half full and sweating; the green fishing line, yellow-looking next to the bottle, loops of it shaken off the spool by Derry's banging; the orange tackle box and scattered around it lures of every color, bright cartoon lures that glowed in the foreground of my vision.

I forced myself to go on talking. "The other woman was Catherine Lambert. Conti had seduced her a few months before the murders as a way of keeping tabs on her brother. He asked her about the goings-on at Lake Trevlac. He probably found out about Geist and his commune from her."

My voice, though mechanical, had a soothing effect on Derry. While I droned on, he lowered his hands, picked up the spool of line, and began to rewind it.

"Catherine made the mistake of telling Conti that George Lambert was planning to dissolve their partnership. That would have cut Conti off from his partner's insurance policy, which was the only resource he had left. So he drove up here to murder George Lambert. He killed the others because they could identify him and because he wanted to make it look like the work of a madman. He'd mistaken Gary Geist for a Charles Manson type and he thought he could frame him. But he didn't know enough about the cult to draw the correct symbol on the cabin wall."

Derry had all the fishing line back on its spool. "That's the way we always figured the bloody cross," he said. He held up the spool. "There's a plastic cover for this thing. There, near your beer. Slide it over, will you?"

Without thinking, I looked to my right. When I looked back to Derry, his hand was in the tackle box. It came out holding a snub-nosed thirty-eight. He pointed it at my chest.

"Stupid of me to quote that suicide note, wasn't it? Grace Conti told you what the original note said, didn't she? Of course she did. I saw it in your eyes. She'd never forget that note any more than I ever will. 'A great evil has poisoned my life. I can't go on living.' I can't have known anything about that note, can I? Can't even have seen it."

"Not if Russell Conti really killed himself."

"Right. You're sharp enough, for a civilian, Owen. I'll give you that. You've wandered all over hell's half-acre on this thing, with me tagging along for company part of the time. But in the end you found what you wanted."

More than I wanted. "You murdered Russell Conti," I said. "You wrote the original suicide note. That's why it was typed and unsigned."

"I wrote the note, yes, but Conti's death was an accident. Not that he didn't deserve it. But I went there that night to scare him, not to kill him."

"That was no accident. You shot him with his own gun to make it look like a suicide."

"Listen a minute. I accidentally shot him with his own gun because that's what I was threatening him with. I wanted him to think I was going to fake his suicide. I knew all about the gun he kept in his desk. We'd tested it against the murder bullets and handed it back when it didn't match. I knew if I put that gun to his head he'd know I meant business."

"Why did you have to scare him? You had a warrant for his arrest."

"I got that warrant by promising Bass, the DA, a confession. I convinced him I could get it, but I wasn't convinced myself. Three years of work on that case, of staring at those crime-scene photos till I had every drop of blood in that slaughterhouse memorized, and I had to beg for a warrant. That's how little evidence we had. I thought my only chance was to scare the life out of Conti."

"A coerced confession was worthless to you. No judge in the world would have let it in the door. You went there that night to execute Conti."

"No," Derry said, leaning forward and showing his small, bent teeth. "I went there for evidence. All Conti had to do was let a piece of it slip. One little piece. What he'd done with the murder weapon. Where he'd stopped for gas. Any little detail and we'd have had him. It would have been his word against mine that I'd ever been in his house. He cried and whined, but he wouldn't talk. His gun had a hair trigger. I cocked it to drive him over the edge, and the damn thing went off right against his skull."

If Derry's gun had a hair trigger, I was a dead man. He was holding it tightly enough to make the barrel quiver.

"I typed the note on his machine and got out of there. When word came the next day that Conti was dead, I got the idea started that there'd been a leak in my department, that somebody had tipped Conti off. It all fit together, or would have, if it hadn't been for his damn wife. As soon as I read the note she said she'd found, I knew what she'd been up to. She'd ruined everything. The case would have been closed if she hadn't been so stupid."

"She was smart enough to spot the flaw in your note. She told me what it was this morning. If her husband had wanted to confess to the murders, he would have come out and said it. Why didn't you just type 'I killed the Lamberts'?"

Derry waved the little gun. "I was scared. I typed what came to my mind. It didn't matter what I put in that note. Grace Conti would have destroyed it. She has you buffaloed, but not me. I know the damage she's done."

"Why didn't you kill Grace Conti, then? Why did you kill Barbara Lambert?" I hadn't made the connection before the words were out of my mouth, but they had to be true. Derry had to have killed Barbara. I'd been looking for

Russell Conti's living accomplice, the one who'd completed Conti's work, and I'd found him. We'd found one another.

"That was an accident, too," Derry said. "I didn't have it in my mind to kill her. She stepped into the street in front of me."

With her answers in sight. Derry had given me a clear picture of that moment on the day I'd met him. I'd failed to recognize it as eyewitness testimony.

I stood up. "Your accidents follow a pattern, Derry. You always borrow something first. Conti's gun. Geist's car. Framing Geist followed a pattern, too. Russell Conti's pattern."

Derry didn't like where I was headed. "Geist was the only suspect left alive," he said. "He was the only one I could frame."

"Is that why you did it? Wasn't it really because Russell Conti had tried to frame Geist and you'd taken up where Conti had left off? Geist thinks the Lake Trevlac murderer is still a player. I think he's right."

Derry was drawing his crooked body in, getting smaller as I watched. The gun he held was unaffected by the process. If anything, it was getting bigger. "I couldn't let that girl reopen the case," he said. "What I did to Conti might have come out. She had to die."

"I'm not buying." I was half drunk on adrenaline and the idea that Conti's continuing presence in the case had been provided by Derry, the relentless pursuer of justice. The Javert. Anthony West had asked how a Javert would react to his quarry escaping into a grave. I thought I knew.

"It still would have made more sense for you to have killed Grace Conti. She's the only one who was a danger to you. She deserved it anyway if she ruined your life. Barbara Lambert never did anything to you. But you can't hurt a hair on Grace Conti's head because Russell Conti wouldn't.''

''What are you saying?''

''That you killed Barbara Lambert because Russell Conti would have. You framed Anthony West because Conti tried to frame Gary Geist twenty years ago.''

I stopped short of saying that Conti would certainly have struck out at me, if he'd been alive and kicking. Derry, or what was left of him, had enough reasons of his own for getting rid of me. It didn't make sense to keep prodding him, but I couldn't stop. I told myself that my only chance was to keep him off balance, but that wasn't why I pressed him. I was awed by the spectacle of the old cop breaking up before my eyes.

''You've become Russell Conti.''

I thought I saw the hammer of the gun move. It was only a tiny motion, but it swung things Derry's way. He watched me stumble backward from the table and bared his tiny teeth.

''Enough talk,'' he said. ''We've got a little trip to make.''

THIRTY-SIX

IT WAS A LITTLE TRIP but a long drive. We took my car. Derry sat in the backseat, low in the backseat to judge from his voice as he gave me directions. He might have covered himself with the old raincoat he'd taken from the peg by his front door. I'd seen him take something else from the peg as he'd pushed me out the door, something that looked like a collapsible umbrella. I didn't think he'd need it. The early evening air seemed unusually clear and fresh, but that might have been a bit of premature nostalgia on my part.

"How much gas you got?" Derry asked when we'd left Trevlac Hills behind us. He leaned over my shoulder to check for himself. "Plenty."

"I filled up back on the turnpike. The attendant will remember me."

"Sure he will. Just like they all remembered Russell Conti. You've been watching too much television."

"Reading too many books," I said to my dashboard.

Derry's directions took us into country that made the Lake Trevlac area seem cosmopolitan. The roads alternated between bad pavement and muddy ruts. I took an active interest in the scenery. Any stretch we passed could end up being the place where I died. I saw many likely choices, little pull-offs littered with beer bottles that had to be parking spots for local high school kids, the spiritual descendants of Samuel Calvert Junior. There were deserted farms, too, with broken-backed barns and hilly land reverting to scrub forest. Perhaps one of them was the farm at which the elder Calvert had been working on the day of the murders. Derry passed them all up.

By the time the sun began to set, the driving and the bouncing on the bad roads had turned my giddy terror into something more like the last weary stage of a drinking bout. When Derry finally told me to stop the car, I did it almost gratefully. We were in a little hollow between wooded hills. The road was narrow and bordered by dried weeds as tall as my window.

"Switch the engine off," Derry said, "and pass the keys back."

I did it, and the insect life around us came on-line immediately to fill the silence. Derry only kept the keys for the length of time it took him to join me in the front seat. Once he was belted in beside me, he handed the keys over.

"It's dark enough to start back now, I think."

"Back where?" I asked.

"You'll see. Just drive. I couldn't wait around at the cabin. Somebody might have spotted your car. Now I can say truthfully that you were there, and you went away. If anyone asks, that is."

"Someone will ask. I spoke with an Atlantic County investigator before I drove up here."

"And told him what? You didn't know anything until I made that slip, and I won't make it again. Turn here. I think you're bluffing anyway. You're not working with anyone. It's not your style. Put your lights on and don't try anything cute like flashing your high beams. Yeah, you're bluffing. You're a loner, just like me."

"Like Russell Conti."

"You're letting me down, Owen. I thought you'd understand if anyone did. You would have gone after Conti yourself. You wouldn't have been able to let it rest any more than I could. You can feel just what it was like for me. I knew Conti was the murderer, but I couldn't prove it. I wanted to hear that bastard say it. I wanted him to admit it to himself."

Without moving my head, I could see the hand Derry was using to grip the dash. It was contorted like a claw. He was close to raving again. He must have realized it, too, because he suddenly stopped speaking. I filled the silence by thinking about what Derry had wanted and what he'd settled for.

It was fully dark when I had another insight. We were barely moving by then. The weedy track in the headlights looked like it could turn into a foot trail at any time.

"I believe you shot Conti accidently," I said.

"Why do you believe me all of a sudden?"

"Because you weren't sure that Conti was the killer. You wouldn't have executed him if you weren't sure."

"I was sure. I am sure."

"No, you're not. You never were. If you had been, you would have spelled it all out in the suicide note. Because you weren't sure, you had to hedge your bet. You had to write a note so vague that it wouldn't be shown up as a phony if the real killer walked in a week later or ten years later. Your doubt is what tripped you up. It's what ruined your life. Grace Conti's blindness didn't keep the case open—your doubt did. You struck the rock twice, and you've been paying for it ever since."

Neither Derry nor Conti answered me. We stayed on the same winding path for a long time. It finally emerged from the woods near a paved road I recognized: Northway. Derry had brought me to Northwood, the Lamberts' old neighborhood. The scene of the crime.

"We leave the car here," Derry said. "Pull it into the weeds. Engine and lights off. We'll sit for a minute until our eyes adjust. The little trail we just took might have been the way Conti reached Northwood unseen."

"He was a city boy," I said. "He'd have gotten lost in a minute."

"He could follow a map. He was an infantry veteran. Korea."

I'd seen a picture of him in uniform in his study and forgotten it. "Was he there the same time as you?"

"In Korea? I was never in Korea."

"You told me you were. When we talked in the restaurant after the funeral."

Derry remembered. His black eyes lost focus, and he slid away from me toward the door. I reached for the gun, but I was too slow. My clumsy try brought Derry back. He prodded me hard in the ribs with the barrel.

"No you don't. Ease yourself out the door."

I didn't move. "You need help, Derry. You know it, too."

"The hell I do."

"When I called you to say I'd found Geist—the man you framed yourself—you said he couldn't have killed Barbara Lambert."

"I was just playing my part."

"You were trying to keep me on your trail until I found you. Until I helped you."

"It's too late to help me. Or yourself. Now move. And no noise. I'm right behind you."

When we were on the dark path, he handed me the ignition keys. "You forgot these. Put them in your pocket."

"Not planning to run me over? What kind of accident will it be this time?"

"Shut up, or it won't be an accident. Start walking. You know the way."

They'd never gotten around to installing streetlights in Northwood. Maybe the residents didn't want their sleep interfered with. The lights hadn't been omitted to preserve the star gazing; the sky was full of stars, and no one but Derry and I was outside to see them. No one was jogging or walking a dog. For the first time I found it easy to believe that Conti had gotten in and out of Northwood without being seen. It was a neighborhood of serious investors who had put all their hard-earned money into privacy.

Northwood's character was one reason I didn't strike out at Derry and yell for help. A better reason was that I wasn't sure I could yell if I tried. Putting one foot in front of the other was as much as I could handle. I couldn't even remember where the Lambert lot had been. I led us to the darkest stretch of the dark road, and that turned out to be correct, literally and symbolically.

"Here," Derry whispered. "We leave the road and climb the hill."

Finding a path through the tangle of the old Lambert lot had been hard enough in the daytime. It was impossible now. We blundered from one thicket to another on our slow way up the hill. Derry stayed close behind me, close enough for me to hear what he was whispering to himself: "It ends where it started. It ends where it started."

"It's not over," I said. "Barbara Lambert's killer is still free."

"He's dead," Derry said. "I avenged the Lamberts. The baby, too."

He'd avenged her years before he'd killed her, but the odd sequence didn't seem to be much more than a technicality. Time seemed to be a technicality. The Lambert murders could have been yesterday or tomorrow or happening right now at the top of the hill. They were happening right now, in fact, all over the country. Patrick Derry was dead and Russell Conti was alive. Or was it Jim Skiles? I wasn't there, stumbling through a forest in Pennsylvania. I was in the New Jersey Pine Barrens, charging deliriously through the woods, pursued by a mad hermit, straining to see the lights of the road that was my last hope, mistaking the wind in the trees for Skiles's crazy laugh.

A gust of wind shook a dead pine next to me, the cracking and creaking sounding very like a laugh. An old man's cackling laugh.

I froze with one foot in the black air. Before me on the forest floor was a rough circle of even denser black. It was the well, the Calverts' old colonial well.

I swung around to face Derry. His right arm was already high in the air. He brought his arm down with incredible speed, his breath coming out of him in a grunt. I heard a sound like the crack of a bat. Then I fell backward into nothing.

THIRTY-SEVEN

I AWOKE IN a darkness so complete that I put my hand to my eyes to make sure they were open. Or maybe I dreamed that I did. I was dreaming vividly between moments of awareness. Again and again, I swung around to face Derry. Each time, he struck me and I fell. Between repetitions of the dream, I gathered bits of information. I was cold. I was wet. It hurt to move. It hurt to lie still.

During one of my longer periods of consciousness, I realized that I wasn't lying down. I was half sitting in something wet and soft. I tried to push myself fully upright with my left arm and passed into dreamland again. I was on the edge of the well. I whirled about and faced, in place of Derry, myself, my own arm upraised to strike me down.

That sight shocked me awake for good. My head slowly cleared enough for me to piece together the little clues I'd been collecting. I was in the bottom of the old well, sitting up to my waist in something that felt like wet leaves but smelled worse. My left knee was not very far from the tip of my nose. My right leg was somewhere beneath me. Both legs and my back hurt when I tried to move. My head hurt, whatever I did. The pain was centered at the base of my skull. Where Derry had hit me, I thought for a time. Then I remembered that I'd been facing him through all the hundreds of times he'd swung at me. The answer to the mystery lay throbbing in the debris to my left. My arm was broken. I'd raised it in time to block Derry's blow, for all the good it had done me. I raised the arm again, very slowly, and rested it across my chest. Then I used my right arm to pull my right leg out from under me. The relief I felt as blood rushed back into it almost canceled out the pain.

I looked up. The opening of the well shaft was visible as a gray circle above me. It wasn't as far above me as I'd expected, perhaps no more than thirty feet. The gray of the ragged circle was so bright compared to the blackness around me that I thought the sun might be up. I wiped the mud from the crystal of my watch and saw by its luminous dial that it was a little after three. Hours to go till dawn. Hours during which I had to stay awake.

The watch dial reminded me of another possible source of light—my old steel Zippo. It was still in my pants pocket. My right-hand pocket, thankfully, the side with the unbroken arm. I thought I'd have to let the lighter dry before it would work, but it lit on the first try. Its flickering light showed me that I was not alone. To my right was the skeleton of a small animal that had fallen into the well in the not-too-distant past. A possum maybe. Somehow I hadn't disturbed a bone of the skeleton when I'd crashed down beside it, not the littlest bone in its long, curving tail. The skull's empty sockets looked me straight in the eye, asking for a plan. I snapped off the lighter and tried to think of one.

Climbing out wasn't an option. I tried to stand once, and the effort produced a light show that eclipsed the gray circle above me. I tried calling out, and discovered, when I drew my first deep breath, that I'd broken a rib or two. The sound I produced was too feeble to rouse any sleeping retirees. My best chance, I decided, was to save my strength until the sun was up.

I passed the time with dream interpretation. It was easy enough to figure out why I'd replaced Derry as the heavy in my replay of the attack at the edge of the well. My subconscious had bought into the charge that I was another Derry, a man broken by an obsession with the unknowable.

Broken spiritually and physically, in my case. It was a difficult accusation to answer given my current dilemma, so I cast around for someone else to blame. Derry came to mind, of course, and Russell Conti. Somewhere between those two monsters was Barbara Lambert. I'd seen her as a victim of my questioning, but I was also a victim of hers. We were even, or very nearly so.

Wondering about the chance that had brought Barbara and me together got me thinking—in a thick-witted, plodding way—of synchronicity, one line of Kate Amato's oddball creed. Synchronicity had dogged me throughout the case. But I'd had the last laugh. I'd demonstrated that all the points of similarity between the Carterets and the Lamberts had been nothing more than accidents after all, that the only thing the old investigation and the current one had in common was me—my fears, my imagination. I'd proven it by falling into a well. There was no parallel to that in the Carteret case. Back then I'd escaped from Skiles's forest trap and run to the comforting arms of Marilyn, carrying the solution to the mystery with me. The memory of that lost night brought me as close to breaking down as anything had since Derry drew his gun.

To focus my mind, I concentrated on Derry and the unlikely fact of his growing up to be Russell Conti. But my mind wouldn't focus. It moved from Derry and Conti to Conti's wife and then to his lover. The two women were another pair whose individual identities had intermixed. Grace had become Catherine Lambert, in name at least, just as Lambert had once dreamed of becoming Mrs. Conti. The two had something else in common, something my bruised head struggled to work out. Each had stunted her life as Derry had, by denying the truth: Grace the fact of her husband's guilt and Catherine her involvement in a horrible crime. Both had seen the truth and looked away.

I hadn't. Not this time. The realization lifted my spirits.

It was my answer to Derry. I wasn't a broken man in the making. Not unless I gave up. Derry hadn't destroyed himself by questioning. His sin had been despairing of the answer.

I rested my sore head against the side of the well, content to watch the circle above me brighten. The show was a slow one without a single plot twist, but I followed it with perfect fascination. I began to see movement and then color, the green of the canopy of leaves. By then I had sounds to accompany the picture, birdcalls and the faraway barking of a dog.

At six on the dot I started yelling. It was still too early, but I was afraid I'd pass out again and miss my chance. The loudest noise I could make didn't even frighten the birds away, but I kept at it, settling into a rhythm of yelling and resting and yelling again.

During one of my rests, I felt a piece of paper in the pocket of my shirt. The Zippo's light told me that it was the receipt for the gas I'd bought on the turnpike. The back of the form was blank, and it gave me an idea. My pen was in my suit coat back in the Chevy. I searched the rotting leaves until I found a stick that didn't crumble in my hand. With it I wrote in watery mud: "P. Derry." The effort made me nauseous, perhaps because I'd used my broken arm as a writing desk, perhaps because the crude letters reminded me of pathetic clues left behind by murder victims in books. I told myself that the exercise would change my luck. Having the note would hold off my death the way having an umbrella held off the rain.

And my luck did change. I'd no sooner finished writing and started yelling again than a little gray-haired head appeared at the edge of the well. It was a woman's head, I thought. It was certainly a woman's voice that called down, "Hello? Pauly? Hello?"

"Help me," I said.

"Pauly?" she asked again.

I lit the lighter and held it as high as I could. "Get help, please."

"I will," she said. "Yes, I will."

THIRTY-EIGHT

THE EMERGENCY ROOM doctor who took charge of me looked like he was still paying off his student loans, but he had a breezy manner that inspired confidence.

"Got you cleaned up finally, I see," he said during one of his many visits to my examining room. "Sorry about your clothes. Even if we hadn't sliced them up, you probably would have tossed them. There's a rumor going around that the well you fell into was really an unusually deep septic tank. How are you feeling?"

"Fine," I said. I was having trouble with sentences of two words and up. I'd been given a shot of Demerol, which had dulled my various aches and pains. The shot had also animated several of the inanimate objects around me. The wall clock was particularly lively. It descended like an elevator every time I looked up at it, but somehow it never reached the floor.

"You were lucky," the doctor said. "Hitting your head on the way down probably saved you. Kept you from tensing up. Neither leg is broken, but the way the right one has swollen I'm betting you'll have some ligament damage. Stretched ligaments if nothing worse. About the third time you dislocate a hip climbing out of the bathtub, you're going to wish you'd gotten off with a simple break. There's no spinal damage that I can see, but you do have two cracked ribs. And, of course, your arm."

He held an X ray up to the light for me to examine. The bones it showed didn't look much more substantial than those of the possum I'd left behind in the well. The smaller of the two bones in my forearm was broken cleanly in two.

The next part of the doctor's lecture revealed that he didn't know how I'd come to be in the well. "Some of the older nurses call that kind of break a nightstick fracture. The term has an interesting derivation. Years ago, they mostly saw these fractures on guys who'd been on the receiving end of a policeman's nightstick. The victim would raise an arm to block the blow, and wham."

He raised his own arm to demonstrate, and I had one last vision of myself on the edge of the well, this one Demerol assisted. In Derry's flashing hand I saw the object I'd mistaken for a collapsible umbrella back at his house. It was an umbrella of solid hardwood, an old-fashioned nightstick.

"We've got an orthopedic surgeon coming to set your arm," the kid said as he slipped the X ray into a manila sleeve. "And the desk people got the question of your health insurance straightened out. Your policy from the newspaper is still in force. Someone named Gleason called to say you were covered for everything except herpes."

My ex-editor was being noble or else he was after an exclusive. I'd give the story to Kate and let her decide.

"The nurse said that Gleason left a message for you." He searched the Captain Kangaroo pockets of his white jacket and came up with a slip of paper. "A Mr. Ohlman is trying to get hold of you. Can you reach that phone on the table? Dial nine for an outside line. Catch you later."

Before I could persuade my hand to reach for the phone, another visitor arrived, Sheriff John Ruba. We'd already had one brief conversation via an ambulance radio. He'd sounded confused then, and from the look of the tiny eyes in his broad, glistening face, I could tell that his condition hadn't improved. He also looked tired and sad.

"The state police found Derry," he said. "The Atlantic City cops have him. He turned himself in a few hours ago for the murders of Russell Conti and Barbara Lambert.

They think that's what he was trying to do. He wasn't what you'd call coherent."

Ruba dug a pack of cigarettes out of his shirt pocket, adding guilty to his other expressions. "What's that cliché about picking the wrong week to quit? You mind?"

I tried to word a joke about the head nurse shooting him with his own gun, but it came out jumbled,

Ruba got it anyway. "The head nurse owes me from way back," he said. Even so, he stood up to close the examining room door. "Join me?"

"Sure," I said. One wouldn't kill me—not if a night in a septic tank and a hundred X rays hadn't.

Ruba lit my cigarette and then his own as he sat down. He looked around for a place to put the spent match and ended up holding on to it.

"The AC cops didn't know what to make of Pat. That's why they were so long getting hold of me. On and off he tried to give his name as Conti. How did that happen to him?"

"Ask a doctor," I said.

Ruba nodded. "Or a priest maybe. I guess at one point Pat claimed to have murdered a cop named Derry. He said he'd dumped his body into a well. No one in Jersey knew what well he was raving about. I would have, if they'd passed the word."

"Would you have bothered checking the well?" I asked, speaking each word slowly and precisely.

"No, I guess I wouldn't have. Not until we'd found your car anyway. You were damn lucky that old lady was out taking the air this morning."

"Did you get her name? I'd like to thank her. She was gone when they pulled me up."

"You don't know who that was? It was Edna Wirt, the woman who lived next door to the Lamberts way back when. I never would have guessed she was still in Northwood. She's the one who ignored the baby's crying all afternoon while the little boy bled to death. What was his name?"

"Pauly," I said, remembering how Edna had called the name down to me. Thanking her might not be necessary. She'd been my second chance, but I might also have been hers.

I handed Ruba my cigarette. He took it and his to a sink, ran water on them, and dropped them into a can marked HAZARDOUS MATERIAL ONLY.

"Rest up," he said. "You and the DA have a lot of talking to do."

I decided to practice my talking using the phone. I thought about calling Marilyn, but she didn't like to be bothered at work. I also couldn't guess what her reaction to the news that I'd nearly been killed would be, whether she'd be proud of me for exposing Derry or mad at me for exposing myself. She'd probably just ask me if I'd remembered to make a wish on my way down the well. I opted for a less challenging conversation and dialed Harry.

"Owen," he said after his male receptionist had put me through. "I've been trying to reach you for two days. Is everything okay?"

"Swell."

"Are you calling from work?"

"No. I've checked into a Poconos resort."

"Uh-huh," Harry said. "You sound like you checked into a Poconos bar."

"What have you been waiting two days to tell me?"

"I heard back from the firm that traced Geist for us. They gave me the name of the person who inquired about Geist before we did. You'll never guess who it was. Not in a million years. Not in ten million."

"Russell Conti."

"Damn," Harry said.

It was good to be alive.

The Drowning Pool

A WILLOW KING MYSTERY

Hard Labor

Willow King, civil servant, romance writer, amateur sleuth and wife of Scotland Yard detective, has a new baby daughter, plus all the worries that come with it. And then some. Not long after her child is delivered, Willow's doctor, Alexander Ringstead, is murdered.

Few women deal with postpartum depression by tracking a murderer, but Willow fears the danger is far from over. Digging into Ringstead's past, she comes to the disturbing conclusion that the killer is very close indeed....

Natasha Cooper

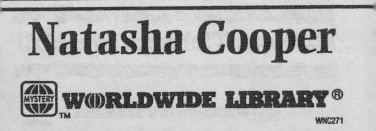

MYSTERY WORLDWIDE LIBRARY®

TM

WNC271

FOWL PLAY

A MOLLY WEST MYSTERY

Birds of a Feather

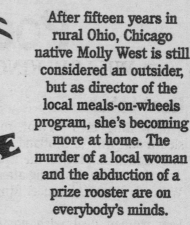

After fifteen years in rural Ohio, Chicago native Molly West is still considered an outsider, but as director of the local meals-on-wheels program, she's becoming more at home. The murder of a local woman and the abduction of a prize rooster are on everybody's minds.

Intrigued, Molly starts digging into the mystery. The trail leads to illegal doings and into the sport of cockfighting. However, the fowl deeds of the ring are minor compared to the blood sport of murder....

Patricia Tichenor Westfall

WORLDWIDE LIBRARY®

WPTW273

Mad Season
A Vermont Mystery

Downhill Slide

Spring. A time for renewal, growth, hope...and mud, at least in Vermont farm country. But something sinister had turned this season into one laced with fear and panic. An elderly couple is murdered in their home. A string of barn burnings adds to the uneasiness about town.

Running the family farm alone, Ruth Willmarth is stuck smack in the seasonal mess and getting deeper by the minute. Another murder hits close to home, and then her ten-year-old son disappears. Ruth valiantly tries to solve the puzzle, which is uglier than anyone dares to imagine.

Nancy Means Wright

DEADLY PARTNERS
A KATE KINSELLA MYSTERY

SEASON OF DISCONTENT

A working holiday to the Isle of Wight is just what nurse-medical investigator Kate Kinsella needs to revive her lagging funds and sagging spirits. It's a missing-person case: hotel owner Nigel Carter has disappeared.

Posing as an heiress interested in buying a hotel on the island, Kate steps off the ferry and into a bizarre murder, then into a jail cell as the chief suspect. With the help of her friend Hubert Humberstone, Kate draws closer to the shocking truth that lies at the heart of a very elaborate deception.

CHRISTINE GREEN

MYSTERY WORLDWIDE LIBRARY®
TM

WCG274